D1490826

Death in a Red Canvas Chair

A Rhe Brewster Mystery

By

N. A. Granger

To Jason —

Happy mystery reading !

N. A. Granger

Copyright © 2013 N A Granger
All rights reserved.

ISBN: 0615763693
ISBN-13: 9780615763699
Library of Congress Control Number: 2013908497
CreateSpace Independent Publishing Platform
North Charleston, South Carolina

Dedication

To my husband Gene, who has taken such good care of me, through thick and thin, and through the writing of this book, with love.

Prologue

The white commercial van drove slowly down the driveway to the left of the elementary school and pulled to a quiet stop alongside the gate leading to the soccer field. The gate was unlocked; he'd made sure of that the night before. The driver looked around, saw no one, then scooted across the front seat. Before exiting on the passenger side, away from the field, he pulled a blue ball cap snugly down on his head, tied a scarf over his mouth and nose, and pulled on heavy rubber gloves. He walked to the end of the van and surveyed the field. Small boys were swarming a soccer ball, flailing and kicking until it extricated itself from the beating and rolled down the field toward the far goal. Parents, predominantly mothers, stood on both sides of the field and cheered their progeny on.

Was she here? He scoured the sidelines. *Yes! There she is - on the far side.* The object of his interest was a tall woman with thick, shoulder length auburn hair, standing on the side lines at midfield, dwarfing the diminutive blond standing next to her.

He waited until the hive of boys surrounding the ball had moved to the far end of the field, then opened the van's rear door and took out a canvas folding chair. He unfolded it and reached back into the van to pull a plastic tarp aside. The stench, which had been bearable while he was driving with the windows open, hit him with an intensity that caused him to gag, but he held his breath and managed to drag the soft, decaying body from the van floor and ease it into the chair. He quickly lifted both to the far side of the van and closed the door. From one of his pockets he pulled a straw sun hat and placed it on the body's head. Sunglasses from his other pocket were forced over the swollen tissue of the face.

Waiting patiently until the action on the field focused the parents' attention was once again on the far end, he quickly picked up the chair with the body and carried them around the front end of the van, through the gate and out to the field. He deposited them at the near end but far back from the goal. After straightening the body and adjusting the hat, he quickly walked away, glancing back at the field only once he'd reached the van. *Good, no one's looking this way,* he thought as he climbed into the driver's seat and turned the key in the ignition with a shaking hand. *God, I hope she finds it. But even if she doesn't, I know she'll get involved. She'll find the killer.* He made a careful circle of the parking lot and drove away, as slowly and quietly as he'd come.

What once had been a vibrant being slowly collapsed into the canvas chair, dripping water and decay, gazing at the soccer game with dull, unseeing eyes.

1

When six year olds play soccer, a tie game has no overtimes ending in sudden death or sudden victory as it is now called. I was enjoying just such a soccer game with other team parents on an early October afternoon. My son Jack, who had previously shown little interest in moving with the swarm of boys around the ball, found himself with the ball in reach and tentatively gave it a kick in the right direction. I yelled from my chair, "Go, Jack!" as he followed the ball, only to be overrun by his teammates and flattened in the box. As our team parents yelled foul, the whistle blew, and the game ended as it had begun, 0-0.

Until that game I'd been leading a more or less ordinary life as wife, mother and emergency room nurse, and because I'd made it a point never to play all three roles at the same time, my existence had been fairly balanced and relatively happy. You might even call it bucolic, since we live in a small town on the coast of Maine. My name is Rhe Brewster. It is pronounced Ree, and it was given to me because my mother thought that the ancient French word for river sounded exotic. Her name is Storm and my sisters are Summer and Sage, so go figure.

It was Friday, and a lazy weekend waited in promise. As kids wandered off the field in pairs and threes and parents jumped to gather chairs, water bottles, and sun umbrellas, I leaned back in my chair, stretched, and took in a deep breath of autumnal air ... then scrunched up my nose at the whiff of something putrid. I turned to my companion in the canvas seat next to me and asked, "Paulette, do you smell that?

Paulette nodded and stood up. "Yeah, every so often I've noticed something nasty. Can you tell where it's coming from?"

"Must be near the field. Maybe a dead animal?"

"Yuck. Whatever it is, I don't want to see it," she replied with a shudder.

This was a typical response from Paulette, my best friend since college, who was repulsed by anything related to muck and blood. We'd been called Mutt and Jeff for years, and while the pint- sized Jeff struggled to collapse her oversized chair, I glanced again at the figure across the field. I'd first noticed it after half time, sitting at the far end of the field, a short distance outside the school fence. The person had been very still during the game, not cheering or yelling. In fact, there'd been no movement at all. There still wasn't.

I stood up and folded my chair. "Can I help you?" I asked with a smile.

"No, I've got it," came the exasperated answer. The chair finally folded and Paulette hoisted it and her bag with some effort.

I looked back across the field. The person was slouched down in a canvas chair similar to mine, the type that holds a can or bottle in an armrest well and is usually a gift from a supermarket, in return for your unavoidable patronage. Well-covered up, I noted, in a long sleeve shirt, overalls, and a wide brimmed sun hat pulled down over the face. *Why had the person sat so far away from the game's action?* I thought for the second or third time. *And why aren't they moving now the game's over?*

"Ready to head home?" Paulette asked.

The players were joining their parents on either side of the field and heading for the field's parking lot, at the other end from the school. Jack ran up to me and I gave him a hug. "Nice game, kiddo!"

"Mom, do NOT hug me in public! Did you see the goal I almost made?" My gangly, tow-headed son smelled of boy sweat and grass, which stained his socks from the knees down.

"Yes, I saw it! I bet next time you'll score!'" I replied as I tousled his hair.

I was hit with a fresh wave of the awful smell and I looked across the field again. The wind was blowing from that direction. Even Jack noticed it.

"Mom, what's that smell?"

"We think an animal died somewhere around here. You want to get your bag?" He headed off to midfield to collect his things. I suddenly had an awful thought about the person in that chair, and that thought was chilling. I hoped I was wrong.

'Hey, Paulette!" I called. She had walked to where her son Tyler was packing his bag. "Could Jack get a ride home with you?"

"Sure thing. What's up?"

"I just remembered I have an errand to run. I'll be by to pick him up in a half hour. Make him take his shoes, socks and shin guards off at the door!" Tyler was Jack's best buddy, and I could guarantee they would be into something rough and noisy as soon as they got home. Hearing the exchange, Jack slung his soccer bag over his shoulder, and without so much as a 'bye', headed towards the parking lot arm in arm with Tyler.

"See you in a bit," Paulette replied. "Can I help?" Paulette knew I was often at my wit's end deciding what to cook for supper, and it didn't help my ego or my waistline that she was Pequod's answer to Paula Dean.

"Nope," I replied. "Be there soon." I made a show of slowly gathering the detritus of my afternoon as a soccer mom and waited until Paulette, the kids, and nearly everyone else were in the parking lot. Then I abandoned my belongings and walked slowly across the field, hoping this was just a dummy someone had left there as a joke, and there really was just a dead animal somewhere.

As I grew closer to the chair, the smell became overpowering and I knew my instinct was right. I'd smelled this before, this odor of death, but still hoping, I called out "Hello? Are you okay? Do you need some help?" No answer. The person was now leaning precipitously to the left, and when I got up to the chair, I hesitated, then bent down to look under the hat. What greeted me was more horrifying than I could have imagined and I jerked back, hitting the chair. The chair and the person in it toppled over. The hat fell off, revealing a dissolving face, opaque eyes. The abdomen was swollen with the gasses released by decay and the hands were covered with sloughing, greenish gray skin. The person – a woman, judging by the long black hair – was clearly dead, really, really, dead.

I quickly walked away, bent over, gagging and starting to shake. I suppose a normal person might have screamed but I'd seen a lot of bad things in the ER, usually with the body still inhabited. This was so much worse that for a minute I couldn't think. *Pull yourself together, Rhe,* I scolded myself, and moved so I stood between the body and the last of the parents straggling to their cars. I pulled my shirt up over my nose, and jiggling with nervousness, I waited until the last car had driven off, then ran back across the field to where I'd left my bag. After fumbling around in its depths, I finally located my cell phone.

Instead of dialing 911, I opted to dial the local police chief. A 911 call would result in an unnecessary trip to the field by the local EMS, with the attendant fire truck and its first responders, plus all the police cruisers in the area. A three ring circus would ensue. The police chief just happens to be my brother-in-law, a bit of small town, borderline nepotism, and I decided he might handle the situation more judiciously.

The phone at the Pequod Police Station was answered before the second ring with a cheery "Good afternoon, Pequod Police. How may I direct your call?"

"Hi, Ruthie. It's Rhe. Sam around?" Ruth Anne Hersh had been the hub for the station since I was a little girl and knew everything there was to know about each and every one of the members of the police force and their families. I really needed to talk to Sam, but there was no way she wouldn't want to know why I was calling.

"Hello, dear. Yes, he's in. Anything I can help you with?"

I gave it to her directly to avoid a circuitous inquisition. "I found a dead body on the soccer field."

"Are you kidding?"

"Sorry, Ruthie, this is no joke."

She paused and then continued, "Hang on, I'll get him, and I'll get the rest from you later." She put me on hold to a country western tune about beer and a pickup truck.

There was a pause that lasted forever, then a click and a familiar voice. "How are you, darlin'?" Sam Brewster was, next to my husband, one of the greatest guys in the world, but he did have some peculiarities. He'd wanted to be a cowboy from an early age, hence the country western music on the police line and the attempted western accent. He also wore a cowboy hat, a string tie, and drove an open Jeep, better suited for a Texas range than a New England town. "Where's this body you found?"

"On the soccer field, right behind Jack's school. I need you out here right now!"

"Are you kidding me, Rhe? A body? Really?"

Lord, he was exasperating. "Yes, really, truly! I've sorta been trained to recognize that. How soon can you get here?"

"Give me 10 minutes. Don't touch anything and stay well away from the body."

"Believe me, I have no intention of getting close to it again. Can you call Marsh?" Marsh Adams is a pathologist at the hospital and an assistant medical examiner for the state's ME. I rattled on, nerves jangling. "You don't need to alert EMS. This woman has been dead for a while, and there is nothing they can do. Come in by the soccer field parking lot, since I'm guessing that the body was carried in from the other parking lot, behind the school. Just get here, okay?" I finished.

"Be there as soon as I can, honey," Sam said as he clicked off. By now, the soccer field and the parking lot were quiet and empty, except for my Jeep. It was also starting to get dark, which didn't help my nerves. I stood for a minute trying to figure out what to do next, then picked up my chair and bag and headed across the field again, where I waited, standing far away from the body. It was creepy there in the growing dusk, keeping company with a dead person, and I jumped around a bit to try to calm myself. It seemed like eternity before I heard several sirens. So much for avoiding the circus.

2

I had hung around for what seemed like ages, waiting to give my statement. To fight the boredom, I watched Marsh Adams and his crime tech do their work. Marsh was a friend of mine of many years, from before the new hospital was built. He'd decided to leave the ER for pathology a few years back; at the time, he told me that he had seen too much pain and suffering in the living and preferred the peace of the already dead. After some catch-up time reviewing pathology, he spent a year in the Maine Medical Examiner's office, returning to Pequod with the title of Assistant to the State ME.

After the initial drawn out procedure of photographing and designating some of the policemen to help with walking a grid, looking for evidence, I called out, "Hey Marsh, can't you work any quicker? You're slowing down with age."

"Watch your smart mouth, Ms. Brewster. This is as speedy as I get!" This with a smile.

Today he had obviously been off call, since he was packed like a sausage into a US Army shirt, stretching the chest and the arms to their limits, and a tight-fitting pair of work out shorts. His bulk comes from lifting weights every day.

"Must have been at the gym when Sam called, right?"

"Your powers of observation never fail to impress."

"Or were you getting a haircut?"

Marsh was sporting a new brush cut, and looked so military I was tempted to salute him. As far as I knew, he had never been married, possibly because of his brusque manner and inability to tolerate fools. In spite of his prickliness, Marsh and I had developed a good working relationship over the years, based on mutual respect.

I overheard Marsh say, "Oliver, get in here and take some close-ups of her neck, will you?" I had often wondered how it was that he and his assistant, Oliver Sampson, got on. Oliver doubled as the town's forensic technologist and came across as an odd duck, quiet but always observing. We'd never really had a conversation in the two years since we were introduced.

I watched Marsh's preliminary examination of the body with interest, while Oliver snapped away at Marsh's direction with a digital camera. I saw him take a liver temp with a long probe and finally, getting impatient, I sidled as close as I could get outside the crime scene tape and asked, "What do you see?"

"Keep your shirt on, Rhe." After a few more minutes, he called back "It's a woman in her late teens or early 20s. Based on her appearance, the most obvious cause of death was drowning, but there is no froth in the mouth or nose. No way would I hazard a guess until I do the autopsy.....interesting though, her body temperature is 88 degrees, way too high for a body in this advanced state of decomp. We've got a real puzzle here, kid."

At that point, he had Oliver roll the gurney to where the body lay and lower it to the ground. The two of them rolled the body onto a plastic sheet and transferred the sheet and its contents to a body bag before loading it onto the gurney. The sound as they zipped up the body bag sent a shiver through me, the finality of death for this young woman.

Pequod is a fairly typical, small coastal town north of Portland, Maine, not the place of even an occasional murder. Many of the town's families have been here for several generations, and when I was young, everyone knew almost everyone else. Even though the expansion of the commuter population to Portland had given the town growing pains in recent years, most of us at the crime scene knew each other through the hospital or the police chief. This familiarity meant I had been able to walk around without anyone questioning my presence. Earlier, I had overheard Sam's two deputies saying that the chair with the dead body appeared to have been carried to the field by one person. While the grass of the field had not revealed discreet shoe prints, indentations from the shoes were clear, as a result of the weight of the chair plus the victim and the softness of the ground. Oddly, Marsh had had to tell Oliver twice to measure the indentations. The results had suggested men's shoes, size 12. I briefly wondered if the person carrying that weight were a really strong woman with large feet. *Not a good image.* Without Marsh telling him to, Oliver had then measured my feet and taken an impression of my shoes to rule me out, since I had been around the body.

After he and Marsh left with the body, Sam finally got around to taking a statement from me and asked me to come to the police station to go over it in the morning. As the darkness surrounding the field became complete, the area continued being scoured by Sam's two deputies, walking an enlarged grid with flashlights. I walked to the side of the field to retrieve my chair and bag, and just as I got there, my phone rang. It was Will, my husband.

"Jesus H Christ, Rhe, where the hell are you? Are you okay?" he practically shouted at me.

"Yes, I'm fine," I replied, and it hit me with a thud that I had forgotten all about Jack and Will.

Before I could explain, Will went on, "I've been calling for the last hour! Paulette called me to tell me she had Jack, so I picked him up and started supper. Where are you?"

"Will, you won't believe this, but I found a body on the soccer field. I called Sam. I've been here the whole time, waiting to give a statement. I'm sorry I didn't hear my phone with all the activity going on."

"A body? Are you okay?" His voice rose with anxiety.

"I'm fine, and I'll tell you all about it when I get home."

"Did Jack see the body?"

"No, no way."

"Can you leave now?" His anger had finally dissolved into a combination of relief and exasperation.

"Be there in a few minutes, honey. I know I should have called you, but I had to stay." Guilt flooded me. "I'm really sorry."

"Sure. I'm just glad you're all right. I was worried," he added a little sheepishly.

"I know you were. Keep supper warm for me - I'm really hungry. Can you hear my stomach rumbling?" I tried to inject a little humor into the conversation, but all I got was a grunt. "Bye."

On the way home, I spent some time kicking myself for getting so wrapped up in what was going on. *But hey, I found a body! You couldn't have a better excuse than that, could you?* And I couldn't help feeling a peculiar sense of ownership of this crime.

When I arrived home, Will had dinner on the table, but his irritation had returned and he grumbled all the way through the meal. Will and I have been married for fourteen years. We had stayed in this area because he got a job teaching at Pequod College, a private liberal arts college on the northern outskirts of the county. Despite his PhD in Psychology, he still didn't completely understand me, and this evening was a perfect example of that.

I volunteered to clean up the kitchen and do the dishes when we'd finished eating, and Will got Jack into bed. A frustrating hour later, after a bedtime story, many stalling tricks and a request for water, Jack was finally down for the night with the lights off and we could finally sit down to talk. Will was anxious to learn what had happened that afternoon, but neither of us wanted to talk in front of Jack. Over coffee and re-heated apple pie from our local bakery, I gave him a rundown of the events at the soccer field. Jack had already told him in great detail about his almost goal. "Are you sure Jack didn't see the body?" he asked, wrinkling his forehead in a frown.

"Well, he smelled it, we all did, but I told him it was a dead animal. And no, there's no way he saw it. I sent him home with Paulette and waited until the parents had mostly left before I went to check it out."

"Would anyone else have seen the body?"

"I really doubt it, everyone was caught up in the soccer game. And I tried to block anyone from seeing it if they happened to look that way. They were all busy getting out of the parking lot, anyway. Even if someone *had* noticed a person just sitting there without moving, well, you know how things are today. They wouldn't want to get involved."

Will made a face and replied, "Everyone but you, Rhe."

I ignored his comment and continued, "I am really curious about the dead girl. She was young, probably college age. Have any of the students at the college gone missing lately?"

"Not that I've heard. Do you know what happened to her?"

"Not sure – the body had been submerged in water for some time and it was pretty gruesome. Marsh's going to do the autopsy first thing tomorrow morning."

"How did it get there?"

"No idea, but the body was apparently lugged onto the field by a strong person - with size 12 shoes, by the way."

"No one saw this person?"

"Hmm…how could someone do that without anyone noticing? You'd think if you saw a person lugging a chair around with a body in it, you might be curious. I think I'll ask some of the parents tomorrow. I need to drive into town and go over my statement with Sam, anyway."

Will took a really deep breath and said irritably, "Rhe, why in hell do you need to put your nose in this? Have you forgotten what happened last time?"

My mind snapped to the robberies that had happened at the hospital the previous winter, when I had indeed stuck my nose in by figuring out who was responsible. We'd received some threats during my investigation, and the threats had profoundly worried Will about our safety, especially Jack's. They'd caused a real rift between us, complete with accusations and arguments. But I hadn't thought about it in months.

"I do remember, but this is different. I'm not hunting a criminal, I just found a body! Anyone there could have found it. It just happened to be me."

Will continued on his tack for a few more minutes, reminding me that I'd promised to stay out of other people's business. *Had I really promised that?*

"Will, this could have happened to anyone. It just happened to be me."

"Right, the perfect person…," he paused and thought for a minute, then reluctantly said, "Okay, I guess it could have been anyone. But will you please leave this alone now?"

I nodded yes, but was thinking the day's events had been far more interesting than anything happening to me lately. All the way home, I'd been trying to figure out how I could help with the investigation without getting in the middle of it. With only two deputies and two patrolmen, Sam's department was stretched to its limits and lacked a designated investigator. I could be an extra pair of eyes and legs. I just had to figure how to do it without upsetting Will. This was going to be a real challenge.

3

Saturday morning was normally our time for errands at the pharmacy and hardware store and the inevitable and boring grocery run. But this Saturday morning promised to be more interesting. Will had papers to grade and a lawn to mow, hopefully for the last time of the season, and I needed to review my statement to the police. I left Jack with Will and headed out, noticing the air had a hint of impending colder weather, brought by an onshore breeze with a faint tang of salt. It made me think about winter, and winter in Maine was not my favorite season. I decided to take a detour down the street to see Paulette, to find out if she had noticed anything during the game.

I parked my Jeep in her driveway and walked around to the side of her house and the door to her kitchen. I admired Paulette's red brick, neo-Georgian home for the umpteenth time. It's a lot like her: neat and organized. Her walkway was already lined with colorful fall chrysanthemums. I guess my house is more like me, a sprawling old salt box, in serious need of yard work.

As usual, I just walked in the door without knocking. Paulette was in the kitchen, doing her Saturday morning baking, and the smell of fresh cinnamon rolls hit me as I entered.

"Well, you finally decided to pay me a visit," she said with a smile.

"The smell of your cinnamon rolls hit me in the driveway and I was helpless," I laughed. "If I eat some, can I ask you some questions about yesterday afternoon?" I sat down at her kitchen table, and Paulette put a plate of rolls in front of me.

"Interesting way to bribe me."

"Did you see the piece in the paper this morning about the body discovered on the kids' soccer field?" I resisted grabbing a roll.

"Was that why you sent Jack home with me? You found it, didn't you? It was that person sitting in the lawn chair! Was that the nasty smell?" Her face contorted in a grimace as she connected the dots.

"Yup, it was. When I went over to see, I'd hoped it was just a dummy, but no such luck."

"Thank God I *didn't* see it. I couldn't have handled it. And certainly the boys shouldn't have seen it!" I knew Paulette had a weak stomach, but I didn't know about the boys. They were into squashing insects and examining road kill at this stage. "Did you recognize the body?" she asked.

"No, but I probably wouldn't have been able to anyway. The body had been in water for some time. Now can I have one of those?" I indicated the source of the wonderful smell.

"Yuck! More than I wanted to know! And only you could say that and ask for food in the same breath. Want some coffee? And tell me more. Just leave out the gory stuff." She poured two cups of coffee and brought them to the table, where the plate of cinnamon rolls was missing one.

I wiped my sticky fingers on a napkin, put sugar and cream in my coffee and told her what I knew. Paulette was not a gossip, except when it came to gossiping with me, probably because we had known each other for so long.

"Dr. Adams said she was about college age, but Will told me there had been no students reported missing from the college when I asked him last night."

"Do you think Sam might know anything by now?"

"I'm on my way to see him to finalize my statement. I'll pump him for more information, and let you know. What I really stopped by for, not that these cinnamon thingies aren't wonderful, is to ask if you'd noticed anything other than the person in the chair yesterday. People, a car, a truck?"

Paulette scrunched her face, closed her eyes and tugged on a piece of her hair, something I'd watched her do many times over the years — a signal she was thinking hard. She'd always had amazing attention to detail, and I was hoping she would remember something. After a minute or so, she said, "I saw a commercial truck of some kind — you know, the big, boxy kind of van with no windows? The kind the phone company guys use. It was light tan, no, dirty white, and was parked behind the school. There was some logo on the door, but who could read it at that distance? Did you see it?"

"No, I missed it. That's a real help, dear, but think harder. Did you see anyone?"

"No, I was more interested in the game and only gave it a glance. What are you planning to do? Rhe, I know that face, and you are going to poke your nose into this, aren't you?

"Aw, geez, Will said the same thing to me last night. I apparently promised him after the last time not to do it again.….but I think I might really be able to help Sam with this."

"Not a good idea, Rhe…."

"Well, I can't help it — I found that body and I want to know what happened to her. I'm just going to do a little sniffing around and see if I can find out anything, you know, ask the soccer parents what they saw. I won't really be involved at all. I mean it." This last part was said with every bit of conviction I could manage. Paulette smirked and shook her head. She knew me too well.

We chatted about the soccer game schedule and the possibility of carpooling before I got up to leave. Paulette handed me a cinnamon roll wrapped in a napkin for Sam and gave me a hug, which is always strange because the top of her head doesn't reach my shoulder. She hugs me around my waist. "I need you safe, Rhe. Be careful, will you?" she called as I left.

I took the roundabout way out of my neighborhood to get to town. The neighborhood is on the south side of Pequod and sits on the original site of a large wood frame summer hotel built in the early twentieth century. Our house stands in what had been the front yard of the hotel, overlooking the ocean. A developer had bought the land and the derelict hotel about 30 years ago, razed the building and slowly sold lots to various builders, calling the whole thing Sea Cliff after the hotel's name. I had explored that old hotel with friends when I was growing up, long after it had been condemned. We were awed at the dining room still set with linen and china, as if the occupants had just gotten up and left. I even went as far as the wine cellar, reached by climbing down two flights of collapsed stairs. It was probably a miracle one of us hadn't been killed during these explorations, but they were far too exciting for me to give up.

The police station is on Main Street in Pequod, one street back from Seafront Drive, the main road along the town's waterfront. Our town fathers were nothing if not imaginative when it came to naming streets. As I turned onto Main Street to reach the police station, I passed the three story, neoclassic, stone monster that was our court house. It was listed as a state historical building for no obvious reason other than it was constructed in the 1880s. I knew it well from jury duty. It dwarfs the police station next door, a banal, 1960s brick box, with a glass entranceway and a cracked concrete parking lot on the side away from the court house. As I entered the station, I noticed Ruthie sitting at the tall reception desk, despite it being Saturday. When Ruthie sits at the front desk, about all you can see is the top of her bun. She is what my mother likes to call an ample woman, with graying hair still showing some of the original bright red, freckles covering her face, and a hearty laugh. I was surprised to see that bun, but on second thought, with the first murder in this town in memory, she was probably needed to field phone calls and e-mail. I announced my presence with a "Hey, Ruthie, how ya doing?"

"So, what did you see?" she asked, getting right to the point. I walked around the desk so I could talk to her face.

"A dead body," I replied.

Her eyebrow went up in a nonverbal 'And?' and her head leaned forward.

"Okay, she's a young adult and was submerged in water for a while before she got deposited on the soccer field. But you already know that, don't you?"

She smiled.

I continued, "Your turn now. Have any young women been reported missing?"

"None in the last several months that I am aware of. Sam is in his office. You need to sign your statement?"

"Yup, and other things," I replied, as I headed down the hall to the left past her desk. Sam was scrunched behind his scarred desk in an impossibly crowded office. There were piles of folders, e-mails, faxes, and letters covering the top of his desk, chairs, filing cabinet and a book case. One nearly dead Christmas cactus sat shriveled up in a pot on the corner of the filing cabinet. I have never understood how he knew where anything was in that office, but he could unerringly retrieve whatever he needed. His clearance system consisted of removing and shredding the bottom layer of papers at one year intervals because he figured if he had not used something by then, they were worthless. The office itself was otherwise undecorated, with bare institutional gray walls, except for a cork board with layers and layers of papers pinned to it.

"You got that statement printed up for me yet?" I asked, going around his desk as he stood to give me a hug. Sam was a huge bear of a man, 6 feet 5 inches and about 275 pounds, so hugs with him were always a physical event. When he was younger, most of the bulk occupied his chest and shoulder region, but in recent years some of it had moved downward, giving him a small paunch that made it harder to get my arms around him. I handed him the napkin-wrapped cinnamon bun.

"A gift from Paulette?" he asked, looking up. He opened the napkin. "There's a bite out of it!"

"I couldn't stop myself. I had two, but it was calling to me on the way here. You need to save me from eating the rest," I insisted with a guilty smile. "So what can you tell me about our dead body?"

"Absolutely nothing. We have no reports of anyone missing with that approximate height, weight, age and hair color. I had one of my deputies run the description through the database of the National Center for Missing Adults. No luck, so we tried the National Center for Missing and Exploited Children. Also drew a blank. I'm just waiting on the autopsy report from Marsh. One thing – we should check out Pequod College."

"Hmm…maybe I could save you some time there. Will said there was no one missing he was aware of, but it's always possible the Dean of Students office has information that's not been made public yet. Although I don't understand why they wouldn't have contacted you."

"You know the Dean of Students?"

"For a long time. This past year we worked on some yacht club dinners together. Would you like me to check with her?"

"Sure, that would be a big help. How soon can you do it?"

"Monday, when everyone's around."

"Good, but nothing more than an inquiry, right? I don't want to have to save your butt in the middle of another criminal investigation."

I was getting reminders from all sides, it seemed.

He handed me a printed copy of my previous night's statement, which I read carefully for errors and finding none, signed it, and I turned towards the door.

"Dinner next week?" I asked. "How about Wednesday? Jack wants to talk about the World Series." He and Jack had attended one of the Series games when the Red Sox were playing in Boston, which had made Sam an instant hero. Plus, Sam was a confirmed bachelor and I knew for a fact that home-cooked meals were rare for him.

"Sure thing, but with this new investigation, we'll have to play it by ear."

I hadn't a clue what I could cook that could warrant his coming to dinner, other than the one thing I had taken the time to learn from my mother: baked stuffed pork chops. I'd only made them for him the last ten times he was over. *Maybe I should try a meatloaf?*

Outside the police station, I weighed my options: a trip to the hospital to see if Marsh had started the autopsy or some visits to team member parents in the hopes someone saw something. Marsh won out. I figured the parents were more likely to be home on Sunday, and a trip to see Marsh was clearly the more interesting prospect. So I climbed back into my old Jeep and drove to Sturtevant, hoping to catch the autopsy.

4

Sturdevant Regional Hospital was named for one of the local gentry who had served in the Maine legislature in the mid 1900s. It had started out life as a single story brick building, and after the county purchased it, two more stories and a patient tower had been added. The morgue was one floor down, in the basement, and could be reached directly through double doors off a back loading dock. I parked in the employee parking lot behind the loading dock and used my employee card to gain access.

There was normally a guard on the doors, because they're needed to admit bodies to the morgue and to sign in non-hospital personnel. Lyle Pendergraff was sitting at his station, behind a Plexiglas wall separating his desk from the corridor. I think he'd been there since before the hospital was constructed, and I had a suspicion that they'd just built it around him. He probably couldn't defend the hospital from a cat invasion, but he knew every employee and delivery person and checked IDs when he didn't. His eyes lit up when he saw me and he waved me in, so his eyesight was still fine.

Inside, the usual smells greeted me – Lysol, embalming fluid, fixative, and dead body odors, an antiseptic olio in chilled air. The two autopsy suites on the left opened by air-tight double doors and when I peered through the glass window of the second one, I found Marsh and Oliver. I pushed through the door, saw the girl's body on the table, and was immediately hit with the nauseating smell of body decomposition. It had been pungent on the soccer field, but in the relatively small space of the autopsy suite, it was overwhelming. I reached for the container of vaporub that Marsh kept on the counter just inside the door and put a good dab under each nostril. Oliver was just replacing the rib cage and approximating the tissue of the Y-shaped incision from each shoulder to the abdomen that marks an autopsy. The flesh was too friable to stitch shut. Various jars stood on a side bench, containing organs and samples of tissue for pathology. Marsh had already changed into hospital greens from the full body suit with face mask that Oliver was still wearing, but had a cloth mask over his lower face and nose. He looked up questioningly from the computer where he was typing notes.

"Hiya, Rhe. I figured you would be here sometime this morning. Did Sam send you?" I could hear him, but his voice was a little muffled.

"No, but he's anxious to get your full report. Can you tell me what you found? You know Sam's going to share it with me anyway." I decided to follow my request with outright bribery. "How about a latte and a doughnut for breakfast next week...?" The best doughnut shop in town, Hole in One Donuts, just happened to be across the street from his gym, and I knew he not only liked their coffee but also was addicted to their lemon-filled confections.

"Well, if you put it that way.... and I know you'll just sucker the report out of Sam," he conceded with half smile. "The body is an 18-22 year old woman, in good physical health, with no apparent premortem injuries or disease. She wasn't drowned, although I'd estimate that she'd been in water for about a day. Based on the kind and state of decomp and initial body temp, she had to have been stored in hot water. I'm thinking hot tub."

Marsh got up and walked over to a light box on the side of the room and flipped on the back light. He slapped up two X-rays. "According to these, she'd suffered a blunt force injury to her temporal bone, with these radial fractures here and here, extending outward from the site of the blow. It resulted in perimortem epidural bleeding, which I found during the autopsy." I knew from my nursing school anatomy that the temporal bones form part of the sides of the skull, and there is a spot on each side of the skull where a junction occurs between the temporal bone and three other bones. At the junction, the skull is thin and rather weak, and a major artery to the outer covering of the brain runs beneath it. The side view of the skull showed a fracture in that area, with secondary fracture lines extending like starfish arms. The artery had undoubtedly been ruptured by the blow, leading to a blood clot that put pressure on the brain.

Marsh moved to the second X-ray and continued, "She was also strangled around the same time. Her hyoid bone is crushed, there is significant subdermal bruising on her neck, and I could just see some petechiae in the conjunctiva of her eyes." The crushed hyoid bone was clearly visible on the X-ray, this one a frontal view of the neck. I remembered that muscles involved in swallowing and speech are attached to this U-shaped bone, and if it is crushed, the airway to the lungs can be blocked. This in turn leads to increased pressure in the veins of the head, resulting in the rupture of capillaries. In the white of the eye, little red spots, called petecheia, appear as a result of capillary rupture.

Marsh went on, "It's clear whoever killed her was strong, given that either injury could be fatal. However, death would not have been instantaneous with the blow to the head, thus the strangulation. A case of real overkill, pardon the pun. I believe the killer was a man, because of the strength needed to crush the hyoid and to move the body around.

"Can you tell from the bruising if the killer was left- or right-handed?"

"Sorry, Rhe, but this guy used both hands."

"Any trace evidence?"

"Nope, the body was clean. The water would have taken care of most of it. Nothing on the chair, either. All we have are the shoe imprints, and some miscellaneous items we picked up from the soccer field – a hair ribbon, a cigarette butt. I still can't figure why this body was dumped in a chair on the soccer field during a game."

I thought for a minute. "It's almost as if whoever did it wanted her to be found."

Marsh nodded in agreement.

"Have you sent anything to the state lab?" I asked.

"I took blood for analysis, but the results won't be in for at least a week. You know how backed up they are." This last was said with a huge sigh. "The samples I took for DNA will take even longer. I also took dental X-rays, so if there is anyone missing, we can make a match that way. Did you hear anything about a missing teen?"

"No to that from Sam, and Will hasn't heard of anyone missing at Pequod. I'll talk to the Dean of Students on Monday, after my shift." I had another thought. "Did you find any jewelry, you know, earrings or a bracelet, on the body? I didn't take a close look after that first one."

"Funny you should ask. There was a gold cross on a chain, which we found in her clothing. It'd been ripped off and apparently fell down into her bra. The cross has the Lord's prayer etched on it, so small that I had to look at it under a microscope. Don't they sell those on TV?"

"Why, Marsh, I didn't think you ever watched TV!" Actually, other than his workouts and his affection for doughnuts, I had no idea what he did with his spare time. "Will you let me know when you learn anything further?"

"Sure thing, but keep your nose clean!"

I held up my hands and exited the room. Marsh was well aware of my predilection for sticking my snubby nose where it didn't belong. At least he didn't tell me not to.

During our entire conversation, Oliver had just stood there watching us silently. He was a study in contradictions - over six feet tall, with a closely shaved, perfectly round head and a gold hoop in one earlobe. With no hair to cover them, it was pretty noticeable that his ears stuck out, sort of like wing nuts, and they were always wired to an iPod. Oliver's face was handsome, but he looked like a teenager, without the normal planes and angles that an adult face acquires. He dressed like a teenager, too, with sagging cargo pants and oversized tee shirts. He was a real charmer, according to some of the nurses. Although he'd been one of the weekend life guards at our local beach club, taking time to work with Jack on his swimming strokes, I'd never had more than few brief conversations with him, during which he'd been rather stiff and shy. One of my goals had been to talk with him some more; he seemed like an interesting kid. But with one thing and another, an opportunity had never presented itself.

Oliver raised a gloved hand in a friendly farewell as I left the room.

5

When I arrived home, I noted the lawn had that freshly mown smell, and when I let myself in the door to the kitchen, I found Will had left me a wrapped sandwich (tuna with pickles, my favorite) on the counter with a note saying "Gone to the softball field. See you around 4. XOXO". While munching on the sandwich, I decided to make some notes on my computer about everything I knew so far about the body, which wasn't much, the only real clue being the chain with a cross. So the next thing on my to-do list had to be a survey of the other soccer parents in the hopes they might have seen something.

After lunch, I headed outside to our pool for a swim. One of the reasons we'd bought this house was the fact that it came with a pool. Swimming is the way I exercise, relax, clear my head, and mull over problems, frequently finding solutions while my body churns the laps. Since it was now early October, we would have to close the pool soon - the heat generated by the solar panels was just enough that I could stand getting into the water and feel invigorated during the swim. Before I entered the pool, I did my routine check of the pH and chlorine balance with a paper dip stick, noting that Will, who doubled as our pool boy, would need to add a couple bags of salt. As I swam up and down the pool, my mind emptying of outside distractions, the thought of the needed bags of salt floated in. Suddenly there was an unbidden connection with Marsh's suggestion that the body had been in a hot tub. I should have asked Marsh if he'd sent a sample of the water out for analysis!

Some homes here have hot tubs, which people use all year round, and like pools, there are a dozen different ways to keep the tub water clean. With that thought, I sprinted to the end of my laps, grabbed my towel, and went back in the house, leaving a trail of wet foot prints and splashes of water from the French doors to our phone. Marsh answered on the second ring.

"Hi, Marsh! It's Rhe. I just thought of something. Were you able to get a water sample from the clothes?"

"Funny you should ask. I did manage to get some water out of the pant cuffs and sent it off for analysis. You know this is a long shot, don't you? There could be tens of hot tubs out there with the same water composition. Plus the sample is undoubtedly contaminated with body fluids."

"Mmmm…hadn't thought of that, but hey, it's a start. Maybe we'll get lucky."

"Did you say we?"

"Thanks, Marsh." I hung up before he could get another word in.

Jack and Will came in around 4:30. Jack was excited because he'd spent most of the afternoon hitting baseballs with his Dad, and Will was really tired from shagging mis-hit balls. Jack had been diagnosed with ADHD the previous year, and sports had become the perfect way to wear him out. As a result, fall meant soccer, winter was basketball, spring was lacrosse and summer was swimming and sailing, and Jack's parents were often more tired than he was.

For supper, I tried a meat loaf recipe. Will said it was tasty, and both he and Jack gobbled it down, but I noticed they covered it in catsup. Jack fell asleep on the couch after dinner, watching a football game. After plopping him into bed, I decided to talk to Will about what I'd done that morning, thinking if I could convince him nothing I was doing was dangerous, he might be less hostile to my investigating.

Will had plopped down in the family room again to catch up on the football game, and I stood in the kitchen, looking at the man I had married, tired, rumpled, and slouched down in the recliner. He was several years older than I and bore a strong resemblance to Sam, including the premature loss of hair on the crown of his head. But unlike Sam, he wore glasses for farsightedness, which magnify his eyes and made him look a little like an owl. What I most loved about him was his sense of humor, his kindness, and his total devotion to Jack and me. We'd married right after he got his Ph.D. from U Mass, and I thought so far we'd made a pretty good couple. We'd had no real conflicts, except for my desire to have another child and his total contentment with just one. It had taken six years and a couple of rounds of *in vitro* to conceive Jack, but I still dreamed of another pregnancy. I used birth control after Jack was born because Will was so adamant, but recently I'd stopped. At 37, I figured I wasn't likely to get pregnant again, and I was tired of taking pills. I'd told Will, but wasn't sure it had registered.

"Do you want to hear about what I did today?" I asked him, coming into the family room and sitting on the couch.

"Not particularly."

His attention was on the game, and gauging by his attitude to my sleuthing the previous year, I'd anticipated he would be less than enthusiastic about my current curiosity about the dead girl. It boiled down to the fact that I thought marriage should allow for personal growth, and Will didn't think investigating constituted a form of growth. He'd more than once expressed his fear of where my talent in this field might lead.

Despite his feigned disinterest, I gave him my description of visiting the police station and the morgue, talking over the game announcer. I got his attention when I mentioned I was going to see Bitsy Wellington, the Dean of Students, on Monday.

Will immediately turned from the TV screen. "Why do you need to talk to her? Did Sam ask you to?"

"As a matter of fact, he did. Just to make sure there're no missing students his office doesn't know about. I know how much you admire her..." This was said sarcastically, since Will had had several confrontations with Ms. Wellington about student academic misconduct, which she was responsible for monitoring. The problem was she'd never met a student she didn't believe. "Do you know where I could find her?"

"The witch should be in her office when you get off work," he said, "and good luck getting anything out of her. She's been dragging her feet on convening an honor court hearing for that football player who plagiarized most of his first term paper. I'm beginning to think she's going to ignore me until the season is over."

"What's the kid's name? Do I know him?"

"Raymond Little. He's a defensive lineman, big kid. I honestly thought he was going to deck me when I told him I knew he'd plagiarized."

"And the reason you didn't tell me was ...?"

"Because he backed off and hasn't approached me since. He's also turned into a model student. I'm sure the work isn't his...it's a quantum leap better than the first part of the semester. I haven't been able to detect any more plagiarism in his work, and believe me, I've looked."

We sat in silence for a minute looking at each other, and I noticed how exhausted Will appeared. His eyelids were drooping and he was slumped in his chair. "Go on up to bed, sweetie, you're falling over. I'll clean up the kitchen."

Will kissed me dispassionately and headed upstairs. I washed the dishes and gave the kitchen a lick and a promise before heading to bed myself. Maybe the meatloaf would work for Sam if I drowned it in catsup.

Sunday afternoon, I sat down with the list of parents of the soccer team and mapped out a tour of their homes. Better to ask questions in person. I took Jack with me because Will had a pile papers to grade and told me he wouldn't have time to spend with him. Jack wasn't too happy about being stuck in a car for the afternoon and asked why we *had* to visit team families. On the spur of the moment, I came up with a great excuse. "Well, I'm going to organize an end of season team party at our house, and thought I'd start now. What do you think? If we can keep the pool warm enough, you guys can even swim!"

"Great, Mom!" He beamed at me, bouncing in his nearly outgrown booster seat in the back. Seeing him in the rearview mirror, it occurred to me for the umpteenth time that Jack was starting to look a lot like his father, tall and fair. We made two stops without my finding out anything new, and then headed to Beth and Stan Smith's. Their son Michael was another good friend of Jack's, and the two ran off to play almost as soon as Beth opened the door. Beth offered me coffee, so I sat in her kitchen, having my third cup of coffee for the afternoon and suspecting I would have stratospheric caffeine high by the time I got home.

"Beth, can I ask you something about last Friday's soccer game?"

"It's about that body on the soccer field, isn't it?" she replied, squinting her eyes in a question. "I read about it in the P and S." Our local newspaper, the Pequod Post and Sentinel, was the butt of many jokes due to its initials and the questionable quality of its national news, but it had good local information, even if the reports were painted in purple prose.

"Was the body there during the game? The paper didn't mention that," Beth asked.

"Yeah, it was. And unfortunately I was the one who discovered it. I've been wondering if anyone else noticed anything. Did you see anything during the game... at the end of the field next to the school parking lot?" Beth looked a little confused, so I continued, "Did you see the person in the lawn chair?

"Yes, I did notice that – was it the dead body?"

"Yup, it was." I paused to let her settle in with the idea. "The Police Chief was thinking maybe some of the other parents saw something that I didn't. Do you remember anything? A car in the parking lot near the entrance to the field? A person?"

"Give me a minute," she replied, taking a long sip of coffee and thinking for a moment. "I did see a white delivery van of some sort next to the entrance,

I think it was just after halftime. I wondered what it was doing there since the lot is closed after school lets out."

"Anything else?"

"Actually I saw someone near the van but at that distance, I could only guess it was a man, mainly because he was pretty tall. Long pants, ball cap, blue I think."

"Beth, you are too amazing! How did you notice all this?"

"Practice, I guess. I've been head of the local community watch program for the last two years, and I just notice things. I know I saw a logo or printing on the van door. I think part of it was a red arrowhead lying on its side. Other than that, just the person in the lawn chair at some point after I saw the van."

"Lucky I stopped to talk to you! You're one great observer. If you think of anything else, anything at all, would you give me a call?"

After a brief chat about the upcoming soccer game and carpooling, I thanked her for the coffee and left without Jack, who'd been invited to stay and play with Michael while I visited the other parents. This made the next three stops easier, but they added little to what I'd already learned. One of them had seen the van, and the other two had noticed the body, but no new details were forthcoming. It was getting late, so I picked up Jack and headed home and texted Sam what I'd learned, before starting dinner.

6

Monday and Wednesday mornings had meant controlled chaos in the Brewster household for some time, because those were the days I'd work the eight to four shift in the ER at Sturdevant. I would get up at 6 to make lunches and breakfast for Jack and Will, and if I were lucky, I'd be in my car heading to the hospital with a cereal bar and a cup of coffee by 7:30. On Tuesdays and Thursdays, Will left early to teach a morning introductory psych class, so I took Jack to school. Will was usually home to meet Jack's bus in the afternoon, unless he had office hours for his students. With this schedule, I had a pretty substantial amount of free time and that meant time to do a little investigating.

Mondays are never quiet in an ER. Injured weekend jocks and people who have waited several days while they've become progressively sicker usually show up first thing in the morning, along with the uninsured, who have to use the ER for their health care. This Monday had been no exception: a badly sprained ankle, a torn ACL, pneumonia, and a particularly nasty motorcycle accident all came through the sliding glass doors early, followed by fevers, coughs, and runny noses. By 4 PM, I was more than ready to put my feet up, but instead of driving home, I went to Pequod College to see if I could catch up with Bitsy Wellington.

Bitsy's office was located in Huston House, where the founder of the college, Millard Huston, and his wife Sarah had lived in the early 1900s. The house had been built in a style called Richardsonian Romanesque and it looked remarkably like the home of the Addams Family. After passing through the heavy wooden front door, carved with animal heads, I consulted the directory and found Bitsy's office on the ground floor at the back of the building. The door for the Dean of Students was open to the hall, probably to encourage students to enter, and I asked the secretary at the desk just inside if I could see Dean Wellington. She glared at me over the tiny little glasses perched on the end of her nose.

"May I ask the nature of your business?" she said.

"Well, it's private and rather important."

"I'm sorry, but I need to inform the Dean of the specific nature of the visit, since she's busy today and her time is limited."

I decided to take another tack. "It might concern a missing student."

After an immediate and brief communication on a phone line, she indicated the door at the rear of the room with a sweep of her arm, saying. "You may go in." *You'd have thought I was visiting the Pope.*

Bitsy sat at a delicate antique wooden desk at the very back of the room, framed by windows looking out over a well-kept garden full of fall flowers. She wore a corporate grey suit, white blouse with a ruffle at the neck, and was perfectly, if overly, made up. Her salt and pepper hair was swept up in a French twist, and not a strand was out of place. I could see she was sitting on a cushion, which I figured boosted her high enough to work at the desk. Her face was much as I remembered, thin and pinched with a narrow nose. If I were a student, I wouldn't come here on a dare.

She looked up from her work, forced a smile, and gritted, "Rhe, what a pleasant surprise! Have a seat. What can I help you with?"

Bitsy and I had grown up together. Her real name was Elizabeth, but because of her small size, we had always called her Bitsy, which she hated. She had been a full-blown bully as a child, for which I blamed her parents, who considered most of the children in town too good to mingle with their daughter. Whether it was swimming lessons or sailing Beetle Cats in and out of the harbor, Bitsy had taken every opportunity to belittle her so-called friends, and I was frequently a target. She hadn't changed much as an adult - subtly pompous and positively unctuous when she wanted to impress someone. She was not married, and I seriously doubted that matrimony would have improved her disposition. With our contentious history, I was really going to have to suck it up to get any information from her, but suck it up I would.

"Actually I am here making inquiries for Chief Brewster." I said this with as much humility as I could muster and gave her a semi-pleading look.

"Your brother-in-law, right? What do you need to know? Something about a Pequod student?"

"You know there was a body found on the soccer field late Friday afternoon?" She nodded.

"I was the one who found it."

"How horrible!" She sat up even straighter in her chair, and as uninterested as she was in me, I could see her antennae twitching.

"The body hasn't been identified yet, and I need to know if there are any female undergraduates missing from campus. Will said he'd not heard anything."

"Well, he's correct. Of course, we would immediately notify the police if any of our students went missing."

"Okay, let me ask you this. How many students live off campus?"

"About 20% have apartments in the area."

"How would you know if any of those were missing, especially if they lived by themselves?"

"Well, I assume their friends might notify the campus police after a day or so. Then I would be notified."

"Is there any way you could check to see if a student living off campus has missed class for several days - at the end of last week and today, for example?"

"Well, that would be difficult and would take some time on my part, since we'd have to look at attendance lists." Clearly she was not going to make this easy for me.

I smiled nicely and prepared to lay it on, "Bitsy....."

"I prefer Elizabeth."

Okay, we'll do it your way. "Sorry. Elizabeth. This information could lead to an identification of the body and would certainly be very helpful to the police. I'm sure Chief Brewster would esteem it a great favor if you could find the time to do this." *Maybe that was too thick?*

She bit. "Well, I suppose it could be done. I can check with the registrar, who'll send out an e-mail to our entire faculty," she grudgingly agreed. "I'll forward whatever we find to the Chief. I expect it will take a day or two."

I ignored the snub, smiled again and asked "Yes, the Chief definitely, but could you let me know as well?" *Definitely pushing the envelope here, but I want to know as soon as he does.*

Bitsy rustled some papers to remind me how important she was, thought for a second, and then said condescendingly, "I could do that if Chief Brewster agrees." She then called her secretary to take my cell phone number on the way out.

"By the way," she added as a parting shot, "tell your husband that I was unable to find anyone to confirm his accusation that Raymond Little threatened him during class, so that whole matter has been dropped."

Why was she telling me this? Why didn't she just call Will? Probably because she knew it would tick Will off. I decided not to reply; it wasn't my fight. Since the audience was over, I exited quickly, murmuring thanks. I gave the secretary my number and practically ran out the front door, feeling enormous relief the meeting had gone relatively well and just maybe something would come of it.

I stopped at the store on the way home and loaded up on spaghetti, spaghetti sauce, and a pound of ground turkey, ever conscious of my husband's weight, not to mention mine. I thought briefly of shopping for the next night's dinner with Sam, but decided it was too far away to worry about.

☙❧

After supper, I dropped into a chair in the family room and put my feet up. I think Will got the hint because he did the dishes, and Jack had returned to the kitchen table, finishing his homework without complaint, a rare night.

"Pretty good spaghetti, oh wife of mine," Will commented from the kitchen sink. "Especially with the applesauce for dessert." This last was subtly sarcastic. Will had a sweet tooth, and I had to body check him to keep him from the cookie aisle of the grocery store.

"Did you learn anything today when you saw Bitsy?" Will asked carefully.

"No, but there are possibilities." I changed the subject. "How did soccer practice go today, Jack?"

"Great! I think we might win this week!" My son, ever the optimist.

After a half hour show on Nickelodeon, Jack went off to bed, Will making sure he actually got there. When he came back, he sat on the coffee table and started to give my feet a rub, one of those small but important pleasures of married life. "So what happened today?" he asked casually, trying to conceal his interest. I gave him a synopsis of my meeting with Bitsy, and he growled at my description of her attitude. I hesitated at the end, wondering whether to relay her last comment to him. I decided to chance it; there was no love lost between them already.

"There's one more thing. Bitsy mentioned on my way out that she'd dismissed your complaint against Raymond Little. She said she could find no witnesses to corroborate your story."

"No witnesses, my foot!" Will sprang up from the coffee table. "He did it in front of the whole class. I bet she just talked to one or two students and intimidated the hell out of them. That pompous, self-serving bitch!"

"What did you tell her when you made your complaint?"

"Just that Raymond had sworn at me and threatened me in class. I asked her to talk to the football coach about his behavior and to initiate a hearing with the school's Honor Court. Well, now I think I'm going directly to the football coach. He probably won't listen either, since Little is a starter, but I'm going to try anyway. I've just gotta find the right time and figure out how to approach him," he said with the frown I knew so well.

We commiserated on our mutual problems with Bitsy for a while. By 10 o'clock, I felt like Will had looked the night before and was ready for bed, and Will had an early class the next morning. We headed upstairs holding hands, so I was not in the doghouse yet. Yet.

7

Tuesday morning was one of those New England autumn days you wish you could bottle - cool with the hint of fall crispness, clear, brilliant blue skies, and increasing flares of yellow and orange in the leaves of the oak, maple and elm trees. There was a fairly strong, salty breeze coming in off the ocean, with whitecaps cresting as far as the eye could see.

After a chilly morning swim, housework and a breakfast bar lunch, I heard the phone ring. It was Bitsy, and she radiated self-importance through the phone.

"Rhe, I have information for you. I've already been in touch with Chief Brewster and he said I could call you. We've managed to find a student who's not been in class since last Wednesday. Her name is Liliana Bianchi. She lives alone off campus, according to the Registrar. I gave her address to the Chief."

"Could you give it to me, too?"

"I'm not supposed to give out that information. You'll have to get it from the Chief."

"Why can't you? You gave me her name, for heaven's sake!" I bit my lip in an effort not to say more.

"Student names are public knowledge, but we are not supposed to give out addresses to anyone who is not family. You will just have to call the Chief." And with that she hung up on me. I stared at the phone and called her some names worthy of Army drill sergeant before speed dialing Sam.

"So what's Liliana Bianchi's address?"

"Nice to hear from you too, Rhe. I take it Bitsy called you?"

"She said she had your permission. So what's the address?"

"Well, since you're being so nice, I'll tell you - 104 Bridge Lane. We're going over there now and you may be there *with* us, but only to look, okay?

I felt calmer now, having taken my righteous anger out on poor Sam. "Sorry, Sam. Bitsy knows how to push my buttons, long story. Since you seem to get on with her so well, could you call her back and ask her for a list of students enrolled in each of Liliana's classes? If she lived alone, it may be hard to locate her friends. But if we could find some students who took more than one class with her, we might have a place to start in tracking where she was last."

"Funny you should ask, I'd just thought of that after I hung up with her."

"One more suggestion? Lay on the charm, Sam. She'll be putty in your hands. See you in a few."

I heard a 'harrumph' on the other end of the line just before I cut him off.

I got the directions to Bridge Road via an online map and left a note for Will. Bridge Road turned out to be a slightly wider-than-one lane dirt road, which wound around in a heavily wooded section of northwestern Pequod. I identified 104 by the crowd of cars parked in front of it: a state forensics truck, Sam's Jeep and a police cruiser with its lights revolving, I pulled to a stop in a cloud of dust.

The house was a single story, old wood frame derelict, probably the hall and parlor type, with the front door leading into a hall with a room on either side. There was a leaning chimney at the left end of the house, and the original white paint was so worn off the house looked gray from the underlying wood. As I approached, I noted the windows were clean and had been caulked and the front door was freshly painted a dark gray, as if the owner, or perhaps the renter, had done some minimal upkeep. The front porch had new boards in some places, although they'd not been painted. Crime scene tape closed off the door.

Sam was standing on the porch with one of his deputies, John Smith.

"Wow, what did you do? Fly here?" Sam asked as I climbed the two creaking stairs.

"Yup, that old Jeep has wings. Do you have a warrant?"

"I got a warrant from Judge Jeffries just in case, after we preliminarily matched the victim's driver's license photo to the body. We didn't have to break in, though. The place was unlocked."

"So when can we go in?"

"Not until the forensics guys are finished, probably by tonight."

"Have you notified her parents?"

"They're coming up tomorrow to try to identify her. I think it's going to be difficult, but they told me she had a gold cross similar to the one Marsh found on the body. They're bringing her dental records. Nice people. Their only child." Sam took deep breath, and I could see the phone call had been tough for him. "They own a bakery in Boston's North End. Not wealthy, though. They told me Liliana was here on a scholarship."

"She have a car?"

"A blue VW beetle. The old Type 1, not the new kind." I knew the last of the old beetles were produced in 1979, and since then had become collector items. I had driven the older version in college and had cried when it threw a rod and had to be junked.

"John checked the impound lots here and in Brunswick, Bath, Freeport and Yarmouth. Found nothing, that right, John?" asked Sam.

"Yessir, but I will check with Portland tomorrow." Deputy John Smith, he of the common Pilgrim name, was so average in appearance you'd hardly notice him. He had brown hair, brown eyes, was of medium height and weight, and had plain Jane facial features. I'd always thought he'd become a deputy to give himself an identity. The one thing that *was* unforgettable about him was his voice - a deep, rich bass, which never failed to surprise me when I heard it. He was also extremely intelligent and never missed a detail.

Just then a silver Mercedes coup came barreling down the road with a trail of dust behind it. It pulled up with a skid in front of the house and in a minute we were enveloped in a gray cloud that left us coughing. When the dust cleared, Bitsy Wellington was teetering toward us on five inch spike heels, her face set and determined.

"Oh Lord, why is *she* here?" I said under my breath.

"That's the same question I think Sam is going to ask her, but maybe a bit more nicely," John tried to whisper.

"Sheriff Brewster," Bitsy barked, stopping at the bottom of the stairs. "What have you found?"

"Nice to see you, Ms. Wellington. We've just begun here. The forensics people are going over the house," he replied amiably.

"Well, I would like to look inside. I need to know what's going on."

"I am afraid that isn't possible. This is an ongoing police investigation, and until we determine whether or not this is a crime scene, you can't enter the house. And we can't give you any information about what we find. In fact, you shouldn't be here."

"As Dean of Students, I have the right to be here. Liliana was one of our students and I have to report back to the President of the college. Certainly if *she* can be here," she said, indicating me with her head, "I don't see why I can't."

"Ms. Wellington," Sam replied with great patience, "Perhaps I didn't make myself clear enough. This is an ongoing police investigation, and we can't release any information until it's concluded. And as far as Rhe is concerned, I officially requested her presence." Since he didn't go on to explain why, I wondered what he was thinking.

"Then what am I to tell the President?"

"Just tell him we'll keep him up to date with the investigation, insofar as we can."

"See that you do." With that, she turned on her heels, and stalked back to her car. She spun out as she'd come, in a gray cloud.

"Well, you got the full Bitsy treatment," I told Sam. "I've gotta go pick up Jack. Will you call me tonight when you're able to get into the house? And let me know when you get the names of the students in Liliana's classes. We," I hopefully emphasized the we, "might find a classmate who had two or more classes with her and might know her. Of course now that you have ruffled Miss Bitsy's feathers, it may take a little more time to get those names."

"If she's as anxious to please the President of the college as it appears, we might get them even sooner," he countered.

I had just turned to leave when it occurred to me he hadn't confirmed his reservation for dinner the next night. "Have you decided to eat Chez Brewster tomorrow?"

"What are you having?"

"Meat loaf."

"Sounds good. I need to talk to you and Will anyway," he added mysteriously. "I'll plan to be there around 6:30. Just please don't make that broccoli casserole again," he said, grimacing and giving me a hug. "You know I love you, but I think your kitchen is an alien planet. You need to take lessons from Paulette." I should have been hurt to the core by that, but I knew he was teasing. Paulette had in fact been trying to teach me, and ketchup notwithstanding, the meat loaf was her recipe.

When I got home with Jack, I suggested to Will that we eat out at our favorite Chinese restaurant. I hoped this would help me avoid talking about where I had been that afternoon. The next night's dinner was already weighing heavily on me for more reasons than the food - I knew Sam was going to talk about the investigation, and Will wasn't going to like it. Plus I was determined to head back out to Bridge Road if Sam called, and he did, around 9 PM.

"Still interested in seeing the inside of the house?"

"Very. Be there in ten minutes."

"Who was that?" Will asked when I hung up.

"Sam. He asked me if I would take a look inside the murder victim's house. The forensics guys just finished up."

"At this time of night? Why are you still involved?"

"I think he wants a woman to look at her stuff. Maybe I'll notice something Sam and his deputies won't."

"I don't want you out there at night." Will's voice was taking on an edge. *Good grief, he'd given me an order.*

I took a deep breath. "Sam and the deputies will be there. How dangerous do you think it can be?"

Will let out a noise that sounded like a bull, just before it charges, then was quiet for several moments. "When will you be back?" he asked.

I went to get my jacket and as soon as my back was turned, pumped my fist in celebration. "Shouldn't be late. Gotta work tomorrow. Don't forget Sam's coming to dinner tomorrow night." I shrugged my jacket on.

"What are we serving?" I could hear the sarcasm in his voice.

"Meat loaf, with lots of catsup." By then I was already at the back door and was outside before he could say anything else.

⤜⤛

Once at Liliana's house, I donned the blue paper booties and white latex gloves offered by John at the door.

"Rhe," boomed John, "you can look but you can't touch. Understood?"

I nodded in agreement and stepped inside to check out the house's layout. Sam was currently in a rather large room on the left side of the hallway, which had the fireplace corresponding to the chimney. There was a black gas insert with fake logs. The furnishings were fairly new, comfortable and colorful, and there was a braided rug on the floor. Probably purchased from a local furniture outlet but definitely not cheap. My overall impression was one of style and tidiness. There was an addition to the back of the house, which could be entered by a door at the rear of the room. It housed a tiny bedroom with an attached bath, and the bed and bath furnishings were Laura Ashley. *Where did Lili get the money for this?* I gingerly opened the medicine cabinet door. No serious meds, just aspirin. No tampons or pads either.

I decided to concentrate on the right side of the hall, where there was a dining room with a table and four chairs, and in front of a side window, a desk and chair. To the back through a wide door was a galley kitchen. Starting in the kitchen, which was well-equipped, I noted there were no dirty dishes and no trash in the wastebasket. The food in the refrigerator was not fresh — out-of-date milk, a browning head of lettuce, soft cucumbers, lo-fat dressing, some sliced cheese. In the freezer there were boxes of Lean Cuisine dinners, a bag of coffee beans, and a carton of soy ice cream. There was also a leaning stack of ice cube trays, and I could see something behind them. I nudged the stack a little to get a better view and discovered what looked like an appointment book. I wanted to grab it, but mindful of John's warning, restrained myself. In the dining room, there were a wireless keyboard and a mouse on the desk by the window, and cords for a computer, but no computer.

I walked back through the hall to find John and Sam and asked, "Did you find anything?"

"Nothing, not even dust," replied John. "Forensics found some finger-prints, but it's clear this place has been cleaned."

"Anything that might let us know where she was and who she might have been with, has been taken care of, it seems," Sam added.

"I agree," I replied. "Did forensics take her computer?"

"There wasn't one."

"Well Liliana definitely had a computer, so it's been taken, either by her or someone else. I think it's a laptop, because there's a keyboard and mouse so she can use it like a desk top. Did forensics find any thumb drives?"

"Not that I know of."

"They did miss one thing. Check in the freezer. There looks to be an appointment book behind the ice cubes."

John looked at me quizzically. "In the freezer?"

"Yup, but I didn't touch it. Would like to look at it tomorrow after it's been dusted, though. So what do you think? Don't ya think this girl has stuff that's way too nice for a college student on a scholarship?"

"I agree, Rhe," John answered, lowering his voice somewhat and glancing around. "Some of this furniture I couldn't afford on _my_ salary. Of course this place might have come furnished."

"Why would a landlord renting a house like this furnish it with such nice furniture? And if she's on a scholarship, why isn't she living in a dorm on campus? Unless she has another source of income that she didn't want people to know about ..." I pondered.

The thought hung there for a minute, then stuck with me all the way home, along with the question of whether the lack of tampons was significant.

8

Wednesday's shift in the ER alternated between quiet and pandemonium. At first, there were just a few babies and children with fevers. Then a case of shingles arrived, followed by a broken arm, a cardiac arrest, and a compound tibia-fibula fracture. At 4 PM, I drove wearily to the police station to look at whatever had been cleared from Liliana's house and examine the class lists. I'd do some checking around campus the next day if I could find some students who had more than one course with Liliana.

Ruthie was not at her desk, so I passed go and went directly to Sam's office.

"Hi there. Any news from forensics?" I asked as I sat down.

"Not much trace evidence and no blood anywhere."

"Identifiable fingerprints?"

"Yup. Most of the prints were Liliana's, but you aren't going to believe this. Some came back to Bitsy Wellington."

My face must have shown my surprise because Sam gave me a satisfied smirk. I had to ask: "How did her prints get on file?"

"Not allowed to tell you that, Rhe, sorry."

"What, and change my opinion of her?" I snorted. "How do you think they got there? Did she maybe go out to the house before giving us Liliana's name?"

"I'd bet my paycheck on that, but why would she? That's the question." Sam frowned, then brightened. "Someone else's prints popped up, too."

"Who?"

"Well, now that we're linked into the FBI's Automated Fingerprint Identification System, it pulled up a heavy hitter from Boston named Bruce Gavoni. I have no idea why his prints would be there either. He's one bad character."

"This just gets stranger by the minute...... Did you get the class lists?"

"I did, but you're going to need to spread them out. You want a room to look at them and go through her stuff?" I nodded, and Sam took me to one of the interview rooms.

The very first things I perused were the class lists. I made note of names that appeared more than once, which classes, and their dates and times. There were three names that appeared twice and one student, a girl, had three classes with Liliana.

Her date book had nothing other than notes indicating when assignments were due, days to pick up dry cleaning, lists of items to be purchased at the local supermarket - nothing even mildly relevant to the investigation and certainly nothing obvious to merit hiding it in the freezer. Then I noticed the initials A/EA next to the Saturday for several weekends before her body was found. Maybe A/EA was something worth hiding, and I made a note to see if I could figure out what it stood for. Just as I closed the date book, Sam stuck his head in the doorway and asked whether dinner was still at 6:30. Since it was now 5 PM, a disaster was brewing.

⌘

I made a record-breaking loop through the grocery store, then raced home with the dinner fixings, calling Will along the way. He had thoughtfully gotten Jack through his homework and was setting the table.

"Are you cooking or is it take-out?" he asked humorlessly. "I thought Sam was coming over." From the tone of his voice, I could tell I was in deep shit.

"He is and I am making that meat loaf - takes 45 minutes, but we can eat by seven fifteen. I bought the rest ready-made except for the green beans. You know Sam is always late, so I've got time."

Silence. Then, "What have you been doing this afternoon? Poking around?" A favorite term of his when he's unhappy with my going places I ordinarily wouldn't and he thinks I shouldn't.

"Please don't be mad. I'm on my way home. We can talk after dinner. I think I have a way I can help Sam. Let's just drop this until we all have a chance to talk about it together, okay? Please?"

"Just get home soon." He hung up, and I knew this was going to be a tough evening.

I bustled in the door, dropped my bag and notes on the counter, and managed to prepare the meatloaf and pop it in the oven in 20 minutes flat. Add to that frozen mashed potatoes, thawed and cooked in the microwave with a dash of garlic, and steamed green beans baked in the oven with mushroom soup, soy sauce, and fried onions, and I had the dinner by seven twenty. Sure enough, Sam was twenty minutes late. My own tardiness was redeemed by the time dinner was over – I knew Sam was addicted to garlic mashed potatoes, Jack loved the green bean casserole, and Will was just happy to have a hot meal on time. Dessert was coffee and an elegant dish of double chocolate ice cream, which Jack was allowed to take into the family room while he watched a show on TV. I had scored with dinner, but it was time to talk.

I handed a copy of my notes on the case to Sam while we were sipping our coffee. He read them over and handed me a picture of Liliana. She was absolutely stunning, making the horror I'd seen on the soccer field all the worse. Long, curling dark hair, brown eyes, and a wide welcoming smile - she must have turned heads. Sam asked me if I had a line on the van.

"No, but that's on my list of things to check out, along with trying to track down any friends Liliana might have had at Pequod."

"Liliana Bianchi?" asked Will, taking the picture. "I had her in my Intro to Psych class last year. She was a beautiful young woman." He stared at the picture for a long time, and I got a chilly feeling that he knew her better than he indicated. "It's a tragedy she's dead, but I don't see why Rhe needs to be involved in the investigation." This last was directed at his brother.

Ignoring Will's comment, I added sadly, "You couldn't tell what she really looked like from the body. Her parents aren't going to have an easy time tomorrow when they come to identify her. I want to help find the person who did this. No one should lose a child."

"This is where you leave it, Rhe! I'm not going to *allow* you to get any more involved," Will practically shouted. He was getting cranked up. I'd never heard him talk to me that way before. Worse, he was spouting off in front of Sam. Sometimes my spouse can really push my buttons, and this time he'd pushed them in a big way.

I jumped up and took a deep breath, feeling anger flush my face, and got ready to let him have it. Sam had been sitting there looking decidedly uncomfortable, but before I could say a word, he slapped the table to get our attention and cut me off. "Actually, Will, Rhe could be a great help with the investigation. She knows a lot of folks in the community and has a real knack for dealing with people."

"But she's not trained as a police investigator. Police get in danger, right? It's part of the job!"

Sam held up his hand. "Wait a minute. She can dig out information my deputies might have a hard time getting, and you know how difficult it's been covering Pequod with only two deputies. Having Rhe to do some legwork for us would really free up John and Phil.'

I sat down and Will continued to glare. Sam continued, "One of the reasons I came for dinner tonight, not that the thought of Rhe's cooking wouldn't entice me," this last was said with a smile that lightened the tension a bit, "is to ask Rhe to join the police department. As an official part-time consultant. That way we can keep an eye on her and what she is doing, and she has a legitimate reason for being out there asking questions."

He paused and then continued, "And we can pay her a little for her time. Wouldn't that help with Jack's sessions?" Jack was seeing a psychologist once a week to help him deal with his ADHD, something known only by the family and Paulette. The fee of $150 an hour, even once a week, carved deeply into our household budget, and we'd had to forego a vacation during the past summer because of it.

Will was about to erupt like Mt. Saint Helens. I knew that Sam's offering to hire me was going to smack him right in the middle of his male pride. After Jack was born, he'd had to face the fact we could not survive on his associate professor's salary and that I would have to work. There'd been more than a few arguments before he eventually accepted we had to be a two income family and I couldn't be a stay-at-home mom. Will stood up abruptly, banging his knees on the table. I frantically tried to make eye contact with Sam to let him know this conversation was going to head south, but Sam persisted, his voice getting louder.

"Don't say it. I knew this was something you wouldn't like. I came here knowing full well how you'd respond. But at least think about it. I really need Rhe. You're my brother for Christ's sake, and even if I *didn't* need Rhe, I'd want to help you. Hell, you're the only brother I have!" With that, Sam sagged back in his chair and waited for his younger brother to have at him.

According to their mother, when Will and Sam were growing up, they were constantly fighting. Sam liked to boss Will around, and Will responded by being obstinate as a mule. As adults, I'd never heard an angry word between them and assumed that with maturity had come mutual respect. I was hoping maturity would win out now.

Will muttered something under his breath that sounded like "Yeah, okay, what's my opinion worth in this house?" then asked gruffly, "Would you like more coffee?" He walked to the coffee pot and stood with his back to us for a long minute, apparently trying to get himself under control, then took a deep breath and got more half and half from the fridge. When he turned back with the coffee pot and the creamer, he was still tense but he'd calmed down. I knew he was angry, but figured our finances were an overriding concern, even if he didn't like it.

His glare softened a little, and he said to Sam, "Rhe and I will talk this over. I'm still not convinced. You'll keep a close eye on her? Not let her get out there on her own?"

"You know I will."

Lord love a duck. This just might work.

Sam left around nine with the remains of the meat loaf, which was novel because he'd never wanted the leftovers before. Will and I went back to the kitchen table. "What are you thinking?" I asked him.

Will was quiet for several minutes. Finally he said, "I'm really not happy about this. I know you. Sam will never be able to rein you in." He sighed, seemingly tired of the argument. "I'm thinking I have the most irritating wife in the world, who doesn't listen to me, even when she knows I'm right. But I love her. If this works, maybe it'll make things easier between us about your extracurricular activities." This last was said with a shake of the head. "I'm really sorry for talking to you like that, but I know you're fearless, and I don't mean that as a compliment. I'm still convinced you're going to get yourself in trouble. Maybe even get hurt." After a long pause, he finally said, "But I guess I am okay with giving it a chance."

We sat in a comfortable silence for a few minutes, and then he gave me that hopeful look he has when he's in the mood, and we headed up to bed without cleaning up the kitchen. Make-up sex with a large dose of gratitude can be a wonderful way to end a day.

9

The next day was chilly and rainy. Fog stood off the coast and threatened to move in, and a few leaves started to drop. I dressed Jack in a slicker and walked him to the bus stop; on the way back, kicking at wet leaves, I contemplated my plan for the rest of the day.

It was pretty simple. Two of Liliana's classes at Pequod met Tuesday and Thursday mornings. The first was at nine, Political Science, so I downloaded a map of the campus and put it in my backpack along with a notebook and a list of the students who had more than one class with Liliana. After slipping on my red slicker and a pair of clunky all-weather shoes, I drove to campus in time to be outside the Poli Sci class when it let out.

The class met in a four story building that was a nice mix of brick and stone, square with no frills. I took the elevator to the fourth floor and stood dripping quietly onto the tile floor and waited. At 9:50, the door opened, and a flood of chattering students rushed out. I was looking for Zoey Harris, a student who had three classes with Liliana, but I had no clue what she looked like. A rather tall, good looking male student came out of the room with two girls glued to either arm, paying rapt attention to his every word. Here was the person with the answer to my problem.

I stepped in front of him. "Excuse me. Sorry for interrupting, but could I ask you a question?"

He gave me the sort of exasperated look he might have given his mother, but answered politely enough, "Sure, I guess… what can I do for you, ma'am?" Amazing. His mother had raised him well.

"I am looking for Zoey Harris. Is she in this class with you?"

"Yeah. She's the tall blonde inside, talking to the instructor."

I gave him my thanks with a smile and as much youth and vivacity as I could muster. *What? He was very good-looking. I'm 37 but not dead.*

It took a full ten minutes for Zoey to conclude her animated conversation with the instructor. When she finally emerged from the classroom, I saw a model-thin young woman, all legs, dressed in a denim skirt so short heavens know what you would see if she bent over. She was wearing cowboy boots, the latest campus fad.

"Are you Zoey Harris? I asked, as she paused to drape her raincoat through her backpack.

"Yeah, and you are...?" she replied cautiously.

With a closer look, I saw she was wearing a good deal of make-up, perfectly done, which seemed strange for a wet day of running to classes. And chewing gum.

"My name is Rhe Brewster. I'm trying to find friends of Liliana Bianchi. Do you know her?"

"Yeah... why do you ask?"

"Is there somewhere we could go to talk? I'm consulting with the Pequod Police Department, and I'm hoping you can help me." It was so nice to be official.

"I guess," she replied hesitantly, but I sensed some curiosity. "There's a coffee bar on the ground floor of the building." We took the elevator down and I tried to make small talk - what was her major, what year she was, if she was enjoying her classes. To all of which she gave one or two word answers. *This is going to be a conversational riot,* I thought.

I bought myself a latte and Zoey a cappuccino, and we settled at a table in a corner. After swallowing her gum, Zoey sipped her hot drink slowly, relaxing into her chair. I asked her a few more inconsequential questions and she opened up, using longer answers. *Who knew caffeine could have this effect on a college student?* After a pause, I gently told her about Liliana, since I doubted she would know about her classmate's death. Zoey's eyes widened and filled with tears, and she set her cup down and covered her face with her hands. It was clear she had no clue what had happened. I let her have a couple of minutes to get her mind around the fact Liliana was dead.

"Mind if I ask you some questions about Liliana?" I asked when her apparent crying had quieted, handing her a napkin for the few tears I saw on her cheeks.

"Yeah, I guess so." She carefully wiped her eyes, then took a sip of her coffee.

"When was the last time you saw her?"

"She hasn't been in class since last week. I think the last time I saw her was in Poli Sci last Tuesday. We usually come down here for coffee afterward, since our next classes don't meet for an hour." She made an involuntary hiccup and asked, "How did she die? Was it an accident?"

"Zoey, I'm really sorry to have to tell you this.... her body was found on a local soccer field last Friday. We only discovered yesterday it was Liliana. I can't give you any more details, but anything you can tell me about her will really help the police in their investigation. Right now, the police are treating it as a homicide."

"Oh God, she was murdered?" Her eyes widened and her hand holding the coffee cup started to shake.

"Yes, and you can see why what you tell me could be important. Did she say anything to you about her plans for the rest of the week or last weekend?"

She took several deep, shuddering breaths. "No, nothing. We just talked about the exam this Friday."

"Are you sure there's nothing else?"

"Well, we always kinda talk about this hottie in our class."

"The tall one with the reddish hair?"

"Yeah, Kelly. He's the quarterback on the football team and a real player, if you know what I mean. He asked me out earlier this semester, but I turned him down. He's a jerk. He hit on Lili right after I rejected him. She actually thought he was nice."

"Did she agree to go out with him?"

"Nah, I'm pretty sure she was already seeing someone. After I warned her to avoid Kelly, I know she didn't go out with him."

"Do you have any idea who she *was* seeing?"

"Not a clue. Lili was pretty quiet about her personal life."

"Does Kelly have a last name?"

"Yeah, Ingram."

"Can you tell me anything about him?"

"Just that he thinks he's the world's gift to women."

"Does he have a temper? Do you know if he ever got rough with any of his dates?"

"I don't think so. He may be conceited, but the only place I've ever seen or heard he's rough is on the football field."

I noted his last name and this information in my notebook. "What else do you know about Lili? Is that what her friends call her?"

"Yeah, nobody called her Liliana." She looked thoughtful for a minute and then said, "I know she was really smart, and I think she was here on a scholarship."

"That's good information, Zoey. Let me ask you this: do you know why she lived off campus? Have you ever seen her place?"

"No, we weren't friendly like that. We talked here on campus because we have a few classes together, but we never went out or anything." Zoey said this rather rapidly and avoided looking at me. I was 95% sure she was lying. "Except for coffee and occasionally lunch, but we always met here. Are you sure you can't tell me anything at all about how she died?" she added, deflecting the conversation away from her relationship with Lili. *Nice touch.*

"No, I'm really sorry, I can't. I'm sure you can understand - the investigation is just getting started. Is there anyone else on campus who knew Lili fairly well? We're trying to make a timeline of her activities and haven't much to go on. Can you think of anyone else I could talk to?"

"Well, there is this one girl. They had a class together and Lili mentioned studying with her, so maybe she knows something. Her name is Tanya Davis."

I had Tanya's name on my list, and she was in Lili's 11 o'clock class. I checked my watch. 10:15. *Plenty of time to catch her.* "Can you tell me what she looks like?" This way I wouldn't have to embarrass myself by asking the first good-looking kid I ran into.

"Sure. She's African American, if that helps. Really tall, not very pretty." A hint of criticism crept into Zoey's voice. I'd already noted that like Lili, Zoey certainly fell in the category of what I called the 'Beautiful People'. It'd been my experience that the beautiful and handsome kids tended to congregate with each other, at least in high school and somewhat in college, so it was not surprising she and Lili hung out together. And I was also pretty sure Zoey had at least a few brains to go with her looks. She was definitely socially adept.

Zoey looked at her wrist watch, which I couldn't help but notice was thin, gold, and looked to be a Patek Philippe. I glanced at her other wrist and saw she had a diamond tennis bracelet, which went with what I had assumed were fake diamond studs in her ears. A little pricey for a college student if they were real. "Is there anything else, Ms. Brewster? 'Cause if not, I need to look over my notes before my next class."

"Do you happen to have Lili's phone number by any chance?"

"Sorry, I don't. Really." Zoey stood up and grabbed her coffee cup.

"Let me give you my cell number in case you think of anything." I tore a page out of my notebook and scribbled my name and number on it.

"Thanks for the coffee. Bye." She grabbed the page, jammed it in a pocket of her skirt, and practically ran from the table, trailing her backpack and raincoat. She stopped by the door to chat animatedly with a couple of girls coming in, and from the looks on their faces, I could imagine the conversation. News of Lili's death would be all over campus by noon.

I enjoyed my latte leisurely, consulted my campus map, and jotted down notes from my conversation with Zoey while I waited for Lili's pre-law class to end. I guessed she was thinking about being a lawyer. Since she had a scholarship, she was probably bright. But then again, maybe it had been awarded on need. By the time I walked to the building next door, the rain had slowed to a drizzle, but the campus was getting foggy - the low sort that hangs on the lawns and moves slowly across the sidewalks. The class was on the ground floor, and I timed it perfectly. A tall black girl was leaving the building as I walked up.

"Excuse me? Are you Tanya Davis?"

"Yeah. You're the policewoman, right?" she replied, looking skeptical. *Wow, news around here travels faster than a speeding bullet.*

Tanya was over six feet tall, toned but not muscular, and clad in the typical college uniform of frayed jeans and a T shirt. Hers said "GEEK is the new sexy" in blazing red letters. She had a bulky backpack slung over one shoulder, to which a blue windbreaker was tied.

"I'm just a police consultant. I couldn't even cuff Dean Wellington," I said with a smile, hoping to break the ice.

It fell flat. Tanya scowled, but at least she was listening. "I heard Lili's dead. I had nothing to do with it. Do I have to talk to you?"

"No, but all I want is to ask you a few questions. I know you and Lili studied together, so you might know something about her that would help us track her movements last week."

After a very long silence, Tanya said, "Well, okay. That bitch Zoey tell you about me? She's a pain in the ass. I don't know what Lili saw in her."

That set me back for a second, but I realized Tanya would never have been part of Zoey's circle, especially as the athlete which she appeared to be. She was just this side of attractive, with a broad face and even features and long, straightened hair pulled back from her face with a red head band. There was a little acne on her chin.

Then it occurred to me I'd never known a college student to pass up free food, so I asked, "How about I buy you lunch? You gotta eat, right?" If coffee had softened Zoey, maybe I could win Tanya over and get her to open up about Lili over some real food.

Tanya thought for a minute and then said, "Sure, but not here. People around here are too nosy. Always up in everyone else's business."

We walked to my car, and I drove us about two miles to an inexpensive restaurant called Moe's, packed with tourists in the summer but quiet now that the kids were back in school. It had fabulous lobster rolls, packed with large, sweet chunks of meat and drizzled with mayonnaise. Remembering that I could put this on my police expense account made it even better. On the way to Moe's, I found out my first impression was totally wrong. Tanya indeed had a scholarship, but was studying math and physics and was one of only seven black women in her class. She was frustrated with the small number of minority students on campus, liked her classes, and had some harsh things to say about Zoey and her friends, who all lived in her dorm.

After eating lunch, which for Tanya was a large plate of fried clams, fries and coleslaw, we got down to business. By that time, Tanya seemed more relaxed.

"How well did you know Lili?"

"Pretty well. We were in two classes together. She was a real sweet girl and pretty smart, you know. Studying with her helped me a lot." After a pause, she said, "I don't get why she had to die! She was so nice to everyone!" Her voice rose sharply, and I reached out and patted her hand to calm her. Despite the fact I had said nothing about how the body was found or its condition, she had figured that Lili's death was not an accident, probably confirmed by the fact I was around asking questions.

"Do you know anyone who had it in for her? Did she have any enemies? People making trouble for her?"

"No, and I don't know anyone who would."

"I take it you've thought about this."

"Well, just since word got around. My boyfriend told me this morning about a body being found, but I never imagined it would be her." She shuddered as she said this.

"How did he find out about it?"

"I think he said he read it in the P & S."

"Have you ever been to her place?"

"Once, last year. We pulled an all-nighter studying for a final. House looked like it was ready to fall down, but inside it was really cool, you know? She has - had - some nice things, you know."

"Do you know how she afforded all those nice things? Zoey thinks she was on a scholarship."

Tanya looked honestly surprised, but then said, "Should've figured that. At first, I thought her parents were rich. Plus she hung around sometimes with Zoey and her crowd. They're all from private schools and have money to burn." Some hostility crept back into her voice. "But Lili wasn't like them, you know? She went out of her way to hang with me and my friends."

"Did she ever talk about her parents?"

"Very little. Just that they were great. She did mention they were using some of their retirement savings to put her through college. That was when I first thought she might not be rich, you know? Said she wanted to help them out."

"Did she say how?"

"Nope. Conversation ended right there. She seemed uncomfortable talking about it, so I didn't push."

"Can you tell me anything at all about how Lili spent her free time? Anyone else I should talk to?"

"No one else I can think of who would know more about her. She lived off campus, and that usually means a lot of time spent driving back and forth and studying at home, you know? There is one thing, though. Lots of times, me and my friends invited her to hang with us on the weekends, you know, for a movie or pizza, but she could never go. When I asked her why, she always said she had to visit her parents. So we gave up asking. Funny though, I've seen her couple of times on campus on weekends during the last month or so."

"Was she with anyone when you saw her?"

"Yeah, some white guy. But I only got a glimpse, you know."

"Could you tell me what he looked like?"

"Tall, dark hair, dressed like a student. It was only for a second."

Darn.

As we drove back to campus, I returned to the question of where Lili's money came from and asked Tanya if she thought Lili had a job.

She looked thoughtful for a minute. "You know, she's been hanging out with Zoey a lot more this year," she finally replied.

"That's interesting. I got the impression Zoey didn't know Lili very well. Is it possible the source of her money was somehow tied to Zoey?"

"Nah, probably not. Besides, Zoey has the reputation of being a tight-wad, you know? She threw a birthday party for a friend last year and collected big bucks ahead of time from the people coming to the party. Rumor was, she didn't pay anything herself and kept the extra. News like that gets around, you know?"

We drew up to Tanya's dorm. As she was getting out of the car, I asked, "You wouldn't by chance have Lili's phone number, would you?"

"No, I don't, and that's funny, you know? I never even saw her use one," Tanya replied.

"Is that so? You never saw her use a cell phone?"

"Nope."

I made a mental note to follow up on the cell phone angle. I also needed to figure out where Lili's money was coming from. "Is there a student employment office here on campus?" I asked as she gathered her windbreaker and backpack.

"Yup, it is in the basement of Tarson Hall. Head down this road and take a left and it's the second building on the right."

"If you think of anything else, give me a call, will you?" I tore another page from my notebook, wrote down my name and cell number and handed it to Tanya. "Anything at all."

"Sure and thanks for the lunch, Mrs. Brewster," she called as she hefted her backpack and headed for the front door of the dorm.

As I watched her walk away, I decided if I heard the phrase 'you know' one more time, I was going to scream.

10

I didn't have to pick Jack up until 3:30, leaving me plenty of time to check out the Student Employment office. Tanya had directed me to Tarson Hall, which turned out to be a bland, one story brick box with parking on the side. After pushing through the front door, I descended a flight of stairs, following the Student Employment signs. I spent no more than five minutes in the office because the anorexic and surly receptionist was completely unhelpful.

"Did you know Liliana Bianchi?"

"No."

"Are there records of students employed by the college?"

"Yes."

"Can you look up Liliana Bianchi's name?"

"No, and furthermore, I can't give out that information even if I find it."

Would she like to suck on a lemon? It might improve her disposition. Another job for Sam. I turned away exasperated.

On my way out, I glanced at the bulletin board, which had a crazy quilt of colorful notices for job opportunities, stapled all over it and on top of each other. Most were hand written or computer printed, but a few were professionally done. One poster in particular caught my eye because of its size and its large, colorful pictures of a cruise ship and a tropical beach. *Nice work if you could get it.*

$\backsim\!\backsim$

Once home, with Jack settled down with a snack and his homework, I entered notes from my interviews with Zoey and Tanya into the computer file on the case and indicated my distrust of Zoey. I closed the page and decided to look for Zoey and Kelly Ingram on Facebook. My husband had created a Facebook profile several years ago, on which he posted the homework assignments for his class, so I used his password and searched their names. Unfortunately, their profiles were marked as private, revealing only barebones information and the standard gray profile picture, so I needed to get them to 'friend' me. Will frequently got friend requests from people he didn't know and half the time accepted them, thinking they were students. So I created an anonymous e-mail, a Facebook profile using my middle and maiden name, and downloaded a picture of an attractive college age woman I'd copied from an online site. I added some comments about Pequod that made it look like I was a student and mentioned Zoey's name in the friend request I sent to Kelly and Kelly's name in the one I sent to Zoey. I hoped to be 'friended' without any question on their parts.

After dinner, I checked Facebook, and no surprise, both Zoey and Kelly had accepted my request. Kelly's page was full of pictures of him with a variety of young women, several taken on an unidentified tropical beach. One of the women looked incredibly familiar, but I couldn't place her.

Zoey's page was amusing, egocentric, and full of gossip with friends about the day's happenings, along with some not so flattering comments about the real me. Apparently I was at least 50, dressed like a model for Goodwill, and wore clodhoppers on my feet. *Really?* In part of a discussion with an Angela Muller, whose name I noted, the name Caribbean Queen came up.

Zoey: "Any decision on the Caribbean Queen?"

Angela: "Not yet, still thinking about summer options. Job hunting is such a drag. I might just take some summer courses and stay on campus."

Zoey: "No way! CQ's hours are really short and the pay is great! You'll meet some awesome people, too."

Zoey was working hard to sell her on it, and it was clear she'd worked on the ship the summer before. As I recalled, that colorful ad on the wall in the Employment Office was for the Caribbean Queen. Given Zoey's link to the Caribbean Queen, I looked for an online site. What I found was essentially the same advertisement I'd seen in the Student Employment office, which read, in large, colorful letters:

"Are you looking for some fun this summer?
Want to spend time in the Caribbean? We are
looking for college students with a sense of
adventure, to work as busboys and housemaids
on our ship, the Caribbean Queen. Lots of free
time to enjoy the sun and sand. We pay roundtrip
airfare to Florida. Call us at ...."

It ended with a Boston phone number and an invitation to contact them at any time by e-mail, using an online application. I decided to fill in their application, using my Facebook name and fictitious identity, then sent it off, with the hope it might lead to something.

⌒⌒

On Fridays, I work 2-10 PM, so my mornings are free. I sent a copy of my notes to Sam and asked him to get employment information on Lili out of the anorexic empress of the Student Employment Office.

Jack had a teacher work day and I'd promised to take him sailing. The day was ideal, and with a nice onshore wind, the weather promised us a fair ride. We kept the Glass Trinket, a 12 foot Beetle Cat, at the yacht club where I'd sailed when I was growing up. Our continuing membership at the club was an annual gift from my sailing-addicted parents. Cat boats feature a gaff-rigged sail and cedar hull with an oak frame, which meant I spent time every spring sanding, caulking, painting and varnishing. A Beetle Cat has two distinct features: a quadrilateral sail, or gaff rigging, raised by and suspended from a pole or spar attached to the top of the sail, and a centerboard, a retractable keel that pivots out of a slot in the center line of the hull. Jack had been introduced to the boat on previous sails, but today I was going to give him a little responsibility. The tiller is a wooden strut, which is fitted to the top of the boat's rudder post and used for steering, and I had Jack sit in the stern and handed him the tiller.

"Jack, I want you to hold the tiller steady. I'm going to lower the centerboard and raise the sail. Do you remember what the centerboard does?"

"Keeps us from sliding sideways? And we can raise it to go over shallow bottoms, like a skim board!" he proudly answered.

"Hold her steady."

We glided away from our mooring buoy. I took over the tiller and the main sheet, the line controlling the sail, and we headed out of the harbor. Will was a solid land lubber who got seasick just walking on a dock, but Jack had taken to swimming and sailing like a true New Englander. I wanted him to become comfortable with the catboat and eventually sail it on his own, which I'd done by the time I was nine.

"Ready about, Jack. Hard alee!" I yelled the words sailors use to let everyone know that the boom is going to swing over and the sail shift to the other side, to ensure no one is knocked in the head or worse, overboard. "What did we just do?"

"Tack, Mom." Tacking means changing course back and forth as you crossed the path of the oncoming wind, so in the face of the onshore wind, we had to take a zig-zag course leaving the harbor. Once out of the harbor, we sped north along the coast in a beam reach, where the wind comes across the beam or width of the boat. As we hugged the shoreline, we could see there were huge homes and estates behind the coastal tree line, atop rocky cliffs. Salt spray splashed and the waves thrummed against the hull. Eventually, we came about, heading south, and came back into the harbor on a quiet and smooth run, with the wind from behind and the sail eased out at a 90° angle to the boat. By the time we moored, Jack's eyes were sparking, our cheeks were ruddy and our clothes were damp from salt spray.

As we ambled to my Jeep, Jack looked longingly to his right and said, "I sure wish the swim club stayed open later than Labor Day. We could take a swim and then get warm in the hot tub." The club where Jack swam in the summer was slightly north of the marina, and it had a large hot tub to warm swimmers between races and also the polar bears who liked to swim in the ocean. *Hadn't Marsh said that the body might have been kept in a hot tub?*

"How would you like to go over there and snoop around?" I asked as I picked up the pace.

"Yeah, Mom. What are we looking for?"

"Treasure? You never know what the wind might have blown in." I rummaged around in the back of the Jeep to see if I could find anything that would hold water. There was a plastic drink cup under the back seat, so thanking the fast food gods, I got Jack into his rear child seat and drove the short distance to the beach club.

The club was an old single story cement square, containing changing rooms and showers and one large room for meetings, land lessons, and a snack shop. It had been closed up for the season and had a deserted and forlorn air, made all the creepier by the fact that heavy clouds were moving in and it was getting chilly. The pool on the ocean side of the building was full and uncovered and was beginning to accumulate leaves and twigs. I left Jack to look in the pool for something interesting, while I made a beeline for the hot tub at the far end. I unhooked a corner of the tub's cover and a fetid odor blossomed out. *Yech,* I thought, trying not to gag. Opening the cover a little further revealed turbid, filthy water. Pinching my nose with one hand, I swooped up a sample into the plastic cup with the other and swirled it around to remove any vestiges of whatever it had held. I dumped the contents on the ground, then took another sample before re-hooking the cover. I knew this sample would not be admissible in court because of how I'd gotten it, but if it contained Lili's DNA, it would give us a starting point.

I drove us home as quickly as I could, while holding the plastic cup between my knees. Ancient Jeeps don't have cup holders. I explained to Jack that the club directors would need to be told about the foul smelling hot tub and that I had a taken a sample of the water to show them. Well, some of that was true.

After settling Jack in with Tyler for the afternoon, with a quick briefing for Paulette about what had been happening, I left for work a little early in order to drop the water sample off with Marsh. Since he wasn't in, I left it with Oliver.

The ER was packed. A patient had come in with a gangrenous foot just before I got there. The smell and his moans permeated the facility and more than a few of the people in the waiting room left.

Because we had only one ER doc available, we called up to Surgery for someone to help out. I didn't recognize the physician who came running in. He was Latino, with smooth caramel skin, dark wavy hair, and a chubby face with full lips and bedroom eyes. All of this was offset by the fact he was generously overweight, reminding me of a hero in an old black and white film who seduces the heroine, but makes you wonder why he was considered such a stud muffin.

"I'm Ed Montez," he said with a warm smile, "the new transplant surgeon, who is apparently getting pressed into service this morning. Is this normal for the ER?" He glanced around as he shook my hand, then pulled on some latex gloves. "No, this is very unusual - we only have one doc here this morning, and he's not long out of residency. I thought we should call someone with more experience."

"Good idea. I guess this happens in a smaller hospital," he said with a deprecating air that rankled me. But after observing him examine the patient with gangrene and then explain the situation to him both patiently and kindly, I decided he was one of the good guys.

Nancy Ennis and I were working the same shift, and we were huddling over an early dinner in the cafeteria when I told her about meeting Dr. Montez. She was ecstatic that another board-certified transplant surgeon had been hired by the hospital's Department of Surgery and the Board of Directors.

"Dr. Montez was hired to organize and expand the transplant division," she said, nodding her head in total agreement with the decision. Her curly hair was bouncing up and down with her nods. "You know the hospital is only doing bone and ACL grafts right now? I think the administration is hoping we can graduate to the big time with organ transplants."

"Is Montez qualified for that?"

"Definitely. He trained at Mass General and did a fellowship in heart transplant surgery at the University of Chicago. You know I trained as an OR nurse," she reminded me. "There've been no openings since I came here, and I'm hoping this new guy will generate a position or two that I can apply for." Nancy had been at Sturdevant for two years and she was bright and ambitious. Her only focus at the present time seemed to be her career, and I felt a little, tiny twinge of jealousy that my own was so set and routine.

"What's happening on the romance front?" I asked, wondering if she might ever contemplate getting serious about someone. I'd noticed she was a magnet for the men we worked with: she had a sweet face with a field of freckles on each cheek and her body had the kind of curves that made men's heads turn. She was also one of the few people I knew who made you smile whenever you saw her.

"Well, I *have* been seeing someone from here in the hospital, but I'm not sure I'm ready to talk about it. You might think I'm a cougar."

"I seriously doubt that! How old *are* you?"

"Twenty-eight."

"Dear heavens, you're a youngster. Who is it? Spill."

"Well… it's Oliver, Marsh's technician."

My mouth must have dropped open, because Nancy quickly added, "He's a really sweet guy and more mature than you might think."

"Does he have a college degree?"

"Sort of," she equivocated. "He has a Medical Assistant Associate Degree. But he treats me like a queen, Rhe, takes me to fancy restaurants in Portland instead of old Moe's, sends me flowers for no reason. We went to New York City for a long weekend and stayed at a fabulous hotel and saw some Broadway shows. The thing is, I don't think I should let myself get serious about him. He's a lot younger and I really want a job in the Surgery Department. And you know that'll play havoc with any normal schedule."

I got the feeling she was arguing with herself. *Where did Oliver get that kind of money on his salary as an assistant to Marsh?* I thought idly. *Maybe he's a rich heir?* I figured she really didn't want my opinion.

"Did you hear about the Pequod student who was brought in late last night?" Nancy asked suddenly, changing the subject.

"No, I only saw the logs for today's patients."

"I heard she was beaten up and she's in ICU. One of the plastic surgeons came in last night to work on her face."

"Look. I know I shouldn't ask, but do you know her name?" Technically, patient's names and injuries are not supposed to be shared, but it's a small town and a relatively small hospital. This sort of information would spread like oil on water.

"Sure, Tanya Davis. Do you know her?"

I bolted up from my chair and asked Nancy to clean up for me.

"Where's the fire?" she asked, puzzled.

"In the ICU," I called back to her as I ran from the cafeteria.

I found the charge nurse for the ICU, Dee Burton, at the nurse's station. She told me that Tanya was stable but had been badly beaten. Apparently, a young man had driven her to the hospital and carried her to the entrance door to the ER, yelled for help and then left. No one recalled what he looked like. I wondered if I were responsible for this. Maybe my questioning had led to the beating. My stomach started to churn.

"Do you know her?" asked Dee.

"Actually, I do. I had lunch with her yesterday. Is there any chance I could see her?"

"She's still pretty sedated, but I think it would be okay if you went in for a minute. I was just about to go in and check her vitals, but you can do it for me."

I treated my hands with antibacterial wash from the dispenser on the wall, then went through the sliding glass door that led to Tanya's room. My eyes were drawn to her head, swathed in bandages, with a cannula for oxygen leading from her nose. She had an IV line in and a heart monitor running. Only her eyes and mouth were visible and her eyes were puffed and swollen to slits. Several of her fingers were splinted, her knuckles were red and raw, and there were dark bruises forming on both arms, which lay unmoving on the sheet. A pulse oximeter was attached to one of her unsplinted fingers. Clearly she'd had one hell of a fight with her attacker.

I approached her bed, checked all the monitors, and seeing that she was doing well, leaned down and whispered, "Tanya? It's Rhe Brewster. Can you hear me?"

Her eyes tried to open, and she said something which I had to lean even closer to hear. "Water." I lifted the cup to her mouth and placed the straw between her swollen lips. She sucked up a bit of water and then motioned with her hand she'd had enough.

"Tanya, who did this to you?"

"My fault, not anybody."

"Did talking to me cause this?"

"No, something else." Her voice was barely a whisper.

"Who did this, Tanya?" I repeated. There was no reply as she drifted back to a drug-induced netherworld, and suddenly I remembered I was overdue in the ER.

As I exited her room, I came face to face with Sam. "I came by earlier but she was still sedated," he explained. "I take it you know her?"

"She's one of the students I interviewed yesterday. Didn't you read the notes I sent you?"

"Haven't gotten to them yet. Is she in any shape for me to talk to her?"

"She's drifting in and out but is sleeping now. I asked her who did it, but all I got was it was her fault. She said the beating's not linked to my talking to her, but she might not tell me even if it were. And she's nowhere near ready for a regular conversation."

"I'll check in on her later then. Her grandfather's coming up from Boston. Maybe he can shed some light on who might have done it. I'll go down to the ER with you." We got in the elevator, and he pushed the '1' button. "I'll have time to look over your notes by tomorrow."

"Good, I have a bunch of things to talk to you about."

"How about lunch tomorrow? Ernie's?" Ernie's is a small Italian place Sam and his deputies frequented, where the food went straight to my waistline.

"Sure, but please don't torture me by ordering pizza."

"No promises. See you tomorrow at noon." He gave me a hug and meandered to the door to the parking lot, stopping to chat with people along the way. He was a popular guy.

And I went back to work full of worry about what Tanya might tell me.

11

One of Jack's favorite treats was being allowed to wait up for me on Friday nights, but getting him to settle down for bed that night was a prolonged nightmare. After a long day on my feet and the mess with Tanya, losing my temper with Jack was just one more log on my personal pyre of maternal guilt and inadequacy.

"I'm a terrible mother," I moaned after Jack fell asleep at long last, and Will and I were finally in bed ourselves.

Will was reading a book and pushed his glasses up on his head to look at me.

"You're both going to be fine. He'll forget all about it by tomorrow morning. You can't beat yourself up every time you two have a bad day."

I leaned back against the pillows. "Will, there's something I haven't had a chance to tell you yet. I think it's why I flew off the handle with Jack tonight."

"What?"

"One of the students I interviewed yesterday about Lili — her name's Tanya Davis - was badly beaten last night. She's in the hospital."

Will, who had resumed reading his book, took off his glasses and gave me a stare. "Yeah, I know her. Tall black girl, very smart. What's your interest?"

"I think she's there because of me."

"How can you think that? What if this was a case of abuse, and not related to you? Maybe she has a boyfriend who got physical with her."

I looked at him, hoping this was true. He continued, "This sort of thing happens at the college more often than you might think. There're students who run counseling sessions on dating abuse in the dorms. I see the flyers all the time."

"You may be right," I answered rubbing my forehead, where a nasty headache was forming. "I could ask Dee to let me know who visits her. Don't the abusers usually feel remorse afterward? Maybe he'll show up."

Will turned and put his glasses and his book on the nightstand. When he turned back he said, "You need to stop thinking the whole world revolves around you, Rhe. Things happen you can't control. You're not to blame for everything."

After what I considered a bad day, his comment really hurt. I stared at him for a minute, then turned off the light and lay on my side with my back to him. Will turned off his light, moved over to cuddle and started kissing my neck. *Great. I have a bad day, he makes an insulting comment and then he wants to mess around.* I wiggled out of his grasp and said, "Look, I have a whopper of a headache coming on and I need to sleep it off. Not tonight."

Silence. Then Will moved back to his side of the bed, turned his back to me and soon was snoring softly. So much for reassurance and support from my husband. Sometimes it felt like I didn't know him.

⊂⊃

Saturday morning I was awakened by the smell of fresh coffee and frying bacon. Will was absent from his side of the bed, and I could hear muffled cartoons voices. I wandered sleepily downstairs and found Jack ensconced in front of the TV. He was attacking a plate of blueberry pancakes with bacon while watching a Disney cartoon. Will was just putting a platter of pancakes on the table for the two of us.

"I thought I was going to have to roust you, sleepyhead," he said, somehow managing to kiss me while pouring me a cup of coffee. "Sit, and we can figure out what we're doing today."

No sorry about last night or how are you feeling this morning? "Not awake yet," I mumbled, sitting down and helping myself to the pancakes. I poured cream in my coffee, added sugar and took a deep gulp, then slathered butter on my pancakes and topped them with warm maple syrup. After several bites, I was able to manage, "Better."

"Jack has a soccer game this morning, remember?" asked Will, joining me at the table with a plate of bacon in his hand.

"Sort of. But I've gotta meet Sam afterward to discuss some case notes I sent him. We're meeting at Ernie's for lunch. Can you and Jack manage on your own?"

"You bet, Mom," piped Jack from the family room, over the sound of animated chatter. "I want a cheeseburger and fries."

"Finish your breakfast first, big ears," I called back. Jack had apparently forgiven me. I turned to Will. "And I plan to check on Tanya this afternoon. That okay with you?"

"Sure, Jack and I will find something fun to do. See you after that?"

He still didn't recognize that what he'd said last night had hurt me. I gave up, he was clueless. "You bet. I'll call you," I snapped, but Will didn't notice.

After breakfast, I made a quick stab at tracking down the white van before we left for Jack's game. I decided to start with the phone book to get an idea of any local businesses that might use vans, thinking maybe one had an ad displaying a logo with a red arrow. There were plenty of bakeries, electricians, plumbers, contractors and handy man outfits, but no arrow logos. I Googled local possibilities, looking for the logo, before expanding my search to all of New England. No luck. Short of driving around looking for white vans, I couldn't figure out where to go with this clue.

⌒⌒

I met Sam at Ernie's a little after twelve in a somewhat better frame of mind. Jack's game had run late and implausibly, his team had won its second game. I settled on a large Italian salad, but salivated over the warm and meaty aroma of Sam's sausage and mushroom pizza. I filled him in on my interviews with Zoey and Tanya while crunching unenthusiastically on lettuce and croutons.

"Sam, it's clear from Zoey's Facebook page she worked on the Caribbean Queen. I went online to their website and submitted a fake application for work. They got back to me immediately with lots of questions and requests for pictures. I'm suspicious, because the whole setup is too good to be true."

"Why would you think that?"

"Well, I know Zoey comes from a well-off family, but Sam, she was wearing a Patek Philippe watch worth several thousands and what I think was a real diamond tennis bracelet. Plus the questions they asked when they contacted me were definitely targeted to young women."

"So what do you think it is?" he asked, taking a large bite of pizza.

"A front...." I hesitated.

Something that sounded like "Ah geez, Rhe, just give me whatever cockamamie idea you've got" emerged from his mouth full of pizza.

I decided to go for it. "Maybe I *am* out in left field, but what if she's involved in an escort service?"

Sam nearly choked. After taking several gulps of water and wiping his mouth with the back of his hand, he gave me a hard look. I knew this would take convincing.

"Look, if Lili was spending more time with Zoey this semester, and if Zoey is indeed working for the Caribbean Queen, what if she dragged Lili into it? That would explain where Lili got the money for the furnishings and house repairs."

"I'm not buying it, Rhe. An escort service with college girls, here in Pequod? If the Caribbean Queen is really a front for something else, I can think of a lot more likely possibilities." He shook his head in disbelief.

"Such as...?"

"Gambling, for example. Maybe money laundering."

"But it's one way to explain Lili's money, and we don't have any other leads. What if the Caribbean Queen is targeting college girls for their business? And their business is creating young, smart call girls. I know it's a real stretch, but I just have a gut feeling maybe we should check it out."

He sat silent for what seemed like an eternity staring at me. I stared right back. Finally, Sam picked up another slice of pizza and said, "I think your idea is nuts, but I have a friend with the Boston PD. I'll ask him to do some digging for me."

"Thanks, Sam, I...."

"If this turns out to be a wild goose chase, I swear you're going to owe me big time," he cut in, pointing the pizza at me.

"And if it really is something?"

"If it does turn out to be a front for another business, I'll see if they can send someone in under cover to check it out. Maybe a fictitious applicant. I have to let Boston handle this. And *do not* go off on your own on this," he said, taking an emphatic chomp.

Too late. "Yes sir." I gave him a salute, mentally kicking myself for the lie. "But you need to do this fast, okay? If Tanya's beating had anything at all to do with Lili's murder, there's going to be a big rush to cover up."

"Not to mention putting you in the crosshairs, again," he mumbled between chews. "Are you going to see Tanya today?"

"Right after this. I'll call you if she's able to talk."

"Another thing," I asked, remembering something I'd thought of right before falling asleep the night before, "Do you know who owns the house where Lili was staying?

"Not yet. I sent Phil over to the courthouse yesterday afternoon to see if he could dig up the owner but haven't talked to him today." Philip Pearce was his other deputy and a digital native who worked miracles with computers.

"Got another request."

"They just keep coming," I heard him mumble.

"There's an uncooperative woman guarding the student employment records at the college. She wouldn't tell me if Lili had been employed through that office. Could you put your considerable weight," said with a smile, "on getting her to open up?"

"Sure thing, I'll just add it to my list, Madam Consultant," Sam said, ignoring the jibe.

"How did things go with the Bianchis yesterday?"

Sam let out a noise halfway between a cough and a burp.

"Just great. They were both basket cases, even before we showed them the body. They made the identification, though I think it was mainly based on the necklace. Neither of them looked very long at her face. The dental records matched, so Marsh released the body. The family has already made arrangements for the funeral – it's on Monday."

"Do you know where?"

"Our Lady of the Blessed Sacrament in Chelsea, 11 AM."

"I was thinking I'd go, because I want to see who shows up."

"I was thinking the same thing," he said, pushing the last of the pizza in his mouth. "We can go together – maybe you can identify a few students and faculty for me. I'm hoping to talk to the parents again afterward, if possible."

"It's a date," I replied, immediately cringing. Sam gave me a weird look but apparently decided not to comment.

"What have you found out about the van Paulette and Beth what's-her-name saw near the field?"

"Beth Smith, and I made a start this morning, but it's going to be difficult. Couldn't find anything online and I may need to just drive around. Really efficient investigational technique, don'tcha think? But I'll keep on it," I promised.

"Well, whenever you get time. And be sure to tell Will where we're going on Monday. Don't you usually work on Monday?"

"I'll trade shifts with someone. Maybe Dee Burton - she covered for me last Friday for the soccer game and I can throw in the offer of an extra shift."

I finished my salad unenthusiastically, listening to Sam complain about some of the town's drunks and homeless he had to deal with on a daily basis. While he talked, I took a good look at my brother-in-law. *Here's a single, good-looking man nearing middle age, who rarely dates or goes out with friends because he's always working. He deserves a life.*

When we finished, I picked up the check for a change, and promised again to call him after I saw Tanya.

⌒⌒

When I got to the ICU, Dee greeted me with a smile. "What? You can't stay away when you're not working?"

"Actually, I am here to check on Tanya. How's she doing?"

"Much better, and her grandfather's here now. She'll be moved to the surgical floor later this afternoon. Do you want to talk with the grandfather?"

'Definitely."

"He's the gentleman sitting outside her room," indicating him with a nod of her head in his direction. "He's really worried because he has to go home tonight."

"Has anyone else come around to see her? A student, maybe?"

"Three young women tried to drop some flowers off this morning. They didn't realize we don't allow flowers in the ICU. They were a little ditsy, know what I mean?"

"Was one a tall blonde, rather pretty?"

"Yup, and there were two others, also rather pretty, but good God, why do they dress like hookers? I wouldn't let my daughter go out looking like that. One of them had a skirt so short I could see all the way to Portland, and one of them was wearing short shorts with cowboy boots!"

"It's the fashion, Dee. You should see what they wear on campus. Did they leave the flowers by any chance?"

"They're out on the desk in the ICU waiting room, if you want to take a look. Oh, and there was a call from someone asking about Tanya's condition this morning. A young man, from the sound of it, and he seemed a little ticked when I told him I couldn't release any information."

I went to the waiting room and checked the flowers for a card. There was one stuck in a plastic holder reading "Thinking of you Tanya! Get well soon!

Love, Zoey, Angela and Katherine." I didn't think this was a group that would beat the crap out of a fellow student, but with girls you never know. And maybe Zoey had a heart, after all. I returned to the ICU and approached the man sitting by the door to Tanya's room. Tanya's grandfather was tall and lanky, dark like his granddaughter, with a full head of grey hair. He was dressed in clean but well-worn clothes and looked exhausted.

"Sir? I'm Rhe Brewster. I know your granddaughter," I said truthfully. "We had lunch together last week."

"You must be the lady from the police that was asking her about the dead student. I'm Aaron Davis," he replied, standing politely and offering his hand.

We shook hands and I asked him, "Do you have any idea who could have done this to her? Did she have any enemies at the school?" While I spoke, I pulled a chair up to his and we both sat down. Mr. Davis took a deep breath, staring at the tiled floor.

"Can't say as she ever mentioned anyone she had trouble with, and I don't know who done this. But I tell you, if I find out who, the beating they'll get from me'll be a flea bite compared to what they done to my granddaughter." His hands were clenched in anger but when he looked up at me, there were tears glistening in his eyes.

"Do you know who Tanya's been dating lately? Does she tell you about the men in her life?"

His shoulders slumped and he said sadly, "You need to know some things about me and Tanya. Tanya's mother passed when she was seven, and since she don't have a daddy, at least one who'd own up to it, my wife and I raised her. Since my Harriet died ten years ago, it's just been Tanya and me. Did the best I could. I'm so proud of her. Got a scholarship, did she tell you? Smart girl. Tells me just about everything, far as I can tell, and 'specially about the young men. She knows I 'spect them to have certain standards, even if she doesn't herself all the time. Last month or so she hasn't said squat to me about anyone she's seeing, and I wonder if it's because she knew I wouldn't like 'em."

I could see through the glass door that Tanya was stirring. When I looked back at Mr. Davis I saw a man in fear of losing the only family member he had left. "Mr. Davis, I'll do everything I can to help the police find the person who did this. I'll be by every day to see Tanya, so if you have to get back to work, don't worry."

"That's good to hear, ma'am. I have to be back at work tomorrow."

"What do you do, Mr. Davis?"

"I'm a carpenter with a company in Portland, and I gotta work to be paid."

"Well, I work here at the hospital and I know the nursing staff. Tanya'll be well taken care of. Let me give you my phone number." I scribbled my name and number on a page from my notebook, tore it out and handed it to him.

"You have my word she'll be safe. Again, I am so sorry."

Mr. Davis folded the paper and put it in his shirt pocket, rose, and extended his hand again. "Thank you, Miz Brewster. You're very kind."

Dee went in to take Tanya's vitals and motioned to Mr. Davis. He walked back into Tanya's room and took a seat by her bed, reaching to hold her hand. This was not the time to ask any more questions and I decided to leave that to Sam. They were talking quietly with their heads close together when I left. I had a brief word with Dee to find out who would be on Surgery the following day and asked if she would cover my shift on Monday, then went down to the main entrance.

As I passed the hospital's information desk, I noticed a young man in a heated conversation with the receptionist. I overheard her say she could not give out any information unless he was a relative, and when he said he was her brother, she broke into a broad smile, which only made him more agitated. The kid looked familiar, so I headed over to the desk. "Can I help here?" I asked.

When the kid turned around, a look of recognition and surprise came over his face. "I know you," he said. "You're the woman looking for Zoey the other day!"

"Yes, I am and I'll bet you're trying to find out about Tanya, aren't you? So the brother routine isn't working, right?"

He flushed, but undeterred, asked me, "So how is she?"

"I'll take this, Rhonda," I told the receptionist, reading her name tag. "Nice to see you again, Kelly," I replied to him, as his name popped into my head. "Kelly Ingram, isn't it?"

"How do you know my name?" he asked testily.

I didn't answer but raised my eyebrows and stared at him. "Care to sit down for a minute?" I headed for a couple of comfy chairs to one side of the hospital entrance.

"No, and you can't make me. Just who the hell are you?" He stopped moving.

"My name is Rhe Brewster, and I'm a consultant with the Pequod Police."

"So?"

"Listen up, Kelly, and let's be a little smart here. It doesn't take a genius to figure out you're the one who called the ICU last night. You're showing a lot of interest in Tanya's condition and I'm thinking you're the one who beat her up." His eyes started to wander around the foyer, giving him the appearance of a rabbit in a trap.

"Well, I didn't, and you've no right to be questioning me!" he said loudly and headed for the door. I raced after him and grabbed him by the sleeve and held on hard when he tried to pull away.

"Look, you can make this easy or I can call Sheriff Brewster. It just so happens he's my brother-in-law."

He stopped, faced me, and said forcefully, "I did *not* have anything to do with it! You can't stop me and I'm leaving!" He tugged away again, but by that time I had a good grip on his arm.

"Okay, go ahead and take off. But as I see it, you have three choices. One, you can sit down here and talk to me. Two, I can call the police station, tell them you probably know how Tanya got beaten and have them pick you up. Or three, you go with me to the police station and tell them yourself. Which would you prefer?"

He thought it over for a minute, then held up his hand. "Okay, okay!" he said resignedly and headed for the chairs.

Once seated, I leaned toward him and asked quietly, "Would you take off your jacket please?"

"Why?"

"Humor me." Under the jacket, he was wearing a tee shirt, and I looked carefully at his arms as he shrugged off the jacket. Not a scratch on them, and I knew Tanya had inflicted some serious damage on whomever had beaten her. His face and neck were clear as well, so I figured he was covering for someone. "You can put your jacket back on. Who sent you here?"

"Nobody, I just wanted to find out how she was doing."

"How did you know Tanya was even here?"

"It got around campus last night."

"Well, if you weren't the one who beat her up, I'm betting that you know who did." I noted his rumpled appearance and unshaven face. Clearly he'd had a tough night. "And I also think you were the one who brought her to the emergency room. True?"

"No! I mean, okay, yes, you'll probably find out anyway. I brought her. But I did *not* beat her up." He got up to leave.

I stood up, blocking his exit and putting my face about three inches from his. "Then in the absence of a name, I'll just head to the station anyway and tell them what we talked about. I figure it'll take them, oh, about 15 minutes, to head out to the college and start talking to your friends. That should make you really popular. And you know what? Whoever did this has some pretty nasty scratches on his arms and probably his face, so it's not going to be a big problem to ID him."

Kelly sat down again, just as a security guard approached us. We had been a little loud, and I was sure the receptionist had called Security.

"Everything here okay, miss?" he asked. I knew the guy, a slightly slow, middle-aged man who wouldn't hurt a fly.

"No problem, Officer Dunster. My younger brother and I were having a little difference of opinion. Everything's fine." Amazingly, he accepted the story, shrugged, and left.

Turning to Kelly, I asked, "So what's it going to be, kid?"

He thought for a minute. "Can you promise me he won't find out it's me who told?"

"I can't promise absolutely, but I'll make sure Sheriff Brewster knows you could be a target."

More silence. Then he blurted out, "It's a member of the football team. He's my roommate. This is gonna get out, I know it. Coach is gonna kill me. Maybe I'll get kicked off the team. I should never have brought her here."

"Kelly, you did a brave thing, bringing her here. I'm proud of you."

"Wadda you know? What a dumb move! If I tell, the team is gonna freak. Will I be arrested?"

I thought about it and then proposed, "Look, I'm not sure if you'll be arrested but I doubt it. You give me the name, answer any questions the police have for you, and you should come out of this without a problem." Kelly groaned, put his palms on the back of his head and turned this way and that. "This may not make you any friends on the team, depending on what they know, but maybe your coach will think you're a stand up guy. Is he that kind of coach?"

"Yeah, he's as straight as they come. And he doesn't take any crap from his players."

"If he *is* what you say, he'll give the team a strong message about abusing women, and you'll be a hero. Well, maybe not a hero, but a good guy. I'd be happy to talk to him for you." I asked again, "Give me the name?"

Seconds ticked by. Finally he said, "Raymond Little. We call him Little Ray because he isn't. And I'm not going back to the dorm until he's been arrested. What should I do?"

"Maybe now's a good time to go see your coach. Maybe he can put you up overnight. Give me his name, and I'll have the police contact you there."

"It's Coach Bernacker. Jim Bernacker. He lives on Hawthorne. Can I go now?"

I didn't know the coach so I took down the information, and then Kelly was off, trying not to run until he got to the parking lot. By the time I reached my Jeep, he was gone. I needed to call Sam, so I leaned up against the driver's side door and dialed. Once I gave him what I'd learned, I'd still have part of the afternoon to spend with Will and Jack.

Sam picked up in his office, and I gave him the particulars of my afternoon at the hospital, along with the names of Raymond Little, Kelly Ingram and Coach Bernacker. I also told him about Raymond Little's threatening Will in class.

"I should've tried to bring Kelly in, shouldn't I?"

"No, you did the right thing. No telling what he would have done if you'd forced the issue. What if he'd decided to whack you and run?"

"Nah, he wouldn't have done that. You know I'm a pretty good judge of character. That kid addressed me as ma'am last week when I met him."

"Still…"

"Look, you should go easy on Kelly. In my opinion, he's basically a good kid who got caught up in something bad and tried to do the right thing. He's terrified that outing Little will have repercussions with the team. And he's definitely afraid Little will come after him. I'm hoping his coach'll take this seriously and protect him."

"I know Jim. He's a good man. He'll handle this right."

"You might want to have the coach there when you talk with Kelly. Will he need a lawyer?"

"Not unless Mr. Davis wants to press charges against him for covering up for his roommate. And he did try to help Tanya by bringing her to the hospital. I'll go on over and talk to Kelly and then see Mr. Davis and his daughter."

"Mr. Davis is leaving tonight to head home, so you might want to do that first."

"Sure thing, Sugar, and I'll send Phil and John to the college to find Ray. You know, you've been a big help today," he said.

I glowed inwardly at his words. "Thanks, boss. Hmmm...do you think there's any possibility I could get a badge or ID of some kind, so when I ask to talk to someone, I can convince them I'm really a consultant?"

"Good idea, Rhe. You'll have to come in and get fingerprinted and have your picture taken." He paused for a second. "And the background stuff will take a little time. Let me see what I can set up for next week. Pick you up at seven Monday?"

"Sure thing, but could we drive Miss Daisy?"

"Who the heck is Miss Daisy?"

"My Jeep. She's gotten so old, I've named her. Driving Miss Daisy, get it?"

I heard Sam give a grunt on the other end of the line. "So just why do we need to take Miss Daisy?"

"Because I'm not into travelling in a wind tunnel for three hours."

And with that, I took off my investigative hat and went home to be a wife and mother.

12

Sunday morning brought Post and Sentinel headlines that a college football player had been arrested for assaulting a female student, no names attached, and that he was being held without bond until a hearing. I wondered why Ray Little's name was being withheld; after all, he was certainly older than sixteen. Visions of Bitsy danced in my head.

Kelly had asked me to talk to his coach, which I did by phone early that afternoon. The coach told me that after he'd consulted with the administration the night before, Little had been placed on leave from the team. The college administration had suspended him for the semester or until his case was adjudicated. According to Bernaker, the team seemed to be taking the news in stride, and Kelly's involvement had been kept quiet, but I wondered how long before that part of it would leak.

My next stop was to visit Tanya. Sam called on my cell just as I pulled into the hospital parking lot. It seemed things were not so good with Mr. Davis.

"I got him to agree Kelly was not involved in the assault and he won't press charges," reported Sam, "but I had to tell him we were bringing in a suspect. It was all I could do to keep him from storming the jail. I finally persuaded him to go home and cool down. I'd hate to have to arrest him for assault or worse."

"He was pretty angry when I talked to him yesterday. Has Little been charged yet?"

"Not yet, but should be by tomorrow if we can get Judge Jeffries to hear the charges and set bail. Are you going to check on Tanya today?"

"I'm at the hospital as we speak."

"Let me know how she's doing."

"Will do. Sam? One more thing. Why wasn't Ray Little's name in the newspaper this morning? The article on the beating only said a college football player. Aren't the names of those accused usually released if they're over sixteen?"

"That surprised me too. I suspect the college brought its considerable influence to bear on the matter. I think you'll have to talk to the editor about that. Not sure he'll be forthcoming, unless you use your feminine wiles."

"Oh hell, I've known Bob Morgan since we were in diapers. I'll try to meet up with him later this week and find out what's going on."

'See you tomorrow at 7 AM?"

"I'll be in the driveway with coffee."

⌒⌒

I was happy to find that Tanya was definitely improving - most of the bandages were off, but her face was still swollen and marked by several lines of stitches. Her jaw, which had been broken, was wired shut. Her broken fingers were still in splints, but I knew she was on the mend when she started talking about getting her nails done. I felt particularly good when she thanked me for getting Ray Little arrested, probably because I hadn't had to get that information from her. Nevertheless, she was going to have to testify at his trial, and the Assistant DA had already been by to talk to her.

"Tanya, where are you going when you're released? I worry if you go back to campus you might run into Ray somewhere, if he gets out on bond. The campus cops can't be everywhere."

Emerging from between her wired jaws, her words came out garbled, and I had to think about the translation. "I'm going home for a few days, then coming back," I was pretty sure she said. "One of our neighbors will look after me, you know, and make this liquid junk I have to eat." She indicated a glass with the remains of what looked like a milk shake. "I'll watch my back. Plus the DA promised he would let me know of Ray's whereabouts."

"How's your granddad doing?"

"He's okay, still mad. He felt better when he found out my friends from the dorm are, you know, organizing their schedules so that someone'll always be with me on campus."

I thought about talking to her about her relationship with Ray, but had a better idea. "I'd like you to get some counseling after you get back. Someone who will accept your college health insurance. Would you be willing to do that?" Tanya didn't answer but hung her head, and I thought I knew why. "Hey, this was not your fault. You shouldn't be ashamed of what happened. And you're not alone."

Tanya shook her head from side to side, still not looking at me.

"Look, the counselor I'm thinking of counsels a lot of young women. Some of them are rape victims. You've had a really bad experience, something you didn't cause, and she'll understand that. And she'll support you. Will you at least give her a try?"

Tanya took a deep breath. "Okay, Mrs. Brewster. I'll give her a try. Just give me a little time."

"Sooner will be a lot better than later, trust me."

She nodded her head twice. "Okay. And Mrs. Brewster? Watch out for Ray. He has a nasty temper, you know, and if he finds out that you're behind his arrest, he'll come after you. And thanks again for everything you did. Really."

She was right about Ray Little. I left with the uneasy feeling he would eventually find out from someone I was involved in his arrest, but soon forgot about it because my last stop before heading home was to see Paulette. I called Will to let him know I was in the neighborhood, visiting with my best friend.

"So where have you been, my high and mighty police consultant?" Paulette asked, looking up her nose at me when I entered her kitchen. "Too busy to reply to my e-mails?" Usually we have coffee once or twice a week to catch up and gossip, but I had been so preoccupied I hadn't even looked at my e-mail.

"I'm really sorry, and yes, crazy busy," I replied, giving her a bear hug.

"Well, we are not amused," she replied into my chest as I hugged her.

Over coffee and a large piece of Boston cream pie, I told her about my week. Our usual half hour stretched into an hour, more coffee, and the temptation of another piece of pie. By the time I finished, any irritation she might have felt was long gone, her eyes shone with curiosity and I had a sugar buzz.

"So Sam doesn't think that the Caribbean Queen is a good lead?" Paulette asked after I finished my summary.

"Nope, but I had an e-mail reply from the Caribbean Queen yesterday, asking me to call their office for a phone interview. You know I can't do that! My voice is pretty distinctive and I sound all nasally, you know, like a duck. Ack, ack, ack." I did my best duck imitation. "No one would take me for an undergraduate." Paulette nodded yes and smiled at my duck talk.

I didn't say anything for a few moments, unsure of how she'd respond to what I planned to ask her. "Paulette, could you call them pretending to be me?

You know you have a great voice and lots of acting experience. What was the name of that last play you were in?"

"Ionesco's *The Bald Soprano*. Which you hated."

"And with good reason. An absurd play by an absurdist playwright. But you were really good."

She raised one eyebrow, giving me a skeptical look. "You are so darned good at buttering up, Rhe. How long have you been planning on asking me?"

"Just since yesterday." That elicited a smile from her.

"And Sam told you not to get involved with the Caribbean Queen angle, didn't he?"

"Yeeeesss," I replied reluctantly. "Sweetie, Sam is waiting for his friend with the Boston PD to follow up, and who knows how long that's going to take. We're going to lose any advantage we might have." A tiny touch of pleading crept into my voice. "And I don't see the problem with looking into the office they have in Boston."

"You know why he warned you off, don't you? You charge into situations like a bull."

"Hey, I work in an ER. Comes with the territory. What do you think? Will you do it?"

She gave me a devious smile and I knew she was in. "Print me the application and I'll make the call."

I wrote down the information I had concocted for the application, and she dialed the number on her cell phone. Even though it was a Sunday, someone answered at the Caribbean Queen office. With an amazing transformation, Paulette's voice became that of a 20 year old, slightly ditzy, college student. She was grinning as she answered their questions.

Suddenly Paulette frowned. "Well...... I don't know when I could do that. Can I call you back? My schedule is a little busy right now. If you need to reach me, here's my cell phone number." She gave them her number, and thanking the person, hung up. "They want me to come in for an interview. So what do we do now?" she asked. I noted that she said *we,* and wondered how far *we* could take this.

"Do you think you could play the role of a college student in person?"

"Well, maybe a grad student with a little makeup and the right clothes. But what if they check me out on Facebook and discover that the picture you posted doesn't look like me"?

"No problem. Lots of Facebook pages have pictures of people who are not the real thing. You can just explain you did it to protect yourself from cyber stalkers."

"So when do you want to do thish caypah?" Paulette sounded like James Bond in *Dr. No* and was clearly relishing her new role.

"Are you sure you want to do this?" I asked. Over the years, we'd spent many cozy hours together, huddled at her kitchen table, drinking coffee, but talking mostly about my life and not hers. It had occurred to me more than once that Paulette was living vicariously through my work and my adventures, and I sensed she was ready for one of her own.

"Absolutely. I can't let you have all the fun."

I considered the "caper" and my week ahead. "Not sure about the timing. I'm going to Lili's funeral tomorrow and we can talk Tuesday afternoon, after I take Dee's morning shift. She's covering for me tomorrow."

We had another cup of coffee and as I helped her clean up our cups before heading for home, I wondered at the fact we shared so much of our lives over a simple beverage. I recalled a quote from T.S. Eliot that had been carved over the door of our favorite coffee shop at college: "My life is measured out in coffee spoons." It seemed that mine was, too.

13

At seven sharp on Monday morning, I met Sam in the driveway, balancing two mugs of coffee and wearing my Sunday-go to-meeting black dress and heels that already pinched my feet. Too bad I couldn't wear black scrubs and flip flops.

"You want to drive?" I asked Sam.

"Sure," he replied and we got into my dented, ten year old, green Jeep Grand Cherokee. At least it had luxurious, albeit sagging and cracked, leather seats.

"Here," I said, handing him a mug before settling myself. "Have some coffee. And I brought breakfast bars, too." I reached into my bag and pulled them out.

He took the coffee and held the mug unsteadily as he started the car. "Thanks, but keep whatever that is," he replied, gesturing at the breakfast bar with his mug. "I'm not into mealy bars of compost, and we're going to stop somewhere to get some real food."

"Hey, these are supposed to be good for you! And filling. At least you'll like the coffee. I put in some of that fancy creamer that you like. I think it's chocolate hazelnut."

"It's actually tastes pretty good," he replied, taking a long slug. "Did Will make it?"

I gave him a dirty look, took off my shoes, and sighed in relief. I sipped my coffee and ate both breakfast bars while we drove out of Pequod to US 1. After connecting with I95, we drove south to Massachusetts, and then picked up US 1 again, which took us into Chelsea. It was a convoluted drive, but less than three hours, which left us plenty of time to make the funeral. Most of the way we just chatted about the usual stuff and people we knew and town gossip. I told him about Dr. Ed Mendez, the new transplant surgeon, and Nancy Ennis' ambitions. Sam knew Nancy, and I had hoped to fix them up at one point, but clearly that time had passed.

We made one stop, where Sam bought two Cajun chicken biscuits and some fries, which he ate with a side of criticism from his sister-in-law. I had a regular chicken biscuit, feeling mildly superior.

'Is there anything new you can tell me?" I asked, while beating a pile of crumbs off my lap.

"Ray Little should be out on bail by now."

"And you're only just telling me this?" My voice hit a high C.

"Since he was being released this morning, you're getting the news as it breaks."

"Who bailed him out?"

"That's where things get interesting. Bitsy Wellington." This last response was muffled by biscuit.

"Did you say Bitsy?"

"None other."

"You're kidding! Bitsy knows Little because of Will's complaint, but why would she bail him out? Maybe if the college were trying to cover up the story of Tanya's beating, she bailed him out at the behest of the college president. What do you think?"

"Possibly, but bail was paid in full last night. As far as I know, there was no lawyer involved, so she must have put up cash."

"Why is that?"

"Because Maine is a no-bail state, which means private agents aren't allowed to deal with bonds. So you either pay in cash or hire a lawyer."

"How much was the bail?"

"I'm not exactly sure, but I think in the range of a hundred thousand. I can check with the bailiff later."

I sat dumbfounded for a few minutes while Sam finished his biscuits. With a bail of a hundred thousand dollars, Bitsy would have had to put up ten thousand in cash. I knew she had plenty of her own money, but why would she do this? Did Bitsy figure into Tanya and Ray's relationship? Nothing was immediately forthcoming from my little gray cells.

"I'm hoping he doesn't decide to go back to campus," Sam continued, after swallowing his last mouthful with the dregs of his coffee. "We discovered that there were two prior charges against him for assault, but both were dropped."

"College students?"

"No, women in his home town of New Bedford."

"Does he know I was involved in having him arrested?"

"Your name never entered in to any conversation we had with him. Why do you ask?

"Because Tanya warned me I could be on his hit list, if he finds out."

"All the more reason for you to be careful. Do you want me to have a regular patrol run by your house?"

"Nope. I don't want to scare Will, and I really doubt Ray would try anything out of his comfort zone, which is campus. Do you think Ray would be stupid enough to go after Tanya again?"

"You never know with these batterers. If he feels as possessive about Tanya as some guys we've seen about their wives and girlfriends, he might. I'll talk to campus security again."

I finished my biscuit, made another useless attempt to de-crumb myself. "Did Phil find out who owns Lili's house?"

"It's a company, and we haven't been able to track down the proprietors. Phil's wondering if it's a shell corporation."

"Speaking of shell corporations, have you heard anything from Boston yet about the Caribbean Queen?"

"Hell, Rhe, I only just called them yesterday afternoon!"

"Just checking. Maybe you could put Phil on tracking down the Queen's owners as well."

"I could, but obviously not right now." A little sarcasm crept in.

"How about her car? Any leads?"

"Still hoping. We've given the description to all the surrounding PDs and also the security people at various airports, including Boston. Maybe we'll get lucky today."

⌒⌒

Chelsea is an inner urban suburb of Boston, a town of about 35,000 residents which developed in the 1800s as an industrial center. Our way to the church wound through a typical Massachusetts working class town of older, multifamily wood frame houses. Our Lady of the Blessed Sacrament was a total surprise. Built of grey limestone in the Romanesque style, it had two octagonal spires on either side of the facade. The facade had a round, stained glass window over the two sets of double doors at the entrance, and altogether the church looked like a something you might see in Europe.

People were already ascending the wide stairs to go in. Cars were parked bumper to bumper on the street and jammed the church's small parking lot, so we ended up having to park on a fairly distant side street.

I put my shoes back on before I got out of the car, and by the time we found our way back to the church, my feet were crying out in agony. While we were parking, a hearse had drawn up in front. A tight cluster of people dressed in black, the women's faces partially obscured by black veils, were ascending the stairs following the casket, which was carried on the shoulders of six enormous pall bearers. I figured this was the family. Sam and I followed at a discrete distance and took seats toward the back of the church. I must confess I spent most of the time during the Mass admiring the colorful windows and the incredible, soaring interior of the church. I also scanned the faces of the congregation and saw two people that I recognized: Zoey and Kelly. They sat together in a group with three young women, probably also students, and I recognized a few Pequod faculty in the pews.

At the end of the Mass, we brought up the rear of the congregation as it spilled out onto the front steps. As soon as the crowd had thinned from around a couple I assumed were the Bianchis, Sam approached them and had a quiet word. When he returned, he said, "They're leaving for the cemetery but have agreed to meet with us at their house after the graveside service. They have invited friends and family back to the house and said we could join them around 1:30."

At that point, Zoey teetered up to us on five inch heels, exclaiming, "Hi, Mrs. Brewster! I didn't expect to see you here!" She politely introduced Kelly and then told us the other three women were members of her sorority: Angela, Christa, and Katherine. Kelly hung back, and since I doubted Zoey knew we'd met before, I greeted him as a stranger. In return, he gave me a look I interpreted as relief. All of the young women were drop-dead gorgeous fashion plates - dresses in a size 0 right from the pages of ELLE, Glamour, and Vogue, with Jimmy Choo or Manolo Blahnik shoes, if I my instincts were right. And the handbags, definitely Louis Vuitton.

I introduced Sam as my brother-in-law and the police chief of Pequod. They all remained tongue-tied and after an awkward pause, Zoey finally asked, "Do you know the family?"

"The Chief met Lili's parents last week," I replied. "I am surprised there aren't more students here."

"They had a memorial service for Lili on Friday at the college, and Lili didn't have that many close friends on campus," Zoey explained.

"Are you going to the house to pay your respects to the family?" I asked.

"Sure," she said breezily. "We know Lili's Uncle Antonio." At that point, Angela gave Zoey a small dig in the ribs, trying to be inconspicuous about it. "Um, we met him a week or two ago when he came up to visit Lili."

"Were Uncle Antonio and Lili close?"

"I really can't say. We just met him that one time, and it was only for a few minutes. At the student center. They were just walking through, I think she was giving him a tour. Really, we don't really *know* him, if you know what I mean."

I gave Sam a sideways look. Clearly, they knew something they didn't want us to know. After saying our goodbyes and turning down the street, I caught sight of Bitsy Wellington. She was standing close to a tall, impeccably dressed older man with a mane of white hair, having a quiet conversation. I hadn't seen her during the service, and she was so intent on what she was saying, she didn't notice me. Near her, waiting with his back turned, was a man I recognized as the Dean of the College of Arts and Sciences. I figured they must have come to the funeral to represent the college administration. I touched Sam's arm and nodded my head in Bitsy's direction, then we headed back to the car. After 15 minutes of driving around, we found a diner and spent the hour or so drawing out our lunch and loading up on caffeine, carbohydrates, and conjecture about what was going on with the sorority sisters and Uncle Antonio, plus the identity of the man talking to Bitsy.

After lunch, we meandered through Chelsea, finding the Bianchi's house on Newell Street. It was an old, two story, wood frame house, with porches upstairs and down, suggesting it was a duplex. It looked tired and neglected, with mold-stained paint and a sagging cedar tree in the front yard shielding the lower half of the house from the street.

We mounted the steps and entered the open front door into a short hallway. The entrance to the first floor apartment was on the right and was also open, emitting a low buzzing of voices. As we entered, Sam nodded toward the Bianchis, who were sitting on a sofa on the left side of the room. Next to Mrs. Bianchi was the white-haired man who had been talking to Bitsy. I noted his resemblance to Mrs. Bianchi, thinking maybe this was Uncle Antonio. Although her face was muddled by grief, his seemed unaffected – handsome with chiseled cheeks, a Roman nose, bushy salt and pepper eyebrows and a thick mustache to match. The Bianchis looked drained, slumped down on the sofa, heads drooping. People approached them to offer condolences, and friends sat in chairs on the left and right, occasionally reaching over to pat their hands.

The living room led directly to a dining room, and women bustled in and out from the kitchen in the back, bringing platters of cannelloni, lasagna, ziti, salad, apple crostata, canollis, and a ricotta cake to the dining room table. We helped ourselves to some of the desserts, and while we were eating, I spotted Zoey and her friends in the kitchen, talking to a young man smartly dressed in what I guessed was an Armani suit. As the man turned and I got a glimpse of his face, I saw he was a younger version of Uncle Antonio, undoubtedly his son. The conversation was apparently unhappy, and each of the young women hugged the young man in sympathy. Their conversation halted abruptly once Zoey looked up and saw us. She and her entourage left the kitchen, saying hi to us on their way by. They all paused to say something to the Bianchis and Uncle Antonio before exiting the house.

When some of the crowd had cleared out, Sam approached Mr. Bianchi and after a few words, both he and his wife and the man I assumed was Uncle Antonio got up and led us through the kitchen and into a small den. The well-dressed young man to whom Zoey had been talking followed us and closed the door. Sam and I sat together on a lumpy sofa that clearly doubled as a bed and the family pulled up chairs.

"Rhe, this is Joseph and Rosalee Bianchi. Rhe's a consultant with our department and is helping us with the investigation into your daughter's death," introduced Sam. I leaned over and shook their hands, offering my condolences.

"And you are?" Sam asked, turning to the other men.

"Oh, this is Lili's uncle, Antonio Moretti," said Joseph Bianchi, turning to the older of the two men. "He's been very good to our daughter. We're beholden to him for his many kindnesses. And this is his son, Adriano."

I switched my attention briefly to Rosalee, as she nodded in agreement. I could clearly see the striking beauty she must have been, before age and grief diminished her. Her dark hair was streaked with gray and she was collapsed into a shapeless black dress, but she had the cheekbones and the flashing eyes of her brother. Adriano was a young god, with olive skin, warm brown eyes, wavy dark hair and his father's chiseled jaw and cheekbones. He was as handsome a man as Lili had been beautiful. Good looks clearly ran on Rosalee's side of the family. Joseph, by contrast, was short and swarthy, with graying hair and stubbly, unshaven cheeks.

"Rosalee and me, we run a bakery," Joseph continued. "I think we gotta a good life, at least until now. Business is okay, but we don't make enough money for Lili's college. Tonio helps out."

"When was the last time any of you saw Lili?" asked Sam gently.

Rosalee finally spoke, in a whisper of a voice, "Last month. She came home to help in the bakery and study."

Joseph nodded and added, "She's a good girl, our Lili. Always coming home to help." This fit with what Zoey had told me about how she spent her weekends.

"Mr. Moretti," Sam said, turning to Uncle Antonio and taking charge of the questioning, "when do you last remember seeing Lili?"

"I dunno, probably several months ago, when she was home." This was said with confidence, and it directly contradicted Zoey's earlier stammerings. Sam glanced at me.

"What do you do for a living, Mr. Moretti?"

Uncle Antonio smiled and said with some pride, "I own several funeral homes here in Maine. Moretti and Sons, perhaps you've heard of them?"

"No I haven't, but Maine's a big state. I take it this is a family business?"

"The 'sons' in the title," he said proudly, "that's for my two sons. Adriano here, he's a junior at Pequod, majoring in business. My oldest, Gabriel, he's working today, already helping me. They're going to take over for me when I retire." He said this with the absolute assurance of a done deal. Adriano remained silent and sat with his head down. He was clasping and unclasping his hands, as if he were trying to maintain control.

"What was your relationship to Lili, other than as her uncle. Do you - did you — help pay her college tuition or room and board?" asked Sam.

"Why do you want to know that?" Uncle Antonio retorted sharply. "Am I a suspect?"

"No, no, of course not, but we need to know as much as possible about Lili's life at Pequod. We never know where an investigation will take us, and it would be a big help to have full knowledge of her circumstances, if you can do that."

Somewhat mollified, Uncle Antonio replied, "I paid her tuition, what the scholarship didn't. Rosalee and Joseph covered her books and the rest."

"Did you know where Lili was living?" Sam continued.

"In a dorm I think." He shrugged and turned to his brother-in-law. "Joseph, where did she live?"

"We never saw where she lived. We never had time to visit. But I gave her the money for the dorm, the amount the college said we had to pay," Joseph answered.

"So you didn't know," Sam continued, "she was living alone in a furnished rental house off campus?"

Joseph looked totally confused and Rosalee dumbfounded. "No, that was not what she told us," Joseph finally replied. "She talked about her friends in the dorm. They're here today. The blond one and those other girls." Since Uncle Antonio was lying about when he last saw Lili, I was watching him closely while this exchange occurred. He certainly appeared to be as confused as his relatives.

"Do you know where Lili's car is?" Sam asked.

"No," said Joseph, "she drove it back to school after her last visit. She always drove it here and back on the weekends. We gave it to her when she graduated high school. A piece of crap, that car, but it ran well. You don't know where it is?"

"No, the car is missing, along with her computer. I assume she had a cell phone?"

"Yes," said Rosalee, "but she paid for that herself with what she earned at the college."

"Do you know where she worked?" I interjected.

"She told me in one of the coffee shops," said Joseph. "Is her phone missing, too?"

"Yes," said Sam, "but I could use her phone number. If the phone's still on, perhaps we could trace it." Joseph recited the number and Sam wrote it down, before turning his attention to Lili's cousin. "Mr. Moretti, may I call you Adriano?" He continued without pausing for an answer, "I need to ask you the same question. When was the last time you saw Lili?" During this entire time, Adriano had not said a word, his whole appearance giving the impression he would rather be anywhere else.

At Sam's last question, he looked up, eyes filled with tears. He choked out an answer. "Same as everyone else. Probably the last time she was home."

"Were you close? I mean being cousins and all."

There was a distinct beat before he said, "Not that close. We saw each other if I came to the bakery on weekends. Occasionally we ran into each other on campus. I didn't hang out with her, she's a year behind me." He was having difficulty getting his words out and his father glared at him. Adriano hung his head again and tears dropped off his face onto his suit jacket.

Silence persisted awkwardly for a minute, then Sam asked the Bianchis, "May I call you if I have any other questions? Would that be okay?" Both Rosalee and Joseph nodded their heads. Adriano and his father did not reply. Sam rose to his feet, repeating his condolences to the Bianchis.

Adriano stood as if to leave, too. He was tall, taller than his father, who said harshly, "Sit down, Adriano." Adriano remained standing, and Moretti repeated with force, "Sit down." Adriano sat reluctantly, with a stare at his father. I stood and followed Sam back to the kitchen. As soon as we left, the door to the den shut abruptly, and I would have given a hundred bucks to know what was being said behind that door. I'd glanced at Uncle Antonio as we left the room, and his expression seemed self-satisfied.

"Well," said Sam, as we walked to my car, "that was particularly uninformative. Except for the phone number."

"Not so," I started to say as we approached the Jeep. What stopped me was seeing a series of deep, jagged scratches, extending from the front to the rear panel of my car, on the driver's side. "Oh, Lord, someone's keyed my car! Will's going to be furious." My voice rose as all I could hear was the ka-ching, ka-ching of the repair bill.

"I thought this was a safe neighborhood," mused Sam, as he examined the damage. "Chelsea's crime rate is pretty low, and I can't see funeral participants doing this."

"So do you think it's random …or some kind of warning?"

"I honestly don't know, Rhe, but it's another reason to be careful when you're asking questions."

We headed north to Maine, talking about the damage to the car, Will's probable response, and our impressions of the Bianchi family. Around 4, we stopped for coffee at MacDonald's and stayed to drink it. While we blew on the tops of our cups and waited for the coffee to cool, it occurred to me I hadn't finished what I was about to say when we discovered the marks on my car.

"Sam, did you notice Uncle Antonio said he last saw Lili when she came home last month? Zoey told us that she'd seen them together at Pequod a week or so ago. So who's lying? My bet's on Uncle Antonio."

"I tend to agree, but without more information we've nowhere to go. Lili apparently told her parents very little about college, and what she did tell them were lies. I'll visit that woman in Student Employment tomorrow to check on Lili's supposed job in a coffee shop."

I thought for a minute, then asked, "Besides the job issue, what other loose ends are there?"

"We have the van."

"Yup, and that seems to be a dead end at this time. We do have the water sample I collected."

"What water sample?"

"You know Marsh thinks the body was kept in a hot tub. He sent in a water sample from her clothing for analysis. I left him a sample from the hot tub at the swim club for comparison. The water smelled really bad, like something had decomposed in it."

"And how did my investigator think to check that hot tub?"

"Just a hunch. Jack and I were coming back from a sail and paid the swim club a visit. I can check on that and her blood work tomorrow, if you wish."

"You'll check on it anyway, whatever I wish," Sam said with a smile.

"Okay, her phone, car and computer are missing," I continued, "but we now have her phone number so it might be possible to track it. Anything else?"

"On a completely separate subject," Sam said thoughtfully, "we have Bitsy bailing out our friend Ray."

"And why was Bitsy talking to the uncle at the funeral? What's the link there? And don't forget about the Caribbean Queen."

"Aw, Rhe…"

I cut him off. "I think you should ask your friends to dig a little deeper into that angle. I'm still not convinced it's the nice little business it appears to be. Did you notice the clothes Zoey and her friends were wearing? There's no way an ordinary college student could afford even the shoes on their feet!' I paused. "Does that about do it?"

He nodded. "Time to get back on the road."

We sat in comfortable silence for the rest of the drive, and despite the coffee, the hum of the wheels and swaying of the car lulled me into dozing all the way back to Pequod. Sam, bless his heart, let me sleep.

To my surprise, Will was rather uninterested in our trip to Boston, asking only a few questions about the funeral, mostly superficial. I avoided telling him about the damage to the car, probably because I knew what would happen. And it did, when he took out the garbage the next morning and discovered the scratches. He came storming back into the house in an apoplectic fit and demanded an explanation. He raged on for several minutes, threatening to sue the police department because Sam and I had used the car on police business, until I managed to get a word in edgewise to tell him the department would pick up most of the repair cost. It was sort of true, since Sam had offered to pay. He calmed down with that, and on the whole, I think he took it rather well.

14

Tuesday I was working to repay Dee, who had worked for me the day before. On my way to the ER, I stopped at Marsh's office in the basement. He was sitting at his desk, looking morosely at a towering pile of files in front of him, but he brightened up when he saw I was carrying two cups of coffee and a bag with the logo of his favorite doughnut shop. He swept the papers off the chair next to his desk, moved the pile of folders to make way for the coffee, and asked me how the investigation was going.

"Not so good, Marsh. We have more or less hit dead end with every lead we've followed. I was hoping you'd have the results of Lili's blood work and the water sample I left for you."

"What water sample?" He opened the Hole in One bag, looked inside, and extracted a doughnut, eyeing it like a starving wolf.

I explained to him where I'd gotten the sample, which I had left with Oliver to give to him, and described what the container looked like. The lemon doughnut had disappeared in three bites, leaving a mist of powdered sugar on the front of his shirt.

'Never saw it and Oliver never gave it to me," he replied, removing a second doughnut from the bag.

"Are you sure?" This was not what I wanted to hear.

"Maybe I missed it. Give me a minute to look around." He reluctantly placed the doughnut on his desk and headed for the autopsy suites. I sat and drank my coffee while he made a tour of the suites, and I could hear refrigerators being opened and shut across the hall. Finally, I heard a key turning in the door of the office next door, and after a minute he came back.

"Well, I can't find anything similar to what you described, and nothing like that was logged in. Perhaps Oliver just forgot. I can ask him when he gets here."

Why would he forget? "So what do you know about Oliver? Do you think he would've deliberately misplaced that sample?"

"I really doubt that. He's basically a good guy, a little quiet, but respectful. After we got to know each other, he opened up. He wants to make something of himself, maybe be a physician's assistant. He's a quick learner, and I think he could do it. Why would you ask?'

"On the basis of a conversation I had with Nancy Ennis, you know she works in the ER with me. She's been dating Oliver. She likes him a lot."

"Well, I can't say that surprises me. He's been very chipper lately. Caught him whistling during an autopsy. But what does this have to do with anything?"

"He apparently spends a lot of money on her, which surprised me. I've gotta ask you a sort of personal question, and I can't explain why just now.'

"Rhe, you always have good reasons. Ask away."

"Can you give me an idea of what Oliver earns between his autopsy assistant position and his time with the forensics job? Enough to support weekends for two in New York City at fancy hotels, Broadway shows, expensive restaurants?"

"I wouldn't think so. I'd guess his paycheck probably doesn't come to more than $1200 a month. He's paid hourly here with no benefits."

"Does he have any other source of income you know of?"

"Do you mean like family money? No, I'm pretty sure he doesn't. So you think he's living beyond his means?"

"Just following bread crumbs, my friend."

Marsh stared at me for a moment. I could see he wanted to ask more questions but decided not to.

"Speaking of bread crumbs," he finally said, dusting off the remains of the second doughnut from the front of his shirt, "I do have the results of Lili's blood work here, along with the water sample that I sent from the clothing. Guess what? She had a significant level of rohypnol on board."

I had seen the effects of rohypnol, or the date rape drug, in the ER, when several rape victims had been brought in by police. It's the drug of choice for rapists because it's a powerful sedative with dissociative and amnesic effects, plus it's tasteless, so it isn't detectable when added to food or drink.

"So she was incapacitated by rohypnol, which means she wouldn't have been able to fight her attacker?"

"Yup," replied Marsh. "And that fits with the fact that there was no skin under her fingernails. One other thing - and I should have spotted it if I had been looking really closely - she was pregnant. The pregnancy was at such an early stage that her beta HCG levels were just starting to tick upward. I'm estimating about five to six weeks." Beta HCG is a pregnancy hormone and can be detected with some accuracy about two weeks after conception with an over-the-counter urine test.

I sat back in surprise. "Would she have known she was pregnant?"

"Probably. Didn't you use one of those tests?"

I flushed. "No, I waited until I was throwing up regularly and had a blood test."

"Well, I missed the implantation site. I did a cursory look at her uterine lining but didn't see it."

That was not surprising. Marsh would have had to go over every inch of her uterine lining with a microscope to find the tiny implantation site of the embryo.

"Would it be possible to recover DNA from an embryo if her remains were exhumed?" I asked.

"Recovery of DNA from exhumed remains is very iffy, Rhe, and the types of tissue from which DNA might be recovered don't include embryonic material. So it would be a long shot at best," he answered.

"Well, okay then." I sighed. Yet another dead end. I looked at my watch and stood up. "Time to get to work. Will you check on the water sample for me? I can get another, since the tub wasn't drained. Just let me know. Thanks, Marsh!" As I left, he was looking hopefully into the bag for a third doughnut.

My shift was full of measled children. Measles seems to pop up every year after school gets underway because some parents don't have their children inoculated, and we were busy keeping the children separate from the rest of the ER population. A dislocated shoulder, two women in labor, and things were lively. Sometime during the shift, the receptionist took two messages for me. The first was from Marsh, letting me know that Oliver had somehow misplaced the water sample, for which he was terribly sorry. The second was from Sam, asking me to stop by the station after work, if I had time.

I finished my shift at 4 PM and decided to swing by the swim club and get another sample of water before seeing Sam. This time I brought along a sterile vial. Although the day was warm and sunny, the deserted club gave me the same sense of anxiety as the last time I had been there, and I hurried from the parking lot to the pool and hot tub. I forced up one corner of the hot tub cover and only a faint smell greeted me. The tub had been drained.

I immediately thought of Oliver. *Did he really lose the sample? Had he come back and drained the hot tub?* I shook my head. *Jumping to conclusions again, Rhe. It's more likely the club caretaker discovered the tub was full and drained it for the season.* I stared at the tub, thinking about whether there might be any parts still containing water, and remembered that hot tubs have filter cartridges. Lifting another corner of the top, I found the cover to the filter chamber and lifted one of the cartridges out with two fingers. I was in luck - the tub had been drained very recently and the cartridge was still moist. I decided to take the whole thing to Marsh and let him recover a water sample. After re-latching the tub cover with the other hand, I carefully carried the filter back to my car, where I was in luck. In my trunk, a black hole that regularly sucks in all sorts of useless items, I found an unopened plastic grocery bag. After struggling to get the darn thing open, I dropped the filter in.

I went directly to the hospital morgue with the filter. Marsh wasn't there, but I had Lyle, the ever-present guard of the back door, watch me place it in one of the refrigerators with a note as to source, date and time. I told him to tell Marsh about it as soon as he saw him, emphasizing how important this was. Then it was time to see Sam.

As I entered the police station, Ruthie gave me a conspiratorial wink and said, "Developments!' I got her gist and practically ran to Sam's office.

"So what's up?" I asked, the excitement making me breathless.

"We found Lili's car."

"Where?"

"Highland Lake. On Sunday, a fisherman spotted a blue VW Beetle in about six feet of water and called it in to the Department of Wildlife and Fisheries. They called the local PD. The car was pulled out this morning. After the plate was run, we got the call."

"Anything in it larger than a breadbox?"

"Nope. Car was empty. But we figure this was a dump job, anyway."

"Do they have any idea how it ended up in the lake?"

"The PD didn't see any obvious tire tracks coming down the hill to the water, just some crushed grass. But there was a good sized rock on the driver's side floor, so we think whoever sent it down the hill must have put the rock on the accelerator and bailed out."

"Where's the car now?"

"Coming here on a flatbed. It'll be in the impound lot in an hour or so. We're going to take a look at it first thing tomorrow, along with those infernal techs who'll make sure we don't destroy evidence."

"Can I be there?"

"As if I could stop you," Sam said with smile. "But don't you work tomorrow?"

"How early can we do this?"

"7 AM?"

"You bet."

⇜⇝

That night, Jack had actually volunteered to go to bed, a first. Will made an early fall fire in our stone fireplace, and we sat in its warmth, drinking our usual after dinner coffee and talking about the case and what had been discovered so far. Even though I did most of the talking, I was really hoping to learn what he thought. It was a total surprise when before I even floated my idea about the Caribbean Queen, Will asked, "Do you think the Pequod students are doing something illegal for money? Perhaps engaging in the world's oldest profession?"

Where did that come from? Sam thought my idea was nuts. I suddenly recalled the long look Will had given Lili's picture and his strange expression the night Sam had come to dinner.

"Why would you think that?"

He looked away for a moment, then said, "Not sure. Maybe the way some of the sorority sisters dress and wear jewelry. I've seen most of them in my class this year and last."

Will's reasoning seemed as flimsy as a Victoria Secret's nightgown, but I hadn't much more when I floated the idea to Sam.

"I proposed that same idea to Sam," I said, "based on the expensive jewelry Zoey was wearing when I interviewed her and the car I saw on her Facebook page."

"What kind of car?"

"A Ferrari, the $200,000 kind."

Will whistled.

I told him what I'd found on Zoey's Facebook page, leaving out the facts I had applied to the CQ for a job and Paulette had talked to them.

"So what did Sam say?"

"That I was nuts. But he did say he'd have a friend on the Boston PD look into it. Maybe Sam's right and Zoey just has rich and super indulgent parents.

But until we get more information from the Boston police, there's not much we can do."

We sat there quietly for a while, drinking our coffee, and then I had an idea. "What about seeing where Zoey goes on a Saturday night?"

Will turned to look at me, eyes wide. "Why on earth would you want to do that?"

"Because maybe that would give us an idea if she's, you know, hooking. You suggested it." *I had him there.* "What if you find out where she lives, and we park ourselves outside and follow her if she goes out?"

Will shook his head. "That's crazy, Rhe. What if we were spotted?"

"Why? Zoey wouldn't be suspecting anything. It could be fun to do a little surveillance together!"

"I don't know. Now you're getting me involved."

"Ah, come on. You could see what I'm doing isn't dangerous. I'll pack us some food and we can get Paulette to watch Jack."

We nattered back and forth for a while more, and finally Will relented, but very reluctantly. We finished our coffee, and just as Will was standing up to take our cups to the kitchen, I took a deep breath, screwed my courage to the wall and said, "Will, I need to talk to you about something else."

"What?" He sat down again, balancing the cups in one hand.

"About the other night, when you told me the world doesn't revolve around me. That comment really hurt. I don't think you even realized it, and that bothered me even more."

"What do you mean? I thought you had a headache."

"I did, but you didn't have to make that comment on top of it. I was upset."

His forehead wrinkled up the way it does when he is concerned about something. "I'm sorry, Rhe. I guess I wasn't thinking. If what I said was really so hurtful, I apologize, but I thought you were being a little dramatic."

"But I was honestly worried my talking to Tanya led to her beating."

"I guess I didn't see that. I'm really sorry, sweetie."

"We haven't been communicating very well lately, have we?"

"No, *we* haven't," he replied.

I deserved that, so I suggested, "How about we work on it?"

"Okay," he replied flatly.

I waited for him to say something more, but he was quiet.

15

The sun was just over the horizon when I reached the impound lot the next morning. I'd decided not to tell Sam about the little road trip Will and I had planned, unless we actually discovered something significant. The blue VW stood surrounded by Sam, his deputies John and Phil, and two forensic technologists. It looked little worse for having been in the lake for a week, with only some mud and algae stuck to the wheels and the bumpers.

"How ya doin' this morning, Rhe?" boomed John.

"Fine, thanks. Have you looked inside yet?"

"Nope, just got here. Techs have cleared the outside."

We all donned gloves and Sam opened one door and Phil, the other. Some murky lake water poured out. One of the techs spent some time looking for the release for the front hood latch, until I suggested he look in the glove compartment. *Voilá*. It contained a collection of disintegrating maps and the hood release. In the trunk, there was a computer, smashed beyond salvage, and a few other personal items - shoes, a sodden sweater, a backpack. Before the crime tech team moved in to remove these items and start taking the car apart, I bent down and looked under the seats on both sides and on the driver's side, I saw a phone.

"Well, lookee here," I exclaimed. "I think I found Lili's phone!" I called a tech over to remove and bag it. "Do you think this can be made operational after all that time in water?"

Phil replied, "It's possible, but only if submersion is limited, which it wasn't. And whether it was on when it hit the water. Still I guess it's worth a try. Let the techs see if there are any prints left on it, which I doubt, and then I'll have a go. Give me a few days."

To look at him, Phil Pearce is the last person you would suspect is a policeman. He's thin as a stick, has hair that looks like it was cut with nail scissors, and his perfectly round face is dominated by a ski slope of a nose, with a bulbous end. He has problems keeping his uniform hat above his ears, but between those ears is a sharp mind he uses to keep up with the latest forensic and police procedures.

The rest of the car yielded nothing of interest. Sam asked one of the techs for a sample of the water in the car and signed it over it to me to take to Marsh. As he handed it to me, I finally noticed that Oliver was not one of the crew and wondered where he was.

⌒⌒

At the hospital, I stopped at Marsh's office, this time handing the water sample from the Lili's car directly to him. "Did you find the hot tub filter I dropped off yesterday afternoon?" I asked him.

"Yeah, Lyle told me about it not more than five minutes after you left. I figured you wanted a water sample from it and that's already been taken care of. Also cut out a large sample of the material to process for DNA, just in case. This filter is from the hot tub at the pool, right?"

I nodded. "When I went back, the tub'd been drained. I took the whole filter because it was still wet."

"Good thinking, kiddo."

"Where's Oliver today?"

"The last time I talked to him was yesterday when I called him about the water sample. He didn't show up for work again today and didn't mention anything about taking another day off."

"You try calling this morning?"

"Right before you arrived, but I didn't get an answer."

"Is this normal for Oliver? Not to come in to work and not to call?"

"Not normal at all. He's usually on time and calls if he's going to be late. I'm a little ticked. We're backed up today with three autopsies."

"It's probably nothing, maybe he's just sick. Why don't you give me his home address and I will swing by later and see if he's okay." I collected his cell phone number as well and tried it myself several times during the morning with no results.

When Marsh had still not heard from him by 4 PM, I offered to make the short drive to the north end of Pequod, where Oliver lived. His home was in an older neighborhood, and I pulled my car to the curb in front of an old, two story wooden farm house, white with green shutters and fronted by a wide porch. On the left side there was a crumbling concrete driveway, pockmarked with patches of weeds and ending at a ramshackle garage behind the house, with two carriage doors. I climbed to the porch and opened the screen door. There was a turnkey of an old-fashioned doorbell embedded in the front door, and when I tried to turn it, the door swung open into the foyer.

There was a muffled noise in the rear of the house, and without thinking, I called out "Oliver, is that you? It's Rhe Brewster." There was no answer, and I hesitated for a second before moving cautiously into the living room to the left of the foyer. At that point, I heard footsteps and a door slam.

A double door opened from the living room to the dining room, and there I saw Oliver. He was slumped in a dining room chair with his head tilted back and blood everywhere. I let out a scream. He slowly rolled his eyes toward me, but at that moment they took on a vacant look, and there was the smell of released bowels. A spray of blood patterned the table and the opposite wall, his shirt was drenched with it and a pool was collecting under his chair. As I approached the table, I saw his neck had been severed almost all the way through to his spinal cord, and blood was still weakly pulsing from the severed carotid arteries. He was dead. I gagged, turned away from the horror and retched on the floor until my stomach was empty.

After my stomach stopped heaving, I spat, wiped my mouth on my sleeve, and made myself turn back to the scene. I stood there, shocked, trying to get my mind around what I was seeing. Finally it registered that the chair on one side of the table had been pulled out and turned slightly, as if someone had been sitting there. At that moment, the screech of a metal door coming from outside, followed by the rumble of a vehicle starting up, pulled my attention away from the horror in from of me. *Someone is leaving.* I ran through the kitchen to the back door and flung it open, just as a white van burst from the garage and accelerated down the driveway.

As it sped by, I glimpsed a triangular logo on the van's door and a man with his head turned away from me sat at the wheel. Across the van's back doors was a scripted *New Living Technologies*. The van cornered onto the street without stopping, tires squealing. I jumped the back porch stairs and ran down the driveway. By the time I got to the street, the van was already too far away for me to catch the license plate, and I stared in frustration as it disappeared. Shaking with adrenaline, I walked to my car, got my phone out and after several attempts to push the right buttons, finally reached the police station.

When I'd finished telling Sam what had happened, I walked over to the front porch of Oliver's house and sat on the bottom step, shivering now, with the bitter taste of bile still in my mouth. All of a sudden I felt exhausted, and I could not get the sight of Oliver eyes out of my head. My head sagged and I had an overwhelming urge to sleep. Just then a deep purple splash of color at the bottom of the stairs caught my attention. Too tired to get up, I skidded my rear down three stairs to get a closer look. It was a match book. Interesting, since Oliver didn't smoke, or at least I thought he didn't, and I hadn't seen a match book for advertising purposes in a long time. It was covered in a royal purple foil, with EA written in silver script. *Where had I seen those initials before?* I leaned sideways against the railing and gave up trying to remember because it was too much of an effort. Without thinking, I tucked it in my jacket pocket, and closed my eyes.

Two hours later, having called Will to let him know what had happened, given a statement, talked to Sam about the van's logo, and watched the EMTs load Oliver's body in their truck to take to the morgue, I headed home, bone-tired but hungry. Strangely, death did not seem to suppress my appetite.

Will was waiting for me at the garage door to the kitchen when I drove in and pulled myself out of the car. Without a word, he gathered me into his arms and I just stood there, feeling safe and warm against his body.

"We mustn't let Jack know anything is wrong," I whispered. Finally we separated and went into the house.

Jack was doing his homework when I came in. "Hi, Mom. Dad said you had to stay late at work."

I gave him a hug and a kiss on the top of his head and with all the mental strength I could muster, pushed the last several hours from my mind. "Yup, and I'm sorry. How was school today?" I asked lowering myself in exhaustion into a chair beside him.

"Great. We're learning about the planets." He went back to his work.

"You hungry?" Will asked.

"Hungry as a bear. I guess you and Jack have eaten?"

"Yeah, I got Chinese. It's in the oven." He grabbed a hot mitt, brought out a cookie pan with some boxes on it, and sat it on the table in front of me, where a place was already set. The smell of garlic and onions and meat was incredible and I attacked the food as if I hadn't eaten in a week.

When every last morsel had been devoured, I leaned back, sighed with contentment and asked Jack, "How's the homework coming, sweetie?"

Jack gave me a sly smile, put his pencil down and announced, "Done, Mom. I was just waiting for you to finish eating. Boy, you sure were hungry!"

"I was. What would you like to do before bedtime?"

"Well…" and then he proceeded to tell me all about a bully at school and what his friends were doing about it. The whole story went on and on, with multiple digressions, until I finally had to interrupt him to get him into a bath.

I left him in the bath and came back to the kitchen for coffee.

"How are you doing?" Will asked.

"A lot better now."

"Coffee's made. I'll pour you a cup and we can talk."

Once we were both back at the table with our cups, he said, "Tell me again what exactly happened. Why were you even there?"

I told him as succinctly and honestly as I could, leaving out only the gore and the fact I'd heaved. When I finished, he got up and went to the sink and stood with his back to me, arms braced on the counter, staring out the window, not saying a word.

There was a long period when neither of us said anything, ominous because I knew what Will was thinking. Finally I said, "The driver of the van did *not* see me - his head was turned away so I couldn't see him. I was in no danger." *But he might have heard me.* "And it isn't as if I knew I was walking into anything, for God's sake. I just figured I'd check on Oliver because Marsh hadn't heard from him." More silence. "Soooo, Saturday night's surveillance adventure is off?" I asked, trying to inject a little levity.

Will finally turned around, arms crossed. "Do you really think it's such a good idea now, Rhe?"

"Aw, come on. We aren't exactly putting ourselves out there, are we?"

Will looked at me and shook his head. "I'll think about it."

At that point Jack came into the kitchen with a towel wrapped around him. 'What are you guys doing? My bath water got cold. Isn't someone going to read me a story?"

After Jack was in bed, I just *had* to Google New Living Technologies. The search turned up three businesses with that name. The first was an architectural design firm, while the second was a company that made equipment for the homes of the physically impaired. The third company's main web page stated its purpose was to create systems for harvesting, preserving, assessing and transporting organs for transplantation. None had logos like the one on the van. I knew Sam would have Phil on the search by now, and perhaps he would find something more. I could ask Dr. Montez tomorrow if he had heard of the third company, since he'd be familiar with sources of tissue for transplantation in this area.

The phone kept ringing off and on for about an hour, and caller ID said it was Bob Morgan, undoubtedly looking for a story for the Post and Sentinel. *Well, I have to see him later this week anyway,* I rationalized as I turned the phone off and left it sitting on the counter.

Later, just before we turned out our bedside lights, Will said drowsily, "I'm going to the nursery Saturday to get the bulbs for your flower garden. It's almost time to plant."

"Jack has a make-up soccer game that morning."

"Oh, crap. I forgot. We'll go."

"No, I can take him. You can come by after the nursery." The nursery was one of Will's favorite places to spend part of a Saturday.

After a minute, Will said, "It must have been horrible for you today. I'm sorry for getting pissed. I don't know what Jack and I would do without you. I want you to know that." Not exactly the apology I was hoping for, especially after our talk the previous night, but it came close. He moved close to cuddle with me, and I was asleep a moment later.

16

I wasn't scheduled to work the next day, so I dawdled over coffee while making Jack his favorite lunch, a peanut butter and jelly sandwich. He ate one nearly every day *because* it was his favorite. Before that, we'd done a year of bologna sandwiches. I decided to drive him to school when I saw a reporter and a cameraman in my driveway. As Jack and I walked out to the car, the reporter stuck a microphone in my face and asked "Were you the one to find Oliver Sampson, Mrs. Brewster?" "What did you see?" "Do you know how he was killed?" while the cameraman clicked away with a zoom lens.

I pushed by her, slapping the microphone aside and screening Jack, who was asking, "Who is she, Mom? Why is that man taking your picture?" Once Jack was in his car seat, I ran around to the driver's side and got in. Bob Morgan was obviously determined to get a story from me. Well, he could just wait.

When we had cleared the driveway, I said to Jack, "That was a reporter from the *Post and Sentinel*, and they wanted to get some information from me for a story. It's nothing to worry about. I'll talk to them later, okay? Right now you need to get to school." I drove away quickly, winding through the neighborhood in an attempt to lose the reporter.

Jack continued with his questions. "Who's Oliver Sampson?"

"He's an acquaintance of mine, Jack. He died yesterday."

"What's an acquaintance?"

"Someone you know but not very well."

"Oh. How did he die?"

"The police are trying to figure that out."

"Are you helping Uncle Sam?"

"Hey Mr. Curious as a Cat…"

"What's curious as a cat mean?"

"It means you ask a lot of questions. Let me ask you one. What about that bully you were telling Dad and me about last night?"

Jack frowned and picked up where he had left off the night before and chattered all the way to the school drop-off line. Thank heavens.

I called Paulette as I left the school and asked her what was on the menu for lunch. She laughed, told me to keep my shirt on, and said she'd see me around noon.

The reporters had made an educated guess about my next move and found me at the hospital, where I went to talk to Marsh. With a show of force which apparently impressed even himself, my rickety and faithful hospital guard, Lyle Pendergraff, managed to fend off the reporter and her cameraman on the loading dock so I could get inside unbothered.

I found Marsh in the autopsy suite, having just finished with Oliver's autopsy. My eyes were drawn to the body bag on the table. Marsh was removing his protective suit, shoulders slumped and face sagging. I put my hand on his arm and asked, "How're you doing, Marsh? I'm so sorry you had to do the autopsy."

"Believe me, if I could've found anyone else, I would've. He was really a good kid." At this point he choked up a little, shedding his usually professional demeanor. "It seemed like life was really working out for him, with what you told me about him and Nancy, and that new motorcycle of his. He was so proud of it."

"There's something I didn't know. Did he ride it to work?"

"Rain or shine. It's a custom Harley Davidson with the body and fenders painted with something he called blue haze, with a silver marble pattern in it."

"That must have cost him some money."

"I don't know motorcycles, but Harleys ain't cheap and I suspect that paint job wasn't either. I thought about it the other day, after you asked me how much he earned."

"Do you know when he got the bike?"

"A few months back, I think." Marsh paused for a minute and then asked, "Did you know he really admired you?"

You could have knocked me over with a feather. "No, I didn't. Why on earth would he admire *me*?"

"He was really impressed with how you solved the hospital robberies last year. He thought of you as a real detective. I think there was a little hero worship on his part."

I was suddenly struck with a deep sense of sadness I'd never gotten to know him, beyond our conversations at the pool about Jack. I asked Marsh what he'd found on autopsy, and it was what I had thought when I saw the body, extreme loss of blood. The only new information was a guess the murder weapon was a wire garrote. One thing was clear: whoever did it was strong and practiced, because of the depth of the wound and absence of hesitation cuts.

After commiserating that we now had two deaths, related by the appearance of a white van, I left Marsh to his paperwork and went to Surgery to see if I could find Dr. Montez. On the way, I tried to call Sam to let him know about the motorcycle. I hadn't seen one at Oliver's when I was there, but I hadn't explored the garage. I couldn't get a signal on my cell phone, typical for most areas of the hospital, and as a rule, employees did not use hospital phones for personal calls unless it was an emergency. So the call had to wait.

Dr. Montez was in the cafeteria having what appeared to be an abbreviated lunch when I finally found him. I slid into the seat across from him, reintroduced myself, and apologized for bothering him. He didn't look particularly pleased to be interrupted, since he was reading a journal article while eating his sandwich. "Dr. Montez, can I ask you a couple of questions? I promise this will be short."

"Fine. Shoot," he replied abruptly, and went back to eating his sandwich with an occasional glance down at his article.

"I was wondering if you knew a company called New Living Technologies. I understand it's involved in harvesting and transporting organs for transplantation, and I figured you might know something about it." I watched his face carefully while I said this and noted that although he had finally focused on me, his attention quickly returned to his sandwich. He paused to take a bite before answering, and I waited impatiently while he chewed and swallowed.

"I've heard of that company," he finally replied. "But the hospital doesn't do business with them as far as I know. At least *I* haven't. Why do you ask?"

"Just something tangential that came up in an ongoing police investigation. Are they a legitimate source of transplant tissue?"

"I wouldn't know. All I can tell you is we get our tissue primarily from the New England Organ Bank, which is overseen by the federal government. Look, I really need to finish reading this article before I head back up."

I apologized again, thanked him for his time, and left thinking here was another instance where I wasn't getting the whole truth. With his background and experience, he should know whether the company was legit.

When I emerged from the hospital, the reporter and her companion had vanished, and it occurred to me they'd probably broken off their pursuit for lunch. I figured maybe this new generation of journalists didn't function without regularly scheduled meals. My iPhone had recorded three voicemails and a text message from Bob Morgan. Again ignoring him, I called Phil, who didn't answer, and left a message for him to call me and another for Sam, describing Oliver's motorcycle.

I drove back to our Sea Cliff neighborhood, my stomach telling me Paulette would have a gastronomic delight waiting for me. She didn't disappoint: lobster salad, fresh sour dough bread, and another one of her waist-expanding confections, a perfect Italian tiramisu. I'd never figured out how Paulette managed to keep her petite shape, but the secret could be worth millions. Over dessert and coffee, we planned our trip to Boston and the Caribbean Queen office.

"So when can you go?" I asked her.

"When are your days off next week?"

"Tuesday for sure. I think I am on nights after that."

"Okay, Tuesday it is. I'll check my wardrobe over the weekend for something young enough. Maybe Sarah can give me the latest on accessories." Sarah was Paulette's ten year old. "What's our cover?"

I could tell Paulette was really enjoying this. "A girls' trip to Boston.' I replied. "There's that Raphael exhibit at the Gardner Museum that we've been dying to see, right?" The Isabella Garner Museum is a small, rare jewel of a museum, which regularly books exceptional travelling exhibits.

"We can have lunch at the museum café and squeeze in some shopping afterward," Paulette added.

"Perfect. What time had you planned to tell the people at the Caribbean Queen you'll be dropping in?"

"How about eleven? We can sit and scope it out beforehand. Do you want me to bring binoculars?"

"Okay, and maybe eavesdropping equipment as well."

Paulette stuck her tongue out at me, and we both giggled. "How about we hit the road at 6:30? Too early for you?" I asked.

"Not a chance. My car or yours?"

Her car was tempting, a very comfortable late model Acura, but if they looked outside to check her out, my old Jeep would be a better fit with a would-be student. "Mine. You need to look like you could use some money," I replied.

⫷⫸

I left Paulette's feeling five pounds heavier and a little jumpy after three cups of coffee. With some reluctance I drove to the offices of the *Post and Sentinel* to get the meeting with its editor out of the way. The *P & S* was located one street back from the police station on Sullivan, housed in a renovated brick warehouse dating from the early 1900s. Following the receptionist's directions, I climbed to the second floor. Bob Morgan's office was on the north end of the building, and he greeted me at the door.

"I'd given up hoping you'd stop by, since you'd done such a good job stiff-arming my reporter. How are you Rhe? It's been what, two years?" He hesitated, looked like he might give me a hug, and finally held out his hand instead, which I shook. I'd forgotten what a mellifluous voice Bob had, and long-forgotten emotions of a teenage relationship made an unexpected appearance.

Bob was tall and had always been rather thin, but now had a small potbelly, new since the last time I'd seen him. He still had the longish brown hair that made him look like a young reporter, and he flashed me the famous Morgan smile, which had attracted girls like bees to honey in high school. He'd had lived up to expectations, too, dating virtually every girl in our class, including me. I'd lasted longer than most, but the intensity of the relationship finally caused me to pull back, something new for him.

"Hiya, Bob," I replied. "I'm well, thanks. I figured I'd get rid of the cubs by coming straight to the lion's den. How've you been?"

"Not bad. The paper's not in the red, which is a real feat, considering the economy." He walked back to his desk in front of one of the large windows lining the office, sat down and indicated a chair in front of the desk. "Have a seat. All of the excitement lately has been great for circulation. And you're in the middle of it."

"Not by design." I noticed with his back to the window, he was surrounded by light and I had to squint a little against the brightness. "How're Will and your son? A son, right?" He was going through polite motions but clearly itching to get to the point.

"They're fine. Jack's growing like a weed. How's Jane?"

"I guess you didn't hear, we got divorced last year." He frowned and looked down at his hands. Bob had married Janie Seaver, one of the girls he had dated in high school, and it had seemed like a solid union.

That truly surprised me, and all I could think to say was, "I'm sorry to hear that."

"Yeah, well, it is what it is." He paused and said, "Let's get down to business. What can you tell me about the Bianchi girl's death and about Oliver Sampson?"

"Nothing, really, because of the ongoing police investigations and the fact that I'm now a police consultant. Which unfortunately means I *really* can't discuss anything."

"Nothing?"

"Nope. But there's something I need to find out from you."

"Hey, tit for tat here. To get something, you've gotta give something."

I couldn't think of anything I could tell him but countered with, "How about I let you know in advance when something's going to happen and then, when this is all over, I can give you the story. Sam's still going to have to approve it, though."

He gave me a funny half smile, thought about it for a few seconds, and said, "Deal. What is it you want to know?"

"Why didn't you release Raymond Little's name in Sunday's article about the beating of the Pequod student? He's over sixteen and it would've made for a better story, along with some of his background." Bob pressed his lips together and frowned. This guy had an ego the size of a hot air balloon when it came to journalism, and I'd just pricked a hole in it. "Well?"

"You're not the first person to ask, Rhe, and the answer is complicated."

"I can handle complicated. Enlighten me."

"Why? Does this have to do with anything the police are working on?"

"It may or may not. I'm not sure."

"Okay, but don't forget I get the story, whether or not this turns into anything."

I raised my right hand. "I swear."

"Well...as you know, when I returned to Pequod the *Post* was essentially on its last legs. Circulation had dropped so much there was basically just enough income for a weekly edition. The manager - Nate Groves, remember him? - was so old he remembered the *Titanic* sinking like it was yesterday. I wanted to take over and make this paper what it should be, you know, modern and newsworthy, but the bank wouldn't loan me the money. That is, until Bitsy Wellington stepped in. Her father owned the bank, and she persuaded him to loan me the money."

"In return for what?"

"Part ownership of the paper. When her father died and left her everything, *she* became the part owner. Hell, she's richer than Croesus, and having her backing meant I could do virtually everything I wanted. Hire good reporters, make it a daily, use color print. And it's become a success, wouldn't you agree?"

I nodded, and decided to go out on a limb. "Did you – do you - have a, uh, close relationship with her?"

"Way too personal a question, Rhe. You know better than to ask."

Maybe that was the reason for the divorce? "Okay, I shouldn't have asked. But is this why you didn't publish Ray Little's name, because she told you not to?"

He nodded and looked out the large glass windows on the other side of his office, staring at the beautiful fall day and the color tinting the trees.

"I hate to mention this, Bob, but where the heck is your journalistic integrity? Or is that a thing of the past?"

He refocused on my face. "It was just a small request, nothing major. We'll use his name when and if there's a trial or he pleads."

"When and if?"

"Bitsy told me with some certainty there won't be a trial. The charges will be dropped to a misdemeanor and he'll be given time served before bail, with probation and probably an anger management course."

"On whose authority?"

"I don't know. One of her many lawyers, I suppose. That's what she told me."

I stared at him, shaking my head. "What's her interest in Ray Little? How does she know him?"

"Haven't a clue and she wasn't taking any questions about it. Believe me, I asked."

"There's a story here, you must know it! Are you *not* going to investigate that, too?"

"Look, Rhe, I've been trying to get out from under ..."

"Literally or figuratively?" I interrupted, irritated at his passivity.

He flushed and continued. "I'm trying to raise enough money to buy Bitsy out. She isn't making it easy - the price she gave me is way more than her share is worth."

"Good luck with that. Bitsy can be one tough nut." I couldn't resist adding, "But of course you probably already know that." I had what I needed, so I rose to leave. "Gotta go. Nice seeing you, Bob."

"I'm holding you to your promise. Don't forget." He gave me a little salute of good-by, placed granny glasses on the end of his nose and focused his attention on some papers on his desk.

I figuratively uncrossed my fingers as I walked out. *There's a snowball's chance in hell you're getting any information from me, Bob Morgan. It'd go straight to Bitsy.*

⌒⌒

For the rest of the afternoon, I indulged in cleaning up the kitchen, collecting dirty clothes to wash that night, and getting in a long overdue swim. Just as I got back from collecting Jack after soccer practice, my phone rang. It was Sam.

"Rhe? I have the plate number for Oliver's motorcycle and had a BOLO put out."

"You move fast for a man your age, cowboy."

I heard a chuckle from his end. "Anything else?" he asked.

"I met with Bob Morgan this afternoon after he called for the tenth time. He even had a reporter and camera person stalking me for most of the day."

"Yeah, he's a persistent son of a bitch, and that's based on experience. I hope you didn't tell him anything."

"Not a word."

"Did you learn something?"

"What we thought. Bitsy quashed the mention of Ray Little's name in the newspaper article. Did you know she owns a majority of the newspaper?"

"No fooling. So that explains it. Do she and Bob have something going on?"

"I had the same thought, but Bob wouldn't confirm or deny. However, he mentioned that Ray Little's probably going to get off with a wrist slap. Apparently Bitsy's lawyers feel confident the charges will be dropped. Sounds like pillow talk to me."

"Yeah, me too. So Tanya and her grandfather will likely be offered money to change her story. I'd better give them a call, because if they take it, it's perjury and if they don't, either or both of them could be in some danger."

"Let me know what you find out, will you?" Just then I got a ding on the phone; someone else was calling me. It turned out to be Phil.

I told him about my conversation with Dr. Montez and that I was more than a little suspicious about his ignorance of New Life Technologies. Phil had found the same three companies I had and was already digging deeper on the third one. We agreed to touch base in a day or so.

17

By Saturday night, Will had overcome his reluctance to tail Zoey and her friends. I knew it was a real concession on his part to support me. We left Jack with Paulette, her family and their two black Labradors, who not only did a great job wearing Jack out, but also caused nonstop begging for a dog.

Around six, we parked down the street from Hamlin Dorm, where Will had discovered Zoey, Angela and Christa were all living while their sorority house was being built. We opened the cooler I'd packed and helped ourselves to roast beef sandwiches on rye with horseradish and mayo, plus some hot coffee. When I'd finished my sandwich, Will handed me the binoculars and I focused them for my eyes, looking at the front of the dorm.

"See anything? Should we move a little closer down the street?" he asked.

"No and no." I put down the glasses and helped myself to another sandwich, taking in a bite of pure horseradish. Instantly my head exploded, my eyes watered and I started to cough and sputter.

"You okay?"

"Yeah, horseradish does wonders for your sinuses. Remind me to eat some the next time I get a cold."

An hour went by, then two. By that time, we had polished off four sandwiches plus pickles and chips and some brownies, and sat quietly, having run out of conversation. We were drinking the last of the coffee. I decided surveillance was about as much fun as watching mold grow on bread and was almost drowsing, when all of a sudden Will said, "See that?"

I jumped. "What?"

He grabbed the glasses and peered. "A car, looks like a Lincoln town car. It's just pulled up in front of the dorm. There's some girls coming out." Will handed me the glasses and started the car, easing closer along the curb with the lights off.

The college had thoughtfully equipped the front of the dorm with halogen safety lights, and once I'd refocused yet again, I could see the girls. "It's Zoey but I don't recognize the others." I also saw short dresses, stiletto sandals, and a little sparkle of jewelry before the girls got into the car and it pulled away.

"Follow them, pahdnah," I instructed Will in my best John Wayne drawl, and he turned the headlights on and drove slowly after the Lincoln. At first Will was hesitant to follow too closely, and the Lincoln got so far ahead we could barely see the taillights. "Pull up closer," I insisted. "Just leave one car between us and them."

We had been tailing for less than five minutes when the taillights suddenly disappeared. "What happened? Where did they go?" I practically yelled.

"There's a turn up ahead," Will replied calmly. "Keep your shirt on." And sure enough, there were the taillights. We were now heading east in a neighborhood of larger homes from what I could see.

How did Will know to turn there? I thought, and almost immediately, the taillights disappeared again. Will made a turn left, once again heading north, without saying anything, and there was the town car again. *He knows his way around out here. That's great. But how?*

On the right side of the road I noticed iron fences and stone walls and lighted, expensive gates. These were probably the seaside estates Jack and I saw on the cliffs when we were sailing. Suddenly the taillights turned right and stopped, and we had no choice but to drive by. The car was in front of an elaborately landscaped, well-lit entrance with a tall double gate of decorative cast iron, with the initials EA scripted into the middle of each half.

Will continued down the road, looking for a place to turn, when I suddenly remembered the match book. I was wearing the same jacket I'd worn when I drove over to Oliver's and reached into my pocket to see if it was still there. It was. And I'd forgotten to give it to Sam. "Pull over, Will, I need to look at something." He pulled the car onto the berm and we stopped.

I flipped on the reader's light on my side of the car and read the initials EA. "Look, hon, I found this matchbook at Oliver's. Look at the initials. Same as on the gate where the car stopped. This must have come from that estate."

Will didn't really look at the match book but said cryptically, "It's possible."

"That means Oliver or his killer could have been at the estate." I sighed. "Or anyone else on God's green earth for that matter. I guess it's not much of a lead."

"How come you didn't give it to Sam?"

"It just skipped my mind what with everything else happening after the murder. You would have probably forgotten, too," I replied a little defensively.

"I think we've done as much as we can do tonight, Rhe. You can tell Sam what we saw, and you'd better give him that matchbook." He put the car in drive and pulled out onto the road, turning the car around.

"Can you just slow down a little as we go by that entrance?" I pleaded. "I want to get a better look. Maybe there's a name." He did as I asked, but other than the EA, there was nothing to see that would identify the estate. The driveway was not visible more than a few yards beyond the gate. I counted the number of gates until we turned right onto the road we'd come in on. Perhaps I could use Google Earth to see the coast in that region and focus in on the EA estate. And I *really* needed to talk to Phil.

As we drove home, it occurred to me for a second time that Will knew something about what was going on. First, his immediate supposition that Zoey and her friends were working as prostitutes – based on nothing really - and then his knowledge of the road leading to the estate. It was not a comforting thought.

"I'd really like to know more about that place. You ever seen it?" I asked innocently.

A pause and then, "No."

"But you knew where the turns were."

"One of my friends from Pequod lives up this way."

"Who?"

"You don't know him. Art Crowell. He's a faculty member in Biology."

"Oh." I didn't think Will was telling me the truth, or at least not all of it, and now Art Crowell was on my list of people to check up on.

We drove the rest of the way to Paulette's in silence and picked up a tired Jack, who got into his PJs and climbed into bed without protest. Maybe it was time to consider getting a dog.

⌒⌒

Saturday morning, a cold rain was coming down, blown into ribbons by the wind. With the soccer game cancelled, Tyler came over to play with Jack, and they sat on the family room rug, surrounded by Lego pieces and their Matchbox cars and trucks. I stood for a while, looking at the ocean through the French doors. The rain was hitting the glass almost directly, and the water sheeted down, blurring the view of a gunmetal gray ocean littered with white caps. I pulled myself away from the view and went into the kitchen for a cup of coffee. Since Will had gone to the nursery and then to the hardware store, his second favorite place to play, I had time to search the internet.

First I looked up Arthur Crowell on the Pequod College site. He was there, an Associate Professor of Biology, but there was no home address. I then checked the phone book, but there was no Crowell listed. Maybe he had a private number. I Googled him, but didn't find anything other than his college affiliation.

Then I went to Google Earth and found the coastline north of Pequod, where I could see the estates lining the cliffs. From my count the previous night, I figured EA was the fifth one from the end of the road, and I focused in on the house. From the aerial view, it appeared large and ornate, with a wing coming off at each end, so the house formed a U around a courtyard facing the sea. There was a large structure at the southern end of the house, probably a garage, since the driveway swung around to the front of it after sweeping by the house. On the sea side, I could see something leading up from the narrow beach at the front of the cliff to the broad expanse at the top. Probably stairs. Just for amusement, I Googled EA and EA house, Pequod, Maine, and to my surprise found a site for East Almorel, with a picture.

East Almorel was formidable stone Tudor-style house built at the turn of the 19th century and was currently privately owned. I could check in the courthouse to find out who owned it, but maybe I'd ask Sam for help with that. Of course, I'd have to tell him why I was interested, and then I'd have to report on Will's and my surveillance. Maybe I'd go to the courthouse on Monday. I also wanted a closer look at it, but was stymied about how I could do that. By Sunday morning, however, I'd hatched a plan.

18

Will had been feeling guilty about not spending enough time with Jack and suggested we take him to a children's museum in Portland Sunday afternoon. "The place has all sorts of activities Jack would like," he said with enthusiasm, "a kid's workshop, climbing sculpture and a giant maze."

"Just right for our energetic son," I concurred.

"Do you want to go?"

His question gave me the idea. "No, I'm thinking this would be a great father-son bonding experience for the two of you." *And give me time to take a look at East Almorel.*

He raised an eyebrow. "You sure?"

"Yup, I'd enjoy a little quiet time."

"Okay, if you're sure."

You bet I am. But a quote from Sir Walter Scott floated into my consciousness, unbidden: "Oh, what a tangled web we weave, when first we practice to deceive." Hopefully this would be my first and last deception.

They left around 1 PM and Will said they'd be back around eight. I waited until the afternoon was just starting to fade, put on a black turtleneck, jeans and a warm dark blue sweater with a hood, grabbed my foul weather gear and headed to the marina. I figured I could sail up the coast, beach the boat south of the house, climb up the stairs to Almorel and have a look around. Nothing to it, except that the wind was blowing around 15 knots and the ocean was rough with good sized waves. Nothing I hadn't sailed in before.

The first part of my little adventure went surprisingly well. The Trinket rode high with only one person aboard, smacking and rolling with the waves. With the Trinket heeled over and the sail close hauled, I took a heading north at a good clip, hiked out on the starboard gunwale. The dark clouds overhead spat rain, and water splashed over both gunwales. I counted the estates as I sailed along, wiping the spray and rain from my face. I sailed slightly past the fifth estate and turned to shore, dropped the sail, and stowed away the tiller, rudder, and centerboard. Using oars I always kept onboard, I turned the bow to the wind and rowed into shore, helped by the wind and current.

I picked a landing spot shielded from the stairs to Almorel by a small promontory and jumped out of the boat as it hit bottom, soaking myself to my knees in the freezing water. Since the tide was still coming in, I set the anchor deep, just above the high water line to keep the Trinket from floating away. My bright yellow foul weather gear came off immediately and was stowed in the boat. In anticipation of a wet landing, I had left the house wearing some fast drying mesh skimmers, but they still squished uncomfortably as I made my way up the beach and around the promontory to the stairs.

From the bottom, the stairs seemed to reach to forever, ascending past packed sand, huge tumbled boulders, and finally a rock cliff. I was panting heavily when I got to the top, where I paused to catch my breath and reconnoiter. I was totally exposed at the edge of the lawn, which stretched from the cliff to the house, a hulking outline against the lightest part of the sky. After hunkering down, I crab-walked quickly to my left, where I would be partially hidden behind a row of wild rose bushes. These stopped at the end of a scraggly string of Eastern white pines that extended all the way to the garage. A thick bed of long pine needles deadened the sounds of my footsteps and thankfully, my shoes had finally stopped squishing. After I traversed the pines and the length of the rear of the garage, I stopped. There were two men's voices coming from somewhere in front.

"Who's parking cars tonight?" one of them asked.

"You are," said the other, with a deeper voice.

"So I get to stand out here getting wet, while you're nice and dry in the kitchen, eating and staring at hookers' tits."

"You bet your sweet ass. And there's prime rib tonight. You can always radio me if you have a problem ....." The voices moved away towards the house. So there were at least two men, but there could be more. For about the tenth time I thought, *What the hell am I doing here? Forget trying to explain why, if I'm caught.*

When I'd sidled around to the front of the garage, I saw one of the doors was open, and I slipped in. I found a Rolls Royce Phantom, a Jaguar coupe, and an empty bay, probably for the Lincoln. In the far corner, gleaming in the dim light, was a motorcycle, painted a brilliant blue with silver marbling. It had to be Oliver's. *What was it doing here?*

I exited the garage and quickly traversed the driveway to the southern wing of the house, with the gravel making a crunching noise under my feet that

I was sure could be heard a mile away. The wing was bordered by the more wild rose bushes, running along its entire length. These provided me with a little cover from the windows while I crouched and crept towards the rear of the house. When I reached the end, I saw there was an open door with light spilling out onto a patio of intricately woven bricks. From the smells and noises reaching me, this had to be the kitchen. Delicious wafts of roasting meat and garlic made my mouth water.

A particularly loud clash of pans, followed by a string of curses, gave me the opportunity to slip across the outer edge of the patio and back to the cover of the rose bushes. When I peeked around the corner, I found that the bushes continued around to the main part of the house. Huge doors interrupted the rose bushes, opening from a large room in the main house out onto another woven brick patio. A huge hot tub stood in its center, surrounded by cushioned chairs and chaise lounges. The hot tub was open and steam rose lazily into the cool night air. The naked couple enjoying its heat and their own did not notice me as I moved to the corner between the wing and the main house.

I shrunk into corner's shadow, then poked my head out and took a quick look through one of the floor-to-ceiling windows into the large room occupying the entire back of the main house. The room was softly lit by two crystal chandeliers throwing shifting shadows on the ceiling. More light pooled from table lamps scattered through the room, alongside comfortable sofas and chairs upholstered in rich reds and deep blues. The floor was a white and gray marble covered by scattered Persian rugs that complemented the furniture. Dazzled by the wealth of the room, I forced my attention to the people in it. I first saw Zoey and the two girls I'd seen the previous night, each sitting with a man, legs crossed and holding a drink. They were certainly dressed for maximum exposure. There were a few equally provocatively dressed Asian girls in the room and by their looks, very young.

The men, by contrast, were dressed in open-neck casual shirts with khaki or dark pants, and most of them I didn't know. But three I did - Judge John Jeffries, Dr. Montez, and Adriano Moretti. Adriano did not seem to be part of the mini-parties going on, but was hanging out at a well-stocked bar at one end of the room.

From time to time, pairs left the room, and couples occasionally wandered back in, with both men and women dressed in silk robes. I was beginning to get stiff and cold, tucked in my corner, when the woman in the hot tub started moaning, and definitely not with pain. The water in the hot tub splashed noisily. *Time for me to make my exit.* I headed back toward the kitchen and decided since it was now fairly dark and the couple in the hot tub was fully occupied, I could cut across the lawn to the row of pine trees at its southeastern edge.

I had almost reached the pines when I heard a shout, "Hey, you! Stop!" I didn't look back but continued running hell bent for leather, in and out of the trees, heading for the stairs. There was a loud crack and something chipped one of the trees. As I bolted from their cover, there was another crack and something whizzed by my shoulder. *How could I have been so dumb? Of course the guards would be armed. No way to talk myself out of this one.*

As I raced toward the stairs, I heard a guard yelling into his radio, "We've got an intruder. Get your ass out here!"

I hit the stairs, taking two at a time and at the midway point, I could hear the guards yelling at each other, with their voices coming closer. About 20 feet from the bottom, where the sand began, I launched myself to the side, off the stairs, and rolled under them, using my arm to erase where I'd landed. My heart was pounding so loudly I could hardly hear the footsteps descending. I clamped my hand over my mouth to quiet my panting and turned my face into the sand.

"See 'em yet?" I heard a man shout, somewhere above me. One of the two guards from the garage, by the sound of his voice. Then the footsteps stopped, and the step directly above me creaked under his weight.

"Can you see anything?"

"No, and I forgot my fuckin' flashlight. You got one?"

"Whaddaya think? I was eating dinner!"

"Well, go get a couple!"

"You go get one! I'm not paid enough to climb up and down those stairs in the friggin' rain and search along that damn beach. It's darker than hell down there."

"You sure you saw someone? You trigger-happy idiot! I think you just wanted to fire the fuckin' gun!"

"The hell I am. I saw someone." A few more colorful phrases followed, mostly having to do with the ancestry of the other guard. The footsteps retreated heavily, back up the stairs. I gasped, having held my breath the whole time the guard stood directly over me. As soon as I could no longer hear him, I dug out of the sand, skied down the rest of the hill, and ran like hell in the deepest shadows along the cliff, checking behind me as I rounded the promontory. There was now some faint light at the top of the stairs. The adrenaline rush nearly lifted me off the sand as I beat it for the shadow of my boat, now rocking energetically in shallow water, but tethered by the anchor. I pulled up the anchor and flung it into the boat. Without pausing to slip on my foul weather gear, I gave the boat a mighty push and rolled over the gunwale into the bottom. As soon as I could get up, I took the oars and rowed as hard as I could until I was far enough offshore to drop the centerboard, replace the rudder and tiller, and then raise the sail.

Getting back to Pequod harbor was no easy feat. I was sailing in nearly complete dark, with only the lights from the estates on the shore and the flashes from the lighted buoy marking the harbor to guide me. Uncontrollable shakes took over as I headed south, with the cold, wet wind chilling me from behind. The familiar three tones of the bell buoys marking the entrance told me when I was finally there.

By the time I reached the marina, my fingers were numb and I fumbled through tying up to the buoy and putting my beloved sailboat in order. Reaching the car, I put the heater on full blast and assessed my situation. It was 7:15. I'd narrowly missed getting killed but still needed to get home, get changed, and pour something hot down my throat. Will finding out what I had just done was not an option.

Will and Jack arrived back at 8:15. They were met by a freshly showered wife and mother, dressed in dry clothes and chugging hot chocolate from a huge mug. I was so happy to see them that they both got strong bear hugs. "You must have missed us," said Will cautiously. "What have you been up to?"

I decided that a half truth was better than a lie. "Well, after you left, I went down to the marina and did a little housekeeping on the Trinket. Ended up taking her out for a short sail."

"In this weather? Are you nuts? Tell me that you at least wore a life jacket!"

"It was in the boat. And the sailing was spectacular. Great wind!"

19

During lunch on Monday, I made a visit to the Medical Examiner's office and found Marsh literally up to his elbows in a body. When he saw me, he stepped away from the table and raised the faceplate of his head gear.

"I got the results of the water samples back," he said. "The water from Lili's clothes and the water from the hot tub have identical components. That doesn't mean the samples came from the same place, but it's suggestive. But here's the clincher. A lot of someone's skin cells had sloughed off in that hot tub and were pulled onto the filter you gave me. The chemicals and heat in the water preserved their DNA."

"And? And?"

"The state lab did me a real favor and rushed the DNA analysis, and it matched the sample I obtained from Lili's body. Her body was definitely in that hot tub. I've already sent the report over to Sam. That was a good guess of yours, Rhe."

I nodded my head at the serendipity of finding the right hot tub and asked, more to myself than Marsh, "So why did Oliver lose the first sample? Until he was killed, I was willing to believe he just misplaced it. Now I'm thinking he deliberately got rid of it."

Marsh shook his head in disagreement. "That's hard for me to believe."

I continued, "I know you don't, but I'm thinking he emptied the hot tub, too. I just can't figure out why. I don't know how he knew Lili and I can't see him as a murderer."

Marsh remained silent and looked so unhappy that I asked, "So how are you holding up otherwise?"

"Okay, I guess. I start interviewing for a new assistant tomorrow."

"I hope you find a good one, Marsh. Replacing Oliver is not going to be easy. I'll see if I can find you a doughnut to help you with it." He finally smiled at that, and just then my phone buzzed with a text message. It was from Sam and I read it on my way to the ER. Short and sweet: "See me ASAP." He probably wanted to talk about Marsh's findings. I could see him after work.

When I walked in, the ER was like a scene from the TV show - utter pandemonium, with patients from a multiple vehicle accident on US 1. It was close to five when I finally left, and I hoped I'd still find Sam at the station.

⌒⌒

As I walked up to Ruthie at the front desk, she gave me a warning shake of her head. "He's in a foul mood," she whispered, which I saw for myself when I walked down the hall to his office. I entered cautiously and said 'hi' and got silence in response. He motioned me to sit down on a chair already cleared off. Something was *really* not good. Sam got up, closed the door, turned to me and yelled, "What in hell were you thinking?"

"What?"

"You know what! What were you doing at East Almorel last night? Do *not* lie to me! It had to be you."

"Why would you think that?" I replied as calmly as I could, while trying frantically to figure how to handle the situation.

"Because the chief of security for the estate called me last night and told me one of the guards fired shots at an intruder, and the intruder had come up from the beach. He couldn't describe the person other than it was a slight male." Still loud. I could see people gathering in the hall outside, through the window in his door.

I took a deep breath and decided I couldn't talk my way out of this one. "Okay, okay, it was me. And I know it was a really dumb thing to do. But please lower your voice."

"Jesus Christ, Rhe. You might have been killed. What on earth were you thinking?" he repeated only slightly less loudly. "And you can't run around lying to Will. I promised him we would keep an eye on you. How's this going to go over if he finds out you went off on your own and we couldn't stop you?"

"Believe me, I know that, and this will *not* happen again. I've got the message. Being shot at is a great deterrent." I paused in the hopes he had run out of steam, then looked at him hopefully. "Do you want to know what I saw?" He took a deep breath, continued glaring at me and sat down. The people outside his window dispersed when he glared at them as well and gave them a dismissive wave of his hand.

"So go ahead," Sam finally replied, after irritably shuffling papers on his desk and then leaning back in his chair, still frowning. "But I'm not sure we can use anything you saw because you were trespassing. Tell me what happened and start at the beginning"

First I told him what Will and I had done on Saturday night and that raised an eyebrow. "So Will thought Zoey and her friends were hookers?" he asked. "Based on what evidence?"

"I don't really know, Sam. I think it was a gut thing." *What else could I say? That I thought Will knew something about Almorel but wasn't telling me?* Then I described how I got to Almorel and reached the back of the main house. He shook his head in disapproval or disbelief as my tale unwound.

"When I looked through the window, I saw three female students from Pequod, along with two or three other young, scantily dressed women, in a room full of older men. Some of the women were Asian, and didn't look older than teenagers, maybe younger. This is definitely an escort service with benefits. Couples were drinking and chatting and then left together to go somewhere else in the house. Some couples came back, and the men were dressed in what looked like silk pajamas. There was a naked couple in the hot tub enjoying more than the water. I was right. Zoey and her friends are earning a lot of money as high class hookers. But I don't know who's behind it, since all I could find out online is that the house is privately owned."

"Well, I'll light a fire under Phil to find that out. And I'll check with the town's lawyer to see if we can use what you saw as probable cause without getting your name out there. If I can get a search warrant from Judge Jefferies, we can raid the place."

"Uh, Sam, I don't think you want to go to Judge Jeffries."

"Why?"

"Because he was one of the men I saw there. Along with Dr. Montez from the hospital."

"Damn it all to hell! And Jefferies is also on the hospital board. You've really opened a can of worms."

"There's more. I saw Adriano at the bar, mixing drinks."

"How in hell is Lili's cousin mixed up in this? I wonder if Uncle Antonio's got his fingers in the enterprise." He paused for a second, thinking, then continued. "If so, the place might be owned by someone out of state. Maybe some of the girls are being transported across state lines to work there. We'll have to notify the FBI as well. Could this get any more complicated?"

"Couple more things."

"Dear God in heaven, what next?"

"Oliver's motorcycle was in the garage there."

"And why would it be there?"

"Well, it wasn't in Oliver's garage, so the killer somehow has to be linked to that estate."

"We can take it into evidence if it's still there when we search the place. Provided I can find a judge who's not getting his rocks off at that house. Maybe Judge Adams. He's 85 and not too spry." Sam frowned some more and then brightened. "I forgot to tell you. Phil's working on Lili's phone, since the techs said it was a lost cause. Get this - it's sitting in a bowl of rice on his desk. Apparently that's a new way of drying phones out. He thinks we can try it tomorrow, once he has put in a new battery."

"So it's not *all* bad news, Sam" I said, hoping to improve my situation with something positive. "And there's more. Have you had a chance to look at Marsh's latest report?"

"Something good after all this?"

"Unbelievably good. You know the water sample I took from the hot tub at the swim club? The one I gave to Oliver that he conveniently lost? Well, I went back, and the tub had been drained, and I now think Oliver did it." Sam rolled his eyes. "Let me explain! I gave one of the hot tub filters to Marsh, who got some water out of it. He had the sample analyzed and he also recovered DNA from the filter fibers. The water composition matches that from Lili's clothes in terms of chemicals, and get this! The DNA on the filter is hers. So her body was in that hot tub for a day or two. You really need to read his reports when they come in," I scolded. It felt nice to have the upper hand for once.

Sam rubbed the bridge of his nose with his fingers, thinking. "That's good news, Rhe. At least we now know where her body was stored. Why do you think Oliver drained the hot tub?"

"Because once I'd given him the sample of tub water, he had something to hide."

"So do you think he killed Lili?"

"No, I don't. Marsh thinks he was a good kid, and I trust Marsh's opinion. Besides, what would be his motive? He didn't know Lili. But Oliver might have been killed because of what he knew or saw. Maybe he knew the killer and knew the body had been in the tub. Maybe he placed it there himself."

Just then I remembered something else that was going to get me in hot water. "Here," I said, reaching into my pocket and pulling out the foil matchbook. "I found this at the bottom of the front porch stairs at Oliver's house. I'm sorry, Sam. I put it in my pocket and forgot about it. I think it comes from East Almorel. See the initials? They're the same as on the gates to the estate."

Sam took the matchbook with his handkerchief. "Good grief, Rhe. Is there anything else you want to spring on me? You realize we probably can't get any prints off this, now that you've handled it."

"Nope, that's about it." I smiled with relief that our little interchange had gone so well. "But what if I give you my prints anyway and maybe you can find ones that're not mine. And Sam, you've gotta believe me, I was scared shitless last night, and I am *not* doing anything like that again. Please, please, don't let Will know. He thinks I went out for a sail in the afternoon, which is true. I just didn't tell him the rest."

"I'll think about that." Sam rummaged around in the detritus on his desktop, found a box, and handed it to me. "Before you leave, you need to have this."

"What's this?"

"A police-issue taser. As a consultant, you can carry one and I want you to have it with you at all times."

"Why?" My stomach started doing nervous sit-ups.

"Because Ray Little was on the Pequod campus yesterday and tried to approach Tanya. Her friends gave him a dose of pepper spray, and he hightailed off, but not before threatening her and telling her he was going to bury the both of you. Obviously he knows you got him arrested."

"Is this going to work?"

"I guarantee it. Use it if he comes anywhere near you. If we can find him first, we can arrest him for the threat. And I *am* having a patrol car run by your house regularly. Don't even think about arguing!"

'I guess I'll have to tell Will at this point. I just hope he understands," I said with a deep sigh.

Sam got up, gave me a bear hug and whispered. "Thank God you were not hurt last night! Where would I go for a good dinner?" He added, "Be careful, honey. You are not invincible."

"Oh Rhe?" he called as I reached the door.

"Something more?" *Oh dear.*

"Have Ruthie take your picture after you're fingerprinted. We've already done the background search, so all you need to do for a badge is pose for the camera and sign some papers."

I stopped and had my fingerprints taken by John, was photographed by Ruthie, who waited until I was making a face before snapping the photo, and then signed five official papers, in triplicate, before finally heading home. I had to figure out how to tell Will about Ray Little.

When I got home, I took the taser out of the package. It was an air taser and seemed relatively easy to use, just pull back the safety slide and squeeze the trigger. It was good up to a distance of fifteen feet, and the package information said that taser victims recovered with no long term effects. Wonderful. Maybe Ray Little wouldn't sue me if I tased him.

I made fried chicken that night, spattering flour and grease all over the kitchen. My guys love their fats. After dishes, homework and playing a video game with Jack, I signaled to Will that we needed to talk. When he came out from tucking Jack in, I was waiting for him at the kitchen table with two cups of decaf and the taser.

He looked at the taser and asked, "Is that what I think it is?"

"Yup," I relied cheerfully. "It's a taser! Sam gave it to me just in case."

"In case of what?" Will's voice got loud.

"Shhh, we don't want to wake up big ears. You remember the guy that battered Tanya? The football player you had the confrontation with - Ray Little?" He nodded in agreement and I continued, "Well, he's been out on bail, and yesterday he tried to get to Tanya on campus. I'm surprised you didn't hear about it."

"I did, and I was going to tell you about it tonight."

I doubted he would have if I hadn't brought it up, but continued, "Sam told me when he gave me the taser. Ray apparently threatened Tanya and included me as well. That's why the taser, hon. And patrol cars will run by the house regularly. I'm a little worried," I admitted.

"You should be worried. You're in it up to your neck."

"But he's after me, not you or Jack. And besides, I don't think he'd come here. Someone would notice him hanging around, don't you think?" In addition to Paulette, the happy homemaker, we had several retired couples on the block who were generally at home and watched anyone new in the neighborhood as a hobby.

Will reached across the table and took my hand with a look of concern. "Do you know what he looks like?" he asked.

At that point, I realized I'd never seen a picture of Ray Little and wouldn't know him from the postman. "Good question. Maybe he has a Facebook page."

"Nope, I've already looked."

"When did you do that?"

"Right after he challenged me in class. I wanted to find out about him before I went to see the high and mighty Bitsy."

"Why wouldn't he have a Facebook page? I thought all kids had one."

"Maybe he figured he was in trouble and took it down so the administration couldn't see it."

"He might be smarter than we're giving him credit for. I guess I'd better check with Sam. Maybe I can look at his booking photo. Are you going to be okay with this, Will? I know this is more than you signed on for. You know this is *completely* unrelated to the Bianchi case, don't you? It was just a coincidence I met Tanya while looking for information about Lili."

Will didn't answer but took a drag of his coffee, put down the cup and examined the instructional booklet that came with the taser. "Let me read about this. Are you sure you won't taser yourself?" he asked with a half smile. I picked up the coffee cups and put them in the sink while he read the instructions and handled the taser.

"I guess we'll just have to get through this," he said finally, when I came back and sat down. "Just be careful. Especially in the hospital parking lot." Starting Wednesday, I would be taking the midnight to 8AM shift, subbing for a nurse who was on maternity leave.

"I will," I promised. "I'm going to park in the back, off the loading dock where the overnighters park. It's well lit, and there's a guard on duty at the door." I looked at my rumpled-haired husband. He was being so reasonable. *How could I have doubted him the other night?*

"Lyle?" Will asked and shook his head. He took my hand and kissed it, and looked at me hopefully. I'm a sucker for that look. We turned off the lights and headed upstairs for a little exercise before falling asleep.

20

At 7:30 AM Tuesday morning, I turned into Paulette's driveway and she was already waiting for me, dress bag in hand, with two coffee mugs and a brown paper bag sitting on the hood of her car. She was wearing tan slacks, a white blouse, and a jacket in muted fall colors, but the rest of her appearance was startling, to say the least. Her normally wavy hair was now straight and had a blue alligator streak with attached feathers on one side. An oversized, bright pink pleather bag hung from her other arm. Her makeup was perfect: thick eyelashes, a dewy, youthful glow to her skin, bright lipstick.

When I got out of my car, she smiled at my astonished look and said, "You wait. The rest is even better!" Just then a warm aroma of something resplendent with sugar and cinnamon hit my nose, and I headed for the paper bag. "Uh uh, wait 'til we're on our way, you glutton," she continued, still smiling.

"Okay, I'll wait," I said with a fake frown, then gave her a hug and grabbed the two mugs and the paper bag, putting them in the Jeep on the front floor.

Paulette opened one of the back doors and laid her clothes bag across the back seat of the car. "We can stop somewhere and I'll change into the clothes for the interview," she explained. "I couldn't leave the house wearing my interview outfit. I can't imagine what Ross and the kids would think! I can wiggle back into these clothes on the way to the museum."

Paulette finally opened the bag as we drove towards route 95 and gave me a warm cinnamon roll, the aroma of which had been torturing me. "So just how early did you get up to make these?" I asked.

"Five AM. And that coffee's yours. It's loaded with the creamer you like."

During the drive to Boston, I told her about my adventure at East Almorel, glossing over the bullet part and Sam's over-the-top reaction. We also went over Paulette's cover story carefully. She was an English graduate student at Pequod, studying part-time, which would make her difficult to locate with respect to the college, and also working part-time as a nanny for Jack. I'd written her a letter of recommendation. She would tell them exactly what she had said on the phone - that she'd seen their advertisement in the Employment Office at

Pequod, and no, she didn't know anyone else at the college who worked for the Caribbean Queen.

We stopped to get gas just outside of Boston, and Paulette went to the restroom while I filled up. "Whaddya think?" she asked when she emerged from the gas station. She was wearing a long-sleeve, form-fitting white blouse, with a bright pink bolero sweater, a tight black skirt that reached only to mid-thigh, and a pair of five inch stiletto heels. Long, dangling earrings hung from her ears and a mass of bangle bracelets took up most of her right forearm.

I shook my head and smiled. "Perfect. Where on earth did you find those clothes?

"PTA Thrift Shop. They were a steal!"

"Can you walk in those things?" I indicated her shoes.

"It's the skirt that's the problem. It rides up my whazoo when I sit down." To demonstrate, she opened the passenger side door and slid awkwardly into her seat, tugging on the skirt.

⌒⌒

The Caribbean Queen office was in an older, mixed use area, with office buildings and homes of various ages and sizes. The older ones dated from the turn of the twentieth century: square, two story clapboard boxes with flat roofs. You could almost imagine horse drawn wagons in the street. But these were countered by some small ethnic restaurants and mom-and-pop stores of various ethnicities. Since we arrived around ten, I had Paulette take a picture of the office with my Canon as we slowly drove by. It was located in a fairly new brick building and appeared to occupy the entire first floor and there was a white van parked in front. Access was by a glass door to the left of a large front window, on which the name *Caribbean Queen* was discretely scripted, with a painting of the ship beneath. There were no apparent closed circuit video cameras anywhere on the block, but nevertheless we parked the car well down the street, choosing a location with a good view of the front door.

Only two people entered and left the office during our hour of surveillance, and I snapped photos of both. The first was a delivery boy wearing a shirt emblazoned with the name of a local coffee shop, carrying paper coffee cups in a tray and a large bag. The second appeared to be another applicant - young, thin, and dressed like a runway model. She emerged about a half hour later.

Just before eleven, Paulette stepped out of the Jeep, pulled down her skirt, and tip-tapped down the sidewalk. When she reached the CQ building, she gave me a surreptitious thumbs-up before opening the office door and disappearing inside. When I lost sight of her, anxiety suddenly hit me like a brick, with the thought that maybe she'd be found out. I reassured myself by remembering Paulette had played many stage roles, both at college and summer stock. She could pull this off, if anyone could.

I'd been sitting in the car for about a half hour, musing on the lack of activity on the street, when a familiar silver Mercedes coup pulled up behind the van. I picked up my binoculars and focused. *What the heck is she doing here? What does Bitsy have to do with the Caribbean Queen? Is there anything this woman is not involved in?* I snapped a picture of her before she entered the office. Then, after a moment of puzzlement, it occurred to me, *What if she recognizes Paulette? If so, the shit's going to hit the fan.*

I tried to think where Bitsy might have met her. They didn't go to high school or college together, and Paulette never went to yacht club functions, complaining about the quality of the food served, so no problem there. But what if she read Paulette's letter of recommendation from me? The letter might be considered just a coincidence, but it could just as easily make her suspicious. I started the car and backed it further up the street and all the way into an alley, just in case. I got out and peered cautiously around the corner, like a turtle with a long neck.

When Paulette finally emerged, she started to walk to where the car had been parked, but stopped when she didn't see it. Then she continued walking in my direction, looking around and smiling when she finally spotted me.

"Hurry up and get in," I cautioned her. "We need to haul ass. Did you recognize the woman who came into the office?" I started the car, blew out of the alley and headed to the left and away from the CQ office.

"It was Bitsy, wasn't it?" Paulette replied, reaching into the back seat for her clothes bag.

"Have you ever met her? Does she know you?"

"She wouldn't know me from a hole in the wall, but I've seen her picture in the paper. She was looking over my application when I left." She peered back through the rear view window. "That's probably her coming out of the office now."

"Crap. I hope she doesn't recognize this car."

"I think we're too far away."

I handed her my GPS unit and told to her hit the directions to the Gardner Museum I'd preprogrammed, before she wiggled out of her skirt and into her street clothes. Fortunately, we didn't see Bitsy's car following us, but I drove nervously, scanning cars in the rear view mirror. The voice of the GPS was annoying calm and flat, and I yelled at it once or twice. Before we arrived at the museum, Paulette had also taken off her feathers and bangles and removed most of her makeup, so by the time we parked, she was looking pretty much like her normal self. The stress and excitement of the morning drove us immediately to the Café, chattering like monkeys as we sat down and were handed menus. Choosing from the mouth-watering luncheon options, we both had the special, an apricot and pistachio chicken salad with asparagus, with a glass of Pinot Grigio to celebrate Paulette's first adventure.

"So tell about the interview," I asked her after a long sip of wine. By this time we'd calmed down enough to have a reasonable conversation.

"It was mostly normal, with a woman interviewer. Andrea Parker was the name she gave. She was in her early 40s, well-dressed, very pleasant. But proper Bostonian…a little aristocratic. Just like we'd thought, she asked what I was currently doing and also about my background. It was easiest just to give her my real history."

"You said mostly normal?"

"There were a few questions that were really off, you know what I mean? She asked about past and present men in my life and how I'd met them – do I go to bars, use online dating services, hook up? She even asked how sexually active I am, nicely of course, but it still threw me for a minute. So I asked her why these questions were important. She told me some cock and bull story about my meeting a number of single men on the cruise ship. She needed to know how I might respond if they made advances. Almost as if she were vetting me."

"So how did you play it?"

"Cool, I think. I figured the cruise ship could be where Zoey and her friends were introduced to the idea of being escorts. So I told her I liked men and had been "doing it" since I was fourteen. You think I overdid it?"

"What I think is, that if this is a legitimate business, you'll never hear back from them. Good job, kiddo!" and I reached across the table and gave her hand a squeeze.

The rest of our afternoon was devoted to the Raphael exhibit and a couple of hours of frantic shopping in Filene's Basement and The Children's Place. Around 6, we called it a day and headed home, deciding to splurge on calories at a Friendly's along the way.

As I threaded our way out of Boston, Paulette asked, "Do you ever think about last year?"

I chuckled. "You mean when my career as Miss Marple started? You got me into this, you know."

"Me? I seem to recall your complaining to me that patient valuables were disappearing at the hospital, and you were going to do something about it."

"Did I do that? Well, if you hadn't called me that night, I never would have had the chance. So it all started with you!" Paulette'd phoned me around 11 PM, complaining of nausea and severe abdominal pain. Her husband was out of town, so I took her to the hospital with what turned out to be a hot appendix and a resulting emergency appendectomy.

"I don't remember much of what happened after we got to the emergency room, to tell the truth. Except for some blessed relief from the pain."

"How could you? You were doped up on pain meds before the operation and a little blotto from the anesthesia afterward." I gave her a smile. "You were pretty funny, actually."

Paulette made a face at me. "But I knew there was someone in my room. I remember asking him what he was doing."

I had been returning to her room with a cup of coffee when I discovered someone dressed in scrubs, rummaging in the drawers next to her bed. "What he was doing was looking for something of yours to steal. I told you all about this right after it happened, don't you remember?"

"Not much."

"The wonders of Versed as an amnesiac. It makes you forget everything!"

"I remember the sound of you hitting the door."

"Yeah, he made a run at me. I had a good headache from that knock." Threatening notes had appeared in my mailbox and on my car soon after that, but I'd never told Paulette about them. The guy had figured out who I was and probably thought I could identify him. Only thing was, I really couldn't.

"That was some plan you came up with to catch him."

"Yeah, not bad for an amateur." After talking with security, I'd come up with a plan they - and ultimately Sam - had agreed to. Disguised and posing as a relative, I pretended to doze in a bedside chair with new post-op patients over the next several days and was finally rewarded by a visit from the thief. I called security immediately, but couldn't resist chasing him into the parking lot, where surprise, surprise, there was a car waiting for him.

"Why ever did you decide to follow him?"

"I don't know. Maybe the devil made me do it." I'd jumped into my car and followed them. They were driving at a rate of speed which would have made Al Unser proud and which my ancient Jeep couldn't match, and anyway, I skidded and ended up in a ditch. By that time Sam had been alerted, and the thief and his accomplice were apprehended a few miles away.

"Well, I'm glad you weren't hurt." Other than an airbag burn on my face and shakes from the experience, I was fine. The car wasn't too badly damaged either.

"Yeah, but living in Will's dog house wasn't much fun." I shook my head remembering the tension.

As we reached the Maine-New Hampshire border, I noticed a black sedan in my rear view mirror, hanging right off my bumper. It reminded me of a car I'd noticed in the parking lot at the museum because it had a completely tinted front windshield and a Maine license plate. Maine has a Variable Light Transmission regulation that allows for only the top five inches of front windshields to be tinted. Plus the other windows were equally dark.

As I watched, the car pulled up even closer, so close that I couldn't see it in my side mirrors. "What is this guy doing?" I screeched at Paulette.

She turned around and looked. "I can't see the driver. Why is he on our bumper? Maybe he wants you to move over?" I put on my right turn signal, waited for a hole in the traffic in the right lane and changed lanes. Unfortunately, the black sedan moved with me and continued to hang on my bumper. This continued for several miles, until I saw a Friendly's sign, decided enough was enough, and got off at the next exit. The black sedan followed. I turned right, found the Friendly's, and drove into the parking lot. The sedan drove by.

"Probably just some nut case heading the same way we are," commented Paulette.

⁂

After a meal of cholesterol topped off by a milkshake, we got back on the road. Within a few miles on 95, the black sedan was back on our bumper and remained there until we turned off on US1 toward Pequod. The sedan followed. US1 is a two lane road and by now, it was dark and the road was illuminated only by headlights, the lights of gas stations and other open businesses, and the occasional halogen street lamp. In a particularly dark part of the road, we felt a solid bump on the back of the car.

"Oh my God," screamed Paulette. "He's trying to drive us off the road!"

"Not if I can help it." I increased our speed as we turned onto the road leading into Pequod. "Can you get 911 on your phone?"

While Paulette fumbled in her purse for her phone, the sedan sped up and hit us again, this time more forcefully, causing the back of the car to skew. Paulette dropped her bag, while I struggled to control the Jeep. The sedan hit us again, this time staying in contact with my bumper and pushing us forward. I held onto the steering wheel with a death grip and tried to eke a little more speed from my car.

I made a decision. "Hang on, Paulette. I'm going to make a turn up ahead at the old post office." Paulette hung on to the strap beside her seat and I slowed, then gunned the car. Pequod had a new post office that had opened the previous year, and the old one was unlit and hardly visible in the dark. I was hoping the driver of the sedan didn't know where the driveway was. The Jeep lurched on its side as I jerked the wheel viciously sharp right, and we skated on two wheels into the parking lot. The sedan didn't make the turn, but I knew it'd be back. The Jeep settled, and I put the accelerator to the floor. We roared to the back of the parking lot, bounced over the edge of the pavement and crashed onto a two rut track leading into the woods. I shut off the headlights, slowed a bit and headed as straight as I could in the dark.

"What are you doing, Rhe?" Paulette squealed.

"Relax. This trail leads back to the quarry. Remember?"

Her voice dropped an octave and she replied, "Yeah. Didn't this trail start where the old PO is now?"

"Yup." I made a guess where the trail bent to the right and put on my dimmers for a moment. Just ahead I saw the bend, turned off the dimmers and went right.

"See any headlights?" I asked Paulette.

"No, but they must be looking. Do you think they'll spot the trail?"

"I don't know. The ground cover has grown over the ruts, but we might have left some impressions. We'd better keep going." After a few more yards, I turned the dimmers on again and drove cautiously around the quarry, turning on my headlights only when I spotted the side road that meandered back into town. Paulette leaned back in her seat, let out a huge, shuddering breath and said, "That was something I didn't bargain for."

"Me, neither." We started to giggle hysterically and nervously chattered nonstop until we reached Paulette's driveway. My knees felt like wet noodles when I got out of the car to survey the damage to the bumper, and I had to lean on the Jeep to walk to the back end. Given the previous dents and dings, the new damage was not particularly noticeable.

"Are you okay, hon?" I asked, walking around to the other side of the car and opening Paulette's door. She had retrieved her purse and had pulled out the phone. "I'm calling Sam," she said, but her hands were shaking so much I had to take the phone from her.

"I'll call him. Why don't you grab your clothes bag and the shopping bags. Don't forget the mugs," I reminded her. I tried dialing but found my hands were shaking too and gave up trying for a minute.

Paulette picked things up, put them down, rearranged the bags, clearly not yet focused. Finally, when she had a grip on everything, she closed the car doors and looked at me with eyes that shone in the house lights. "Haven't you called Sam yet?"

'I'm trying to calm down enough to punch the right numbers. And figuring out what to tell him."

Without even listening to me, she continued, "I'm <u>still</u> shaking. It was kinda like being on a rollercoaster. I was really scared, but now that it's over, I'm feeling, I don't know, higher than a kite. Is this why you've gotten into doing what you do? The adrenaline?" she asked.

"Not exactly. I would have preferred a more sedate ride home. But we did make it in record time." We both giggled again, still nervous, then got quiet, looking at each other.

"Did my interviewing at the Caribbean Queen have anything to do with this?" Paulette asked thoughtfully.

"I hate to say this, but I think so, and I was the target. You would have been collateral damage."

"But why, Rhe?"

"I must be getting too close to something that has to do with the Caribbean Queen, and I'm probably not the safest person to be around right now." After I moment, I added, "I'm sorry I dragged you into this, girlfriend."

"Believe it or not, I'm glad I was there with you, Rhe." She smiled at me. "You can obviously take care of both of us ...you're something, you know that? Do you want to come in for a while? I can make some coffee."

"I really think I need to get home. Here, take your phone." Her hands were full, so I tucked it into one of the shopping bags. "I'll call Sam on mine when I get there. See you tomorrow?"

"You bet," Paulette replied. "And I had a wicked good time, despite everything."

Dear God, I thought. *I've created a monster.* "Are you sure you're okay?" I asked again. Paulette was still trembling. "Go in the house, lock all the doors and windows, and make yourself a strong drink."

"Coffee?"

"No, you numbskull, scotch or bourbon!" I hugged her again.

"Whatever will Ross think if he finds me in the kitchen with an empty liquor bottle?" she asked, muffled against my middle.

"Just do it! That's straight from Miss Marple."

Paulette shifted her mugs and the various bags and shuffled with her load to the back door. I watched her until she was safely in the house and I heard the lock clunk.

I too was still nervous, holding on to the steering wheel tightly with freezing hands as I drove home, looking behind me in the rear view mirror. I called Sam before I went into the house. I had to tell him what Paulette and I had been up to, and on the heels of my misadventure at Almorel, his response was not pleasant. I got a "What the hell do you think you are doing?" again, and "What am I going to do about you?" again, and all manner of ill-tempered growling. I did manage to squeeze in a description of the car and part of the license plate I'd noted in Boston. I also told him I'd seen Bitsy at the Caribbean Queen office and had a snapshot to prove it.

More growling. "I want to see that picture now, Rhe. Can you send it to me?"

"Sure, as soon as I hang up."

"Are you sure it was her? No, don't answer that." He paused for a minute, then said, "You realize Paulette could have been hurt as well. Jesus, Rhe, you've put her in danger now, too. For tonight at least, I'm sending over patrol cars to sit on both your houses. Maybe tomorrow as well. And guess what? *No* objections!" His voice got louder and ended in a bellow.

"Yes sir," I replied meekly.

"How do you think the driver, whoever it was, knew how to find you?"

"Good question. Paulette asked the same thing. I'd hate to say Bitsy was involved, but I'm getting so paranoid that I'm beginning to wonder if there's a tracker on my car."

"I'll check it for you tomorrow when I see you." A long, quiet pause ensued, during which I could hear his breathing calm. Then "I'm good and mad at you, Rhe, but I'm really glad you're okay."

"Me, too, Sam."

∽∼

I decided to bite the bullet and tell Will what had happened as soon as I put away my purchases and said good night to Jack. I left out the part about Bitsy. He listened without interruption, storm clouds gathering in his look. When I finished he said quietly, "Rhe, this has *got* to stop. You and Paulette could've been killed. It's way past time for you to bow out of the investigation." His face told me there was no arguing with him, and to tell the truth, I was sufficiently scared to agree with him.

"Sam is sending patrol cars to sit outside here and Paulette's tonight."

"Good. I think there should be one here every night until this – whatever it is - is over." For once, we were on the same page.

Later, as Will and I were getting ready for bed, I asked him if anyone had called for me today. "Bitsy called me at my office around noon and asked where she could find you, he replied. "She said she had something to tell you about Lili. I told her you'd gone shopping in Boston. Why?"

"No reason. Did you happen to tell her where I'd be?"

"I might have mentioned the Gardner while we were chatting. What's this about?"

"Just that I thought I saw her in Boston today. Getting out of a car like hers. But if she called you from here, I must have been mistaken. No problem."

Fat chance I was mistaken. Bitsy was behind this, but there's no way I could prove it, I mused. *She's like a huge, ugly garden spider spinning a web with some distorted pattern I can't figure out. Was it just a warning or a real attempt on my life? Either way, I needed to be really, really careful.*

21

Wednesday morning, I called the police station. Sam was out but Phil, his computer-savvy deputy, was there. I checked in with the patrolman in the car outside my house, and he told me he would be following me to the station. When I arrived, Phil was in his office, typing away madly on his keyboard and looking up and down at the computer screen. He didn't stop until I sat down next to his desk and asked him if Lili's phone was working.

"I was just about to find out. Figured to get an audience, but you'll do." He smiled, picked up a phone sitting on his desk, pulled a new battery from his desk drawer, and inserted it.

"I'm not at all sure this is going to work. The phone was in the water a long time and everyone's betting it's ruined," he said, shaking his head in doubt. He pressed the power button and held it down. All of a sudden, the screen lit up with the network logo and the phone chimed. "Well, wadda ya know?" His face lit up with pleasure.

"You're a genius!" I crowed.

He beamed at me. "No, just a long shot with instructions I Googled."

"So what can you get from Lili's call list?"

John scrolled down the list. The usual - parents, Zoey, Tanya, Kelly, a bunch of other names I didn't recognize, but two others I did: Antonio and Adriano Moretti.

"Moretti senior was paying her bills, we'd expect his name to be there. But Adriano - why would she be calling Adriano? Can you pull her phone records and see where she called during the last two weeks before she died?" I asked.

"Sam started working on the court order for the LUDS last week after you guys got her phone number." LUDS are local usage details, a record of local calls made and received from a particular phone number, and require a court order even when the police are asking.

"How soon should he get it?"

"We should have had it Monday, but today, for sure. Should I call you?"

"Absolutely. Have you learned anything about East Almorel."

"Found some interesting stuff. The estate, the Caribbean Queen outfit, and New Living Technologies are all part of the same shell company. It's called Palestra. Based in Boston, but I can't find an address."

"Okaaay.....are there any more parts to this shell?"

"It looks like there are companies within companies, and it's getting pretty hairy. I think I'm going to need some help to go any further. So I called a friend at the FBI office in Portland. He's my best option since there's no state bureau, and it could be right up his alley since we might be looking at interstate commerce. He's going to work on it tonight. I'll let you know if he finds anything."

I thought of the previous night's ride from hell. "Phil, do you think you could find a tracking device on my car?"

"Sure thing, but why?"

"Just a hunch. Can you do it?"

"Where's your car?" Over the next fifteen minutes, Phil manually inspected my Jeep, looking under the vehicle, in the wheel wells, and in the trunk and glove box. When he didn't find anything, he used a GPS detector, again finding nothing. "Do you want to tell me what's going on?" he asked when he was through.

"It's probably nothing," I equivocated, "but Sam suggested I have my car searched, so tell him you didn't find anything when you see him."

☞☜

When I got home, again followed by the police car, I made a couple of sandwiches and brought them down the street to Paulette's. There was another police car parked on the street in front of her house, with a uniform I didn't recognize. He rolled down his window as I crossed the street and politely asked if I was going to the McGillivray's house.

"Yes, I am," I replied. "I'm Rhe Brewster, Sheriff Brewster's sister-in-law. Do we really need *two* units on the street? It's starting to look like something from the Godfather."

"Just following the Chief's orders, ma'am, but there'll be just one car starting tonight. We're short-handed. Make sure you signal us if you see anything suspicious."

"Thanks, Officer...." I read his name tag, "....Burns. I feel safer with you here."

The door to Paulette's kitchen was locked for the first time in memory, but after I knocked, she came running through the kitchen, unlocked the door and let me in, giving me her usual around-the-waist hug. Another first - no enticing smells in her kitchen. I pulled back, looking down at her with some concern and asked, "How're you doing?"

"Better than last night, but still a little shaky. You'll never guess who I just got off the phone with! Guess!" I made a huge show of thinking about it, and shook my head. "The Caribbean Queen office! They want me to work for them this summer. Not bad for a 30-something actress!"

Now it was my time to hug her. "Great work! Um......you do know you're not going?"

"Of course, you idiot."

"Well, you seemed a little excited about it, and I wondered what you were going to tell Ross when you left for the summer." I got a smile from that.

"What did you bring?" Paulette asked, reaching for the napkin covered plate.

"A couple of ham sandwiches."

"What, no tuna fish?"

"I'm into change. Got some coffee?"

Paulette whipped up some chipotle lime mayo to make my sandwiches tastier. After I devoured mine and was looking longingly at the remains of hers, she asked, "Have you thought any more about what happened last night?"

"Yeah, I talked to Sam about it and told him I thought this wasn't just some stranger, but someone deliberately targeting me. I just couldn't figure out how that car found us. I had Phil scan the Jeep for a tracking device this morning. Nothing."

"So it was a nut."

"Well *I* think she is. And a dangerous one."

"You mean Bitsy."

"Yup. She called Will yesterday to find out where I was, supposedly because she needed to talk to me about Lili. Will said he's pretty sure he mentioned the Gardner museum, and that's where I first saw that car."

"Oh, Rhe, this is serious. Can Sam question Bitsy?"

"Why? There's no proof she's involved. And if she is, it might make her even more dangerous. I also saw Phil this morning. He's been doing some digging and found out that the Caribbean Queen, East Almorel, and the company with that logo, New Living Technologies, are all parts of a shell company called Palestra. But where does Bitsy fit into all this? That's the real question."

We gaggled more about our previous day's adventure before I left, both of us telling the other to be alert and careful.

≈≈

That night, I kissed a sleepy Will good-by and headed for the hospital a half hour early, in order to catch up with the status of the ER before my shift began. The unit on our street followed me and the driver waited while I parked behind the hospital, climbed the loading dock steps and had the back door handle in hand, before giving me a beep of his horn and leaving. Just as I opened the door, I noticed a white van parked in a shadow at the far end of the dock. My pulse picked up a pace, and despite knowing it wasn't the safest thing to do, I walked down to take a closer look. Sure enough, there was a New Living Technologies logo on the door. I took pictures with my cell phone and sent them to Sam with the location and the message "URGENT, check this out, now at hospital" and retreated to the loading dock door quickly.

I entered as usual, showed my ID to the guard, not the faithful Lyle for once, and walked down the corridor to the elevator. I could see a man coming from the other end of the hallway. He was huge, well over six feet tall and at least 250 pounds, all snugly packed into a tee shirt, flannel-lined jeans jacket and wide denim pants. A dark blue watch cap was pulled down over his hair, partly covering his ears. As I approached him, he turned slightly away, so I really didn't get a good look at his face. As soon as I passed him, he made a headlong rush to the back door. I yelled at him "Hey, you! Mister! Can I ask you a question?" He didn't stop and banged through the door. By the time I had hot-footed it to the loading dock, the white van's motor was starting up and it peeled out in reverse, leaving tire marks on the pavement. Before I went back in, I called Sam's phone and left a voicemail to let him know I'd seen the van's driver. The guard at the desk told me the driver had had a valid vendor license and had logged in under New Living Technologies.

I wanted to see if any transplants were scheduled for the next day, but I was already late and was swept up into a maelstrom the minute I arrived in the ER. There'd been a fire in an apartment building on the north end of town, where the houses were old and burned liked tinder. Because of the sheer numbers coming through the doors, the ER was crowded with ER docs, plastic surgeons, a pulmonologist and an orthopaedist, as patients were evaluated, given emergent treatment and triaged to the various hospital departments.

By eight AM, I felt like a zombie, and when I left, there was a patrol car waiting in the parking lot for me. Good ol' Sam didn't miss a beat. Will had opted to take Jack to the bus instead of driving him to school and was waiting in the kitchen when I came in the door from the garage. "Looks like you had a hell of a night," he commented, giving me a hug and then stepping back to take a good look. "I heard about the fire on the 11 o'clock news. You smell like you were in it. Was it as bad as it looked?"

"Worse," I replied, dropping my bag on the counter and thumping my bottom into a kitchen chair. I put my head down on the table and caught myself drifting, despite the warm aroma of coffee brewing.

"Come on, I'm giving you a boost upstairs." Will pulled me up from the chair and pushed me from behind to get me up the stairs to our bedroom.

"Do you want to take a shower before bed?" he asked solicitously and turned toward the bathroom.

"A shower sounds nice," I said, but dropped on the bed instead. It felt like lying on a cloud and I sank in. I sensed Will taking off my shoes and covering me with a blanket. That was the last I knew until around 2 PM, when I woke with a start, rolled over on my back and spent a few moments getting myself oriented. *What was that smell?* I thought for a brief moment, before remembering the fire and figuring out it was me. After a really, really long, hot shower to get rid of the reek of smoke from my skin and hair, I dressed and headed downstairs. The note on the table said "Good morning or maybe good afternoon? Tuna sandwich and diet Coke in the fridge. Sam called – call him. See you tonight. Bringing supper home with me. Will".

While munching on the accompanying pickles, I called Sam. "Did you see the van?" I asked without a hello.

"Hello to you, too. And yes, we got the picture and tried to locate the owner from the license plate, but it's just that shell corporation that Phil unearthed. Palestra?"

"That's the name, and I'm going to show Paulette and Beth the picture I sent you to confirm it's the logo on the van they saw. It's certainly identical to the one on the van at Oliver's. Do you think you can find it?"

"Since we can't locate Palestra, I put out a BOLO. Call me if Paulette ID's it as well."

When we finished talking, I walked down the street to see if Paulette was home. One faithful police car was parked midway between our two houses, and Officer Burns was at the wheel. I waved at him. When I got to the back door, it was unlocked and I smelled cookies. Paulette was back.

"Bad night at the hospital last night, huh? I saw you pulling in this morning. Did you get some sleep?" Paulette asked as I came in.

"About six hours, amazingly. The ER was a zoo, but we didn't lose anybody. I don't know about the people flown to Portland."

"I heard one died when I turned on the TV this morning, and the *P & S* had its usual blazing headlines." She poured us each a cup of coffee and I groaned as a plate of peanut butter chocolate cookies magically appeared.

"You're obviously feeling less nervous today," I remarked. 'You didn't lock the back door."

"I don't want the door locked when the kids come home, and yes, I'm feeling better. To what do I owe the pleasure of your company?" This, with a real smile.

"I have a picture I need you to look at. I took it with my cell phone last night at the hospital." I powered up my iPhone and pulled up the photo of the van.

"Not anything gory from the ER I hope," Paulette said, taking my phone. "Hey, this is the van I saw at the field, I'm sure of it! Where did you find it?"

"Parked at the loading dock when I went in last night."

"Did you see the person driving the van?"

"Yeah, I did, only not really."

"Care to explain?"

"When I was walking through the hospital basement, I saw this huge guy heading for the loading dock doors, not dressed in hospital scrubs. He shot past me with his face turned away, so I never got a good look at him. I ran after him, but he was in the van and heading out of the parking lot by the time I got there."

"Have you told Sam?"

"I have. It's the van I saw at Oliver's, but we wanted you to identify it as well."

Paulette looked at the picture on my iPhone and nodded a yes. Then she gave me a look of concern and tugged on her hair before saying, "Rhe, think about this. You're a target now. I don't care if you think the van driver didn't see you at Oliver's. The driver saw you last night, and the hospital could now be a dangerous place for you." Since I had already gotten the "be careful" speech from everyone else, it occurred to me maybe I should just record one to save people the trouble. I had the message and it troubled me plenty.

⌒⌒

Beth Smith also ID'd the van when I stopped by to see her after lunch with Paulette, and I left a message for Sam that the New Living Technologies van was definitely the one at the school on the day I found Lili. I was sitting at my kitchen table with a yet another cup of coffee later that afternoon when the phone rang. The caller ID showed it was Phil.

"Hi, Phil! What's up?"

"Darn it, Rhe! I keep thinking you're a psychic when you answer like that. I have some information for you. You won't believe it!"

"Shoot!"

"Well, you know the search the FBI was doing for me? It turns out that one of the owners of the shell corporation is Antonio Moretti. He has his fingers in a whole lotta pies. He not only runs a funeral business, but is also an owner in the Caribbean Queen, Almorel and New Living Technologies. How does a guy like Moretti get involved in a tissue bank?"

"Hmm... his funeral homes could be a great source of body parts, if he were inclined to break the law. Just think, Phil, is there an easier way to obtain tissues for transplants than from a mortuary?"

I knew that the selling of body parts had become a huge issue in recent years, driven by the need for organs for transplantation. Ligaments, skin, and bone were also in short supply. Tissue and organ donation is supposed to be regulated by the FDA, but in truth, the regulation was lax and the demand was great. In the last few years, there had been a number of stories in the national news about tissues and organs being purloined from bodies, mostly in mortuaries. The lack of sterile conditions in a mortuary and the fact that the tissue and organs were never screened for any transmittable diseases, including cancers, put the recipients at grave risk.

"What's Sam going to do about this?"

"Nothing until after the Almorel raid. I hear it's scheduled for Saturday night. There's going to be a meeting with the FBI on Tuesday, to do a post-mortem on the raid, but this latest development is sure going to make that meeting more interesting. Sam told me to ask if you can be there. Are you working that day? We're meeting at 10AM."

"You're in luck. My day is free. I'll see you there."

22

I left Will with a good night kiss at 11:30 PM and headed for my shift at the hospital. When I pulled out of the garage, I noticed that there was no patrol car out front. I called Sam. "Hey, how come there's no patrol car on the street here?" I asked.

"Sorry Rhe, I had to pull Burns off to manage a car accident just north of town. Just stay inside with the doors locked, and I'll have someone back there soon."

"Sam, I'm working the 12-8 shift and I'm on my way to work right now. I can't wait."

"Crap, why didn't you tell me?"

"I didn't think I'd need to. Don't worry, I have my taser and I'll park close to the loading dock."

"I'm heading over to the hospital now. Stay in your car until you see me."

"Is that really necessary?"

"Yes, it is and don't argue." He hung up.

It felt good knowing I'd be back on days the next week, and I felt even happier when I didn't see a white van parked at the loading dock. The closest parking spot to the loading dock was at the edge of the lot about 100 yards away, not ideal but well lit, so I parked and waited for Sam. Eleven forty-five came and no Sam. Eleven fifty-five, and still no Sam. I called and got his voice mail, left a message that I was waiting. By midnight, I knew I couldn't wait any longer and felt ridiculous just sitting in my car, with the back entrance to the hospital so close. No cars had driven in since I'd arrived, and I figured I was as safe as I'd ever be. So I took out my taser, turned off its safety and made one last look around outside the car before getting out, bag over my shoulder, taser in one hand, car key in the other. I was locking the car when I heard footsteps crunch on the pavement behind me. I spun around to see who it was, taser at the ready, but not fast enough.

Someone behind me wrapped his arms around my middle, pinning me to him, arms at my sides. Before I could scream, a hand clamped a cloth tightly over my mouth and nose, and the sickly sweet smell of chloroform filled my nasal passages. I twisted my head from side to side, trying to remove the cloth from my face, but the hand didn't budge. I kicked at the person holding me, stepping on his feet, but it was like being held in a vice clamp. I tried to fire the taser still in my hand, aiming for his legs, but missed and lost hold of it. I had to be hurting him because I heard a string of colorful curses, but struggling caused me to breathe harder, and in a short time I was dizzy, moving became more difficult, and my knees buckled. My eye lids drooped, shutting out my surroundings.

Chloroform is nasty stuff, but it's about the only anaesthetic effective in a short amount of time, and the cloth over my mouth was soaked with it. I remember being released and falling to the pavement and have a vague recollection of being lifted, with a lot of unrepeatable words about my weight, then nothing.

Ever so gradually, I became conscious of lying on a hard floor. A few more minutes, and I could feel being bumped around but was still really groggy. Whatever I was in, it was moving fast, and after being thrown against the side on a sharp turn, the road got smoother. *Highway?* It sounded like it. I looked around and found I had been dumped in the back of a van or large SUV, and my hands and feet were bound with something wide and unyielding, with my arms behind me. Something was also covering my mouth. *Probably tape, maybe duct tape.*

Then came a stabbing headache, and all of a sudden I felt nauseated. I rolled on my side and then remembered the tape. *I can't throw up*, I thought. Inhalation of vomit is a nasty way to die. I began to panic, hyperventilated, flailed around, and the nausea became worse. Frantically, I rubbed my face against the floor in an effort to dislodge the tape.

"Hey, Miz Brewster. You okay back there?" A sarcastic, deep voice registered though my panic.

Where had I heard that voice before? The distraction took my mind off my nausea for a moment, and finally my brain kicked in. I began a monologue to myself, the same one I'd given to frightened patients over the years. *Calm down. Calm down. Breath slowly, deep breaths, in and out, in and out. Do not give in to the nausea. Fight the fear. You can do this.*

I took my own advice, breathing in and out slowly through my nose, and continued rubbing my face on the floor. It was covered with a thin rugging, which gave me some traction, and I finally managed to dislodge one corner of the tape from my mouth, taking some skin with it. The absurd thought that I was going to have some scabs and a nasty rug burn to show for it came to mind, but then I thought maybe I wouldn't be alive to worry about it. With just a little more air coming in, I began to feel better.

"Yo, Miz Brewster! Can't answer me?" the deep voice chuckled. "Well, you've stuck your nose in where it didn't belong for the last time!"

I heard another, higher voice, warning, "Shut up, Ray. That's not professional."

"Like that's important?" replied the one called Ray. "Who the hell cares?"

I'd heard that other voice, too. I rolled the voices around in my mind and finally recognized them. These guys were the guards at Almorel! My heart sank. *Ray, Ray. Where had I heard that name before? Ray Little? Couldn't be. Ray Little was African American.* And then it dawned. This *had* to be Tanya's Ray Little. Because I had never seen a picture of him, I assumed he was black. Ray had to be the big white guy I'd seen in the hospital basement Friday night. I was a victim of my own prejudices. Since I'd never taken the time to find out what he looked like, I'd missed my chance to tell Sam I'd seen him. But Ray obviously knew who I was, plus he had a wicked ax to grind. *Was the other man Bruce, the guy whose fingerprints had been in Lili's house?* It must have been Bruce who killed Oliver, since the person driving the van had not been the enormous size of Ray. I was in deep, deep trouble. I resumed my calming mantra, telling myself to take deep breaths in and out.

The ride continued for a while in silence, and I wondered where they were taking me. Certainly not anywhere in Pequod. I struggled silently with the tape around my wrists, pulling and twisting as much as possible while fighting the occasional bump in the road. Gradually my head cleared.

"Hey, Bruce, what are we supposed to do with her, once we get there?" I heard Ray ask.

"Leave her in the freezer. Mr. Moretti will figure out what to do tomorrow. By then she'll be a popsicle, and no one will have to worry about her no more." He chuckled at his own wit.

Hearing that, my fear returned in a tidal wave. *Focus on something else, Rhe. Think of Jack, think of Will.* Then it hit me. Who would know where to look for me? By now, I was sure the alarm had gone out. Surely Sam had reached the parking lot and found my car. *My bag, did I still have my bag?* I looked around, and there it was on the other side of the van. *Sam wouldn't know I'd been snatched. He'd just think I'd gone in to work without him. The taser, I'd dropped the taser. He'd see it!* But I spotted the taser next to my bag.

The ER would eventually notice my absence and someone would call home, looking for me. Will would freak and call Sam. Sam would go back to the parking lot, but he'd have no idea where to look for me. I could see Will taking Jack to Paulette's and driving around frantically. Tears came, but the fact that crying made it harder to breathe killed my pity party pretty quickly.

We were now apparently on a road with a series of traffic lights, because of the stops and starts, and then the van made a series of rights and lefts that had me rolling from side to side. Finally the van turned right, drove for a short while, swung around and backed up. We had reached our destination. The rear door of the van - I could now see it was definitely a van - swung open, and two men, one large and the other slight, confronted me.

"How do you want to handle this?" asked the one I had identified as Ray.

"Go prop open the side door," said Bruce. "Then we lift her highness out and get her inside. Here are the keys." Ray disappeared for a minute and I heard the screech of metal on pavement. While he was gone, I twisted and wiggled my way to the front of the van, thinking wildly I could worm my way over the seats. I heard Bruce order Ray, "Get in the van and pull her towards the door. Then you can take her arms and I'll grab her legs and we'll lift her out."

Suddenly, big hands grabbed my ankles. "Where do you think you're going, Miz Smarty Pants? Gonna try to drive away?" Another sarcastic chuckle. "Lookee here, Bruce. The bitch managed to get the tape off part of her mouth!"

I tried yelling "Don't call me a bitch" at him, but the remainder of the tape muffled my words into something unintelligible.

He chuckled, "You can try to scream all you want, bitch,'cuz no one's going to hear you." With that, he forcibly jerked me to the rear of the van, pulling up my jacket and scrub top. Ray then grabbed me roughly under the arms, while Bruce tried to lift my legs. Ray was doing all the lifting and my legs dropped.

"You're a useless son of a bitch," Ray complained. "All you're good for is giving me orders. Here, I'll carry her." He got out of the van, stood me up, and lifted me onto his shoulder like a sack of potatoes.

"Watch who you're calling an SOB, you dumb fuck. Remember who takes care of business for Mr. Moretti. You're just along for muscle." The menace in Bruce's voice was unmistakable, and Ray stopped talking. I got my first good view of Bruce, upside down, and he didn't *look* menacing. Short, wiry, thinning hair combed over a flaky scalp, a homely face to which time had done no favors, and ears that looked like jug handles. *Jughead.* I almost laughed.

I continued to struggle, dangling over Ray's shoulder, and managed to rub one of my stud earrings off against his jacket. I hoped Bruce wouldn't notice. Ray banged my head going through the door, stunning me into submission, and said "Oops! Did that hurt?" *Yes, it hurt like hell, but I'd never tell you.* Then he lugged me down a thickly carpeted corridor, where I caught a glimpse of a room filled with caskets. This was one of Moretti's funeral homes! Probably in Portland. We got in an elevator and descended one floor. The elevator door opened to cooler air and the smell of embalming fluid, and from my vantage point I could see the floor was scuffed linoleum. The mortuary. We stopped and I twisted around to see the front of a large, thick metal-sheathed door. "Open it, puhlease," Ray mocked Bruce, "and get a move on. She's a ton of cement. What have you been stuffing your face with, bitch?"

Bruce laughed, pushed down on the handle and yanked the door open. He flipped the light switch on the outside wall and fluorescent light filled the freezer. Ray dipped his head as he walked through the door, scraping my back on the door frame, and then dumped me unceremoniously on the thin rubber mat covering the floor. I looked up to see his toothy grin and glanced at Bruce, who was standing just outside. I made pleading noises and shook my head from side to side, knowing full well that it wasn't going to do any good.

"Forget it, you're here for the night. Enjoy your nap!" Ray laughed. "Let's get out of here. I'm hungry! What do you think cook has whipped up for tonight?"

"Is that all you think about?"

"Well, not all..." He looked at me with a leer.

"Forget it. Mr. Moretti said not to touch her."

Ray shuffled out of the freezer and shut the door with a thud. I heard the handle snap. "Have fun trying to get out of there," I heard Bruce yell. Something metal clanged on the lock. The muffled sound of Ray's voice came through the door. "Aren't you going to shut off the fuckin' light?"

"Hell no!" came the reply. "I want her to enjoy her surroundings!"

"Do you think there'll be coconut cake....?" and the voices faded.

I struggled to sit up, not easy with your hands behind your back, and looked around. The freezer was about ten by ten, with shelves on three sides. Various items wrapped in plastic were on the shelves, but it definitely wasn't time to investigate because it was damned cold. All I was wearing was my scrub suit and a thin, flannel-lined fall jacket. I scuttled over to the freezer door, put my back against the wall, and bent my knees. One thing swimming and the occasional yoga class had done for me was keep me limber, and I had an idea of how to free myself. I was bound at the wrists but had managed to stretch the tape a little, so I pulled my shoulders down as far as I could and wiggled my hands under my rear end. It felt like I was wrenching my arms out of my shoulder joints. Gradually I worked my bound arms over my rear and up behind by knees. From there, it only required some contortion to get my legs through the circle of my arms.

What I needed to do then was free my wrists and remove the tape from around my ankles. First I tried ripping the tape with my teeth, but gave up when I couldn't make a dent. The shelving around the freezer was cheap metal, though, and based on similar freezers I'd been in at the hospital, the edges were probably sharp. I hopped over to one shelf, felt the edge with my finger. *Sharp enough.* I began sawing the tape around my wrists, back and forth, over the edge. Eventually the tape tore enough for me to rip it the rest of the way with my teeth, but not before I dug deep, bloody scratches in my wrists. Then I unwrapped the tape around my ankles.

The exertion of freeing myself had kept me fairly warm, but once I was free, the bitter cold enveloped me again. "How are you going to stay warm, Rhe?" I asked myself out loud.

My eyes drifted to the contents of the shelves and I inspected them more closely, slapping my arms around my upper body as I did. I was in a freezer full of body parts. Legs, arms, joints, and individual tissues were all shrink-wrapped and in plastic bags with some sort of numerical identification system. So I was right. New Living Technologies was supplying body parts and tissue for transplantation or surgical practice. If my hospital had been using some of these tissues, some of the patients could have been in infected with God knows what. I had to get out of there to let those patients know. *But most of all, I need, need, need to be with Jack and Will.*

By now I was shivering, and I started to think about how to stay warm. I knew the head was the greatest area for heat loss, and I had to find a cover for my head. I went to the largest frozen body part on the shelf, ripped the plastic bag with my teeth, removed it and placed it over my head and the back of my neck, tucking it into my jacket collar. The smell from the frozen tissue had permeated the bag, but it wasn't bad, and definitely tolerable if it kept me alive. What I needed next was some insulation. I opened other bags and unwound the plastic shrink wrap. I hated removing my scrub pants and jacket, but had to do it in order to wind the plastic wrap around my arms and legs. At this point it hardly mattered that the wrap had been encasing parts of dead humans. This human wanted to live. The plastic bags I inflated and sealed, then stuffed them in my pants and the body of my jacket. After I pulled my arms out of my sleeves, I burrowed them under the plastic bags and crossed them in front of me against my shirt, to try to conserve body heat.

With that done, I did feel warmer, and I started walking, pacing slowly back and forth in the freezer. Will and I had done some winter camping the year we were married, and we'd taken a winter survival course. I remember the course instructor saying that vigorous exercise was not recommended in a freezing situation. You could quickly become exhausted and the exercise would squeeze out whatever warm air was trapped inside your clothes - in this case, my jacket, pants, and the plastic bags and wrap. So now the question was: Could I keep this up until someone found me? Surprisingly, Dumb and Dumber hadn't thought to remove my watch, and when I checked the time, it was 2 AM. So I was looking at another six to eight hours minimum before anyone might show up. Then the problem was whether it would be Antonio Morettti or someone else who found me.

I knew from my nurse's training that hypothermia had five stages. The first was shivering, and I'd already been doing that for a while. Shivering burns the body's energy stores and produces heat. I was adding to that by pacing and I tried some isometrics from time to time. I had to delay reaching the second stage for as long as I could, because then body temperature drops below 95° F and the shivering becomes intense.

I kept up walking back and forth, but after a while, it felt as if the cold were invading my body, taking over my muscles and reaching into my bones. I pushed on, thinking about Will and Jack and pretending that we were trotting on the beach, calling to Jack to keep up with me. I managed to stick with just shivering for what seemed like a long time. Eventually I found myself getting tired and realized that my shivering had become more pronounced. I kept on, slower now, pacing back and forth across the freezer floor, pausing to do a few isometrics until I had to give that up because it was taking too much effort. Time passed. My mind focused on staying moving, staying alive. I *would* see my husband and son again. Pacing, pacing. My world shrank to a ten-by-ten square, back and forth, corner to corner, squeezing my arms inside my jacket. I recited the Pledge of Allegiance, the beginning paragraphs of the Constitution and the Declaration of Independence, the Gettysburg Address. I even started reciting the twenty-third Psalm, but decided it was too morbid for someone who was going to live. Instead, I sang pop songs and watched with detached interest as my breath clouded the air.

My small, square metal world faded, and I turned inward, becoming conscious only of my breathing and the effort to move my legs and squeeze my arms. My muscles stiffened and moving became difficult, but I kept going. Finally my walking became erratic, coordination jerky, and I struggled to move the muscles of my face. I gave up talking out loud. By the time I reached stage 3, I knew my thinking would become muddled and I'd probably start feeling warm and lethargic and want to lie down. But I still knew where I was and what I was doing and why. I made a mental list of food we needed at the store, and recited it. I went over ER procedures in my head.

After what seemed like an eon, walking, walking, I began thinking that I was just walking down the street to my house. I must have gone out on a really cold day without my parka, but I'd be home soon. *Why don't I just sit down for a little and rest? Home is just down there and maybe Paulette will come along. When I get up, I'll walk the rest of the way.* My knees buckled and I fell to the cold, so cold floor. *It was nice, resting,* I thought, *and it's warm here in the sun. No! Get up Rhe! You're reaching stage 3, get up! Don't give in.* I struggled to sit up.

I just sat there, weighing the effort of getting up against just lying down again and resting. I was so tired. I thought I heard voices, yelling, muffled. A door opened and someone was yelling my name. The voice wouldn't stop, and then something warm was being wrapped around me. I opened my eyes slowly and tried to focus. *What's Sam doing here? Is he taking a walk with me?* I could feel myself being lifted onto something flat and hard, but not cold. Then I was moving, lights overhead, an elevator ride, more lights and then a jarring lift into a bright space. *Where was I?* I could feel things being removed from around my arms and legs and then some areas of wonderful warmth, under my arms, behind my knees, in my groin. My hands and feet started to feel like they were being stuck with knives. *Someone pricked my arm!* There was a siren blaring. I wanted it to stop, I wanted to sleep. An oxygen mask was placed on my face. *Where was I going?*

Finally the siren stopped, and there was more jarring and lights, bright lights. I heard a lot of voices, and a warm blanket covered me. The oxygen I was breathing in was warm. Pads were placed on my chest, and I could hear the beeping of a heart monitor. I slowly got warmer, at first with painful prickling spreading to my upper and lower limbs, then gentler prickling, like getting in a hot tub after a cold swim. It felt wonderful. I became more alert, and I heard Will's voice, "I love you, Rhe! Stay with us, you hear?" His hand wrapped around mine.

It was all so very nice and warm and comforting and I would have slept, but they kept poking me, taking my temperature, taking my blood pressure, making me warmer. Finally, I just opened my eyes and looked at Will, who hadn't let go of my hand, and said, "Where am I?"

"Maine Medical Center, dear," replied another voice. I looked around and discovered I was in a treatment room, and it was a nurse answering me.

"You're okay, Rhe. Thank God. You're in the ER," Will explained. "They're warming you up. You were an ice cube when Sam found you. And you looked pretty funny all wrapped in plastic. Smart girl, my wife."

I smiled. "How did he find me?"

"I'm going to let him tell you. Right now I'm just going to sit here with my wife and enjoy her being alive. ...."

"How's Jack?"

"He's fine. He's with Paulette, and they'll be here later today to see you."

"Today? What time is it?"

"Seven AM, Saturday morning. You hung on for almost six hours."

"What did you tell Jack?"

"Just that you got lost and got very cold and Uncle Sam managed to find you. We can figure out what to tell him later when he asks more about it."

"Which you know he will," I replied with a smile. "I'm tired. Do you have to keep me awake? I had no idea how exhausted you could feel after hypothermia."

"We need you awake, Mrs. Brewster," replied the nurse officiously, "while your temperature comes back up. Just to make sure there's been no damage to your brain, skin or motor functions. You should know that."

Ouch. I knew that. She may be right. My thinking is not quite what it should be. I'm a little muddled. But I couldn't help it and started to close my eyes again.

"Hey, Rhe," said Will, squeezing my arm. "Keep your eyes open."

"But I walked all night!" And so it went for another hour or so.

During that hour I managed to wring out of Will that I'd just reached stage three when Sam found me and that there was an EMS truck already on the scene. The rest of the story would have to wait until I was debriefed by Sam. I pleaded, he was firm, and I finally let it go.

As it turned out, I made a rapid recovery and was released from the hospital late Saturday afternoon. Will drove me home with a two car, Portland police escort. I guess I was so happy it didn't occur to me until later that Sam wasn't there. Paulette and her family, Will's and my parents, and Ruthie were all there to greet me. It was overwhelming, and after tears and hugs all around, I was happy to be put to bed, have a gourmet dinner by Paulette brought to me on a tray, read my son a bedtime story, and finally, finally be allowed to sleep. When I roused briefly in the middle of the night, Will was curled around me like a second skin.

23

The insistent sound of a phone ringing pulled me out of a deep recuperative sleep. "Who on earth would call at this time on a Sunday morning?" I groused. "It's 6:30 in the AM for Christ's sake!"

Will groaned, rolled over, grabbed the phone and handed it to me. "Probably Sam," he mumbled. "He was driving me crazy last night calling about you."

"Sam? This better be good!" I answered crossly, becoming painfully aware of the scabs forming around my mouth from the tape and rug burn, the bandaged cuts on my wrists, and the deep ache in my shoulder muscles. "Might I remind you I've had quite an experience these last 24 hours? Don't any of you sleep?"

"Not this past night, kiddo. Rhe, I'm really sorry. I know you need to recuperate, and I hate asking you to come down here and wouldn't if we didn't really need you. We took a number of people into custody last night, including the two guys I think kidnapped you. We need you for a lineup."

"Where did you find them?"

"At East Almorel. We raided the place last night, remember?"

Remembering the scheduled raid smacked me awake. I'd totally forgotten. That was why Sam hadn't been there last night. "Did you call Bob Morgan to let him know about the raid?"

"I did. He was out there himself with a photographer. Check the newspaper this morning – there's a headline occupying the top half of the front page. We also arrested a Pequod College student. She's hysterical and wants to talk to you."

"Give me a minute." I sat up and pushed the hair out of my face. "Okay, I'm with the program. Who's the student?"

"Zoey something. You saw her at Almorel the evening you did your reconnaissance."

My reconnaissance. "Funny, Sam. Anyone else I know get arrested?"

"Judge Jeffries wasn't there, and neither was Dr. Montez. But we did pick up Adriano Moretti. He hasn't said a word except to ask for his attorney, who's due here around 10. Are you up to this?" he asked with concern in his voice.

"Let me get some coffee."

"I can send a patrol car to get you."

I looked at Will and said, "They're going to send a patrol car to get me in a few minutes."

He groaned and said "I'll drive you."

To Sam I said, "Will's going to drive me. Be there in a half hour, but you'd better have something for me to eat." Will got Jack up with a promise of breakfast at MacDonald's, made me coffee, and the three of us drove to the police station.

The station was filled with people when I arrived, and Ruthie had obviously been called in to man the desk. She gave me a desperate look as I walked by her. I could hear her patiently but forcefully explaining to three lawyers at the same time that they could meet with their clients once an interview room became available. Sam met me in the corridor.

"So where's my breakfast?" I asked him with feigned irritation.

"It'll be in my office right after the lineup. You feeling okay? Up for this?" He was staring at my scabs.

I nodded. "Actually, I'm feeling pretty good. Just a little tired. Let's do this."

"Okay, if you're ready, we're going to do two lineups, and see if you can identify the guys who grabbed you. I'm sure after those idiots get lawyered up and figure out what they're going to say, they'll swear you coerced them into driving you to Moretti's, where you locked yourself in the freezer to frame them."

"Did you know one of them is Ray Little?'

Sam shook his head in warning. "I don't want you to say anything to me until after the lineups, okay?"

We went down the corridor to the back of the station. Along the way, Sam stopped in Phil's office, gave him a breakfast order and some money and told him to get something for himself, his other deputy, John, and Ruthie while he was at it. We then went to a room with a one way window, where I stood, then Sam went out into the hall and gave some instructions to John. The door of the room, which I could see through the window, swung open and six men walked in, single file. They turned and faced the window to some inaudible commands. I couldn't help it, I started to shake involuntarily. Ray Little was the second from the left, and I indicated that to Sam. How could I forget him? A huge, hulking young man with a mean and threatening scowl on his face. I guess he was oblivious to the shit he was in.

The men filed out and a second group of six filed in and faced the window. Bruce was the last one on the right. He looked completely nonthreatening and nondescript, but I knew better. "That's him, Sam," I said, "at the end on the right. I'm not likely to forget that face."

"Okay, that's it for now. Let's get some breakfast," said Sam. We stopped in the break room on the way back to his office and got coffee and then took in the fast food feast laid out on his desk: pancakes and syrup, a bagel with cream cheese, scrambled eggs and bacon, hash browns, an egg and sausage biscuit, orange juice and milk. I whistled. "Quite a spread! You're sharing this with me, I hope?"

"You bet," Sam replied, reaching for the egg and sausage biscuit.

I took the scrambled eggs and bacon, the hash browns, and the bagel and cream cheese, figuring I needed some energy after my night in the freezer. "You can have the pancakes," I offered graciously.

Sam smiled. "Glad to see your appetite hasn't been affected." Then his face drooped and he looked me straight in the eyes. "It's my fault you were taken, Rhe. I can't tell you how sorry I am. I promised I'd get to the hospital to walk you to the door and I wasn't there."

I could hear his unspoken words, *You could have died.*

"Sam, you know I would never blame you. How could we know Ray and Bruce would be at the hospital?" I reached across his desk, took his hand, and we just sat there holding hands for a few minutes. "It was my own stupid fault for not waiting, and even if you'd been there, those two goons would have just figured another way to get to me. So let's just forget about it, okay? And you saved me! So tell me how you found me. Will said I needed to ask you. He said he didn't really know the details." I dug into the scrambled eggs.

Sam inhaled the biscuit in three bites and started stabbing at the pancakes. In between bites, he said, "I got to the hospital parking lot at 12:05 and found your car, figured you'd already gone into work, but decided to check in the ER. When I discovered you weren't there, I went back out to the parking lot to look for anything that might tell me what happened, but other than the door of your car being unlocked, there was nothing. I called Phil, to see if we could track your phone, and then called Will. I can't say it was a pleasant conversation. I had to threaten him with being locked up to get him to calm down and stop him from going out and searching on his own." Sam sat back at this point, pancakes having disappeared, and sipped his coffee.

"My phone! And I was cursing Ray and Bruce for putting my bag in the van with them."

"Those idiots actually did you a favor, but we don't have the technology to track a phone GPS. So we called our friends at the FBI. They were already involved in our planned raid, so they were pretty receptive. It did take an hour or so, but they managed to pick up your phone's signal in Portland. Problem was, the signal was moving and heading north out of Portland by that time. So we asked if they could find out where your signal *had* been and that took a good while longer. But they finally found the last place it'd been before leaving Portland. I was already on my way to Portland when they called and gave me an address. Then I had to call the Portland PD, and they had to get a court order to allow us to enter the funeral home. That took more time. But they met me at Moretti's with the paper work and an EMS bus about 30 min after I got there. My God, I was freaking out, sitting there waiting."

"How did you know I would be there, and not still in the van?"

"I didn't, but the FBI was still tracking the phone and John and Phil were heading to East Almorel, based on their information and a pretty good hunch. While I was waiting, I looked around and found an earring I thought was yours outside the side door of the funeral home. Figured you were playing Hansel and Gretel. Man, I was relieved when I found you in that freezer. Wasn't sure you recognized me - you were pretty cold.

"Oh, I'd know that cowboy voice anywhere."

Sam smiled. "After I reported to the FBI we'd found you, they made the decision to wait and scoop up your travelling buddies at Almorel on Saturday night. Moretti showed up at the mortuary around 9 on Saturday morning, and the FBI took him in. But without any concrete evidence he'd been involved in your kidnapping, they had to let him go this morning. That kept him from warning anyone we were onto him before the raid."

"So how did the raid go down?"

"What you might expect - yelling and shrieking from the girls, two naked couples running in from the hot tub with towels flapping, and general commotion. The cook tried to hide in a walk-in fridge.."

"I can sympathize."

"...then threw pots at us when we pulled her out. Ray and Bruce made a run for it but didn't get far. That Ray is one strong guy. It took three agents to get him under control. At least he and Bruce were smart enough not to draw their weapons. Adriano gave us no trouble, just walked outside and waited to be cuffed."

"Sounds exciting."

"Yeah, but I was calling Will every five minutes about you. He finally stopped answering my calls. I need to sit down and explain everything to him, so we're on the same page. He doesn't seem to be angry...."

"He isn't."

After some silence while I finished my share of the breakfast, I sat back, feeling a little queasy from all the grease. "Just wish I'd realized it was Ray in the hospital basement Wednesday night."

"It probably wouldn't have changed anything....he was gone well before I could have gotten there. How about more coffee and a doughnut to finish this off? You look like you could use some sugar, Sugar." Big smile.

Queasiness forgotten, I asked "What kind of doughnuts are you offering?"

"The usual, but maybe there's chocolate one left for you."

"At 9:30? Fat chance!" We ambled down to the break room, where I refused to choose a doughnut from the several dented and dried ones left in the box, a first for me. We refilled our coffee cups. The coffee had been sitting there heating since early that morning and by now was likely to take the enamel off my teeth, so I diluted it with water and added a ton of powdered creamer.

As I took a first unenthusiastic sip, Sam regarded me carefully and said, "Rhe, you've been here most of the morning. Do you want to go home? You look whipped."

"I think I should see Zoey first." My maternal instincts must have kicked in, because I really wasn't all that enthusiastic about dealing with her.

"That would be great, if you're up to it. She doesn't have a clue about the seriousness of the situation. She keeps asking when she'll be released. We tried to explain to her she needs a lawyer, but she kept saying she didn't need one and insisted on talking to you."

"I'll talk to her, but beyond persuading her to get a lawyer, I'm not sure what else I can do."

"That would be plenty."

24

As I followed Sam out of the break room, whatever energy I'd had suddenly drained away, as a result of the emotion of the line-ups and the double-whammy of the large breakfast. He led me to the corridor on the other side of the station, where Zoey was being held in an interrogation room. I wasn't sure what I could do to help, but since I was partially responsible for the raid on East Almorel and her being arrested, I felt I should do something. At the last door on the left he knocked, and we entered. Zoey appeared to be sleeping, with her head on an old wooden table in the middle of the room. As we came in, she jerked up, half rising from her chair, panic on her face until she recognized me. After her night in jail, Zoey looked almost clownish. Her hair was tangled, makeup smeared, and there were black lines down her cheeks where her mascara had run with her tears. Her nose was red and runny, and there was a puddle of either snot or saliva on the table where her head had been.

"Mrs. Brewster, please!" She focused immediately on me. "Tell them they have to let me go! I haven't done anything wrong!" I reached across the table and handed her some tissues from my bag. Zoey took several, blew her nose, and while I walked around the table to sit beside her, attempted to straighten her skimpy halter top to make it less revealing. I pushed her discarded platform sandals out of the way before turning my chair to face hers and taking my seat.

When I did, she noticed my face for the first time. "Oh God, what happened to you?"

"Just a little run in with a rug and some tape," I replied. "Nothing to worry about, really."

Sam sat on the opposite side and began by saying, "You've been mirandized, Miss Harris, so I'll ask you again, now that Mrs. Brewster is here, do you want to waive your right to an attorney?"

"I, I, I don't know," Zoey stammered.

Trying to convey as much sympathy as I could, I faced Zoey, placed my hand on her arm and said, "Zoey, you're in a lot of trouble. The police know that East Almorel is a…." and here I stumbled, trying to decide whether I should smack her with the truth, "…high class brothel. They know you have been providing sex for money and that makes you a prostitute." Zoey's eyes filled with tears that ran down in the black rivulets on her cheeks.

Sam continued, "Prostitution is illegal in Maine, and you're going to be brought before a judge on that charge. You can ask for a lawyer and you have the option of pleading not guilty, if that's what you want. Do you realize the seriousness of the situation?"

More tears and snuffling followed, but after soaking a few more tissues, she nodded and said, "It just started out for fun..."

Sam interrupted, "Anything you say without a lawyer present can be used against you."

"I understand that, but what if I give you information? Will that help me?"

"It won't hurt, and you can ask for leniency in your sentencing."

"Sentencing?" she shrieked. "You mean spending time in jail?"

"Yes," Sam replied calmly. "The maximum sentence is a year in jail and a two thousand dollar fine. However, with this being your first offense and if your information is helpful, your sentence might get reduced to probation. This might keep you from being dismissed from college. I'd feel a lot more comfortable if you had a lawyer present and signed the form giving up your rights to remain silent."

"I don't know any lawyers," she replied, hanging her head and starting to cry again. "My parents are going to have to know about this, aren't they?" A tear dripped off the end of her nose.

"You're an adult, Zoey," Sam replied, "and you can handle this by yourself if you can manage the financial aspects. If you are unable to pay, the lawyer will be paid by the court system, but court costs and any fines incurred you *will* have to pay."

Zoey sat there for another few minutes, bawling into her hands and shaking with the effort. Gradually her sobs slowed and finally stopped. She wiped her eyes and face and blew her nose again. She straightened up, and looking at me, said with an air of resolution, "Call me that lawyer and bring me the form." When she asked if she could have makeup from her bag, I knew she'd made her decision.

I'd remained silent during this entire exchange, but decided at this point I could interject. 'Would you like something to eat, Zoey? Coffee?" She nodded wordlessly.

Sam motioned me out into the hallway and told me he had just the person in mind to represent her and could probably get him here within an hour. He okayed my getting her some food from the station break room and told me to see Ruthie about getting Zoey's makeup. In ten minutes, I was back in the room with coffee, one of the dented doughnuts, and her makeup kit.

"Thanks, Mrs. Brewster," Zoey said in a tiny voice. She used the contents of the makeup kit before eating. I had brought her brush, and by the time she had brushed out her hair, she was looking much like her college self. I asked her if there were anything else she needed, but she shook her head and calmly munched on her doughnut, so I left to go out into the pandemonium in the reception area. Only to be greeted by relative quiet.

Ruthie was glowering, and the lawyers were sitting in chairs, texting, talking quietly with the person sitting in the adjacent chair, or intently reading something. I could see some out in the parking lot, talking on their phones. Ruthie had restored order, it was clear. "Who's Sam going to get to represent Zoey?" I asked her.

"My nephew." she responded, with pride in her voice. "Just graduated from the University of Maine and passed the bar. Got hired by Lamb and Schultz here in town to handle local criminal cases. You know those two," referring to the aforementioned Lamb and Schultz, "are too old for all this excitement. It'd probably give them a heart attack."

"I had forgotten your nephew went to law school. Somehow I thought he was still an undergraduate. Time flies."

"Sawyer's a smart boy, and I'm sure he'll do a good job."

At that moment, a young man came bursting through the front door, spotted Ruthie and broke into a huge smile. "Auntie Ruth! It's so good to see you!" he exclaimed and went around the desk to give Ruthie a hug.

"What did you do? Fly here? We just called you! Sawyer, this is my good friend, Rhe Brewster. She's a consultant with the department, and is a friend, sort of, of the young woman who asked for a lawyer."

"I was actually having breakfast at the Pie and Pickle. Nice to meet you, Ms. Brewster." He extended his hand, which I shook. Very firm grip. His eyebrows went up as he saw my face.

"My face is fine, Sawyer, and pleased to meet you, too. Is your last name Hersh?"

"No, it's Smith. Lawyer Sawyer Smith, easy to remember," he replied with a bigger smile. Sawyer was neatly dressed in a blue button down dress shirt, sharply creased pants, and had apparently shaved not long ago. There was a tiny bit of a red scab just under his chin, where he'd apparently nicked himself. He was not handsome, but with carrot red hair, freckles and blue eyes, he certainly got your attention.

"Let me get Sam and take you to the interview room to meet your client."

Ruthie found Sam for me, and on the way down the hall, we told him the circumstances of Zoey's arrest, and finished outside the room by letting him know what Zoey had agreed to thus far. "Do you have any problems with this?" Sam asked.

Sawyer shook his head, "No, you've done everything right so far, and I think I can get any sentence argued down to probation, especially if this is a first time offence and she gives you helpful information."

"Good," replied Sam, and we entered the room. Sam introduced Sawyer, and Zoey's face lit up when she saw him. He looked like a senior in high school and exuded so much youthful eagerness, I could see where Zoey might like him. She shook his hand, and Sawyer sat down next to her and explained he would be paid by the court to represent her unless she had money of her own.

"I have some," she replied quietly, looking away in discomfort, "from what I've earned." We left them alone to confer for a few minutes, and while we were waiting outside, I told Sam I thought it would be inappropriate for me to be involved in any interrogation. He thought for a minute, then asked me what I would like to find out when he questioned her. When we re-entered the room, Zoey had signed the form relinquishing her right to remain silent.

When we were all seated, with Sam and me across the table from Zoey and Sawyer, Sam hit a button on the tiny recorder he'd brought in and warned all of us the interview was being recorded. He stated the date and time and the names of the people present and continued, "Miss Harris has agreed, in the presence of her lawyer, to waive her right to silence." Sam looked at me, nodded, and began the questioning. "Zoey, I want you to tell us in your own words how you became involved in the, uh, activities at East Almorel."

Zoey replied in an almost child-like voice, "I guess it started when Dean Wellington was at my high school recruiting for Pequod. She talked to me and one of my friends about the fact we could earn money and have fun on summer breaks, working on the Caribbean Queen. When I got here, she set up an appointment for me at their office in Boston."

Sam and I looked at each other with the same surprised expression, and he immediately pressed the stop button on the recorder and said, "Counselor, Miss

Harris, I need to talk to Mrs. Brewster in private for a minute." He motioned me to follow him out to the hallway.

"What in hell is Bitsy doing in the middle of this?" he hissed.

"Shhh, keep your voice down. This explains why I saw her at the Caribbean Queen office in Boston last Tuesday. She's actually pimping for the ship and East Almorel. What a racket. She picks out young women while she's recruiting for the college!"

We re-entered the interrogation room, and Sam picked up where he had left off. "Tell us more about how you were recruited, Miss Harris."

"Well. Like I said, Dean Wellington got me the job on the boat. Kristen and me – she was with me last night – both interviewed in Boston and got hired. During last summer, we cleaned the guest cabins, changed sheets, pulled down the covers at night with the whole chocolate thing. I got lucky because I waited tables when I wasn't housekeeping. Kristen had to clean the public toilets. We had lots of time off, though, and there were unattached men on the boat who paid us a lot of attention and we spent time with them."

"What did "spending time" with these men entail?"

Zoey blushed and looked down at her hands before speaking. "Well, sometimes, you know, things got personal."

"How personal? Were you intimate with them?"

"Sometimes."

"Did they tip you when you did?"

She thought for a minute and frowned. "I guess they did, because we always had more money in our paychecks after a hookup."

'So how did you end up at East Almorel?" Sam prompted.

"I got a call from the Caribbean office about a month after I got back. They asked me if I'd be interested in more work and would I come in to talk about it. That's when I met Antonio Moretti. He said to call him Uncle Antonio, and he was very nice, asking me all about Pequod and how I was doing, and then he asked if I would like to make some money. Actually lots more money. A thousand a weekend. He told me he was looking for young women who were pretty and had a sense of adventure. The men I would meet were older and look-ing for company for an evening and I wouldn't have to, have to, you know, if I didn't want. That I would just be a companion for an evening. At first, I didn't want to do it, but the more I thought about it, the more I thought how great the money would be. And if I didn't have to do, you know, what was the harm?"

"And did you have to?"

"Yes. That became very clear the first night I was taken to East Almorel. It was glamorous and all, but the men were mostly a lot older and demanded that I do things I didn't want to do and got angry if I didn't. When I complained to Uncle Antonio, Mr. Moretti, he told me if I didn't do what the clients wanted, he'd tell my parents what I was doing."

"Did you recruit anyone?"

"No, I didn't. Really. Dean Wellington had arranged a job on the boat for two other girls a year ahead of me, and Uncle Antonio recruited both of them."

"What was Adriano doing at Almorel?"

"He was sort of the manager, I guess. He made sure everyone had whatever they needed - drinks, food, whatever."

"Was Lili one of the girls at East Almorel?"

"Good God, no. *No.* She knew nothing about it. Besides, we used to call her "Lili-white", you know, least likely ever to hook up or put out. But she was Adriano's girlfriend. I never saw her at Almorel, but I saw them together plenty. I'm sorry I didn't tell you, but you see why I couldn't? He was pretty wild about her, bought her lots of nice stuff, and she was definitely in love with him, too."

"Why do you say that?"

"She'd been talking about running away with him. I think there was pressure from family, them being first cousins and all. She didn't know about the other stuff, Almorel or what Adriano was doing there. She just said her parents and Uncle Antonio would kill her if they knew how far her relationship with Adriano had gone."

I looked at Sam. Finally we knew the father of her baby.

"Do you know the guards?"

"Yeah, and they creep me out. The smaller one's Bruce. He's been there the longest, and he's Uncle Antonio's man. I don't like him, he's always looking at us girls in a weird way. I see him peeping at us a lot. The big guy Adriano hired recently. I don't know his name. He looks like he's popping steroids and he has a short temper. I was in the kitchen getting a snack, I think it was last weekend, and he and Bruce were there yelling at each other about a prowler on the property. The big guy was reading out Bruce about not wanting to go down to the beach and take a look. Then all of a sudden Bruce pops out a knife and holds it under his chin, and the other guy got real quiet. Then they both went out looking."

"How long have you been going to Almorel, Zoey?"

"About two months, starting when I came back to school."

"Did you meet men named Jeffries or Montez at Almorel?"

"No, we were never told their names and the men, when they gave us a first name, well, I'm pretty sure it wasn't real. Maybe if you had pictures, I could pick them out."

Sam turned the recorder off, and we left Zoey with Sawyer to work through what would happen next. Out in the corridor, I looked at my watch and saw that it was 11 AM.

"Is Adriano's lawyer here yet?" I asked Sam.

"I was just going to check on that. Stay here for a minute." He returned with an older man, tall and beautifully dressed in what was surely an Italian-made suit with a silk striped power tie. He was carrying an ostrich skin brief-case, distinctive by the all-over raised bumps on the leather and its two to five thousand dollar price tag. The lawyer had a sharp face with a long chin, and his haircut must have cost a bundle. Long but not overly so, with just the right amount of gray at the temples to make him look mature and powerful.

"This is Mr. Moretti's lawyer, Mr. Rimmer. Mr. Rimmer, this is Mrs. Brewster, a consultant with our department who was involved in the investigation of the, uh, situation at Almorel."

Mr. Rimmer looked at me impassively with cold, hard eyes as he shook my hand. If the scabs on my face registered with him, he gave no sign of it. He radiated menace, and as he released my hand after holding it tightly for just a moment longer than necessary, I shuddered involuntarily. "Nice to meet you, Rhe." *Not Mrs. Brewster. How did he know my first name?*

Sam took us to an interview room off the same corridor. Adriano was sitting at the table, rigidly upright with a stony look on his face. Before Sam could open his mouth, the lawyer said, "Adriano, the family has hired me. Do *not* say a word. I'll have you out of here shortly."

Nevertheless, we all sat down, and Sam started his recorder, once again noting the date and time and people present. "Mr. Moretti, I am going to ask you some questions. You may answer them or not, as your lawyer advises. When I'm finished, he can talk with you about your arraignment and bail. Have you been Mirandized?" Adriano nodded yes.

"Can you please state that?"

"Yes, I've been read my rights," Adriano replied.

"Good, then let's proceed. Do you understand you've been arrested for promoting prostitution and patronizing prostitution of a minor, according to the laws of the state of Maine?"

Adriano looked at his lawyer, who said, "Do not admit to anything." Adriano remained silent.

Sam then continued, asking him if he could describe the nature of the activities at Almorel. Silence. He then asked a series of questions concerning how he came to be at Almorel, if he was the owner or knew the owner or owners, how he had met the young women arrested, and if he knew where they came from and their ages. To all of these questions, Mr. Rimmer shook his head and Adriano remained silent. Sam asked about the guards and who had hired them. More silence. Then he asked Adriano if he knew Oliver Sampson and how his motorcycle had come to be in the garage. Rimmer continued shaking his head.

And for this he's paid the big bucks? I thought.

Finally, Sam asked, "Did you kill Liliana Bianchi?"

Clearly, this question had been totally unexpected. Rimmer jumped to his feet and said, "That question is completely out of bounds! Mr. Moretti, please come with me." He got up and headed for the door, but surprisingly, Adriano didn't follow him. Instead he spoke for the first time.

"I didn't kill her," he said, his face suddenly pinched with grief and tears forming in his eyes. 'I did not kill Lili," he said again, this time with anger, pounding the table with his fist. "I did *not* kill her. I *loved* her. I loved her so much!"

"Mr. Moretti, shut up," yelled the lawyer.

"I will *not* shut up." Shouting now, he exclaimed, "I! Did! Not! Kill! Her!" With each word, his fist hit the table again.

"Mr. Moretti, I am reminding you again not to say anything!" Rimmer was sounding like a one note piano.

"What's there to say? She's dead!" Adriano shouted back at him.

Sam looked thoughtful and then asked, "Do you know how she died?"

Adriano looked at him and said, "No, and I don't want to know."

"She was drugged, had her head bashed in, and was strangled to death."

"I don't want to hear this!" Adriano turned his head from side to side in agony.

"Then her body was put in a hot tub for two days before being dumped on a soccer field."

"Stop it!" Adriano screamed. He jumped up from his chair and Sam rose, thinking he was going to run out. But all he did was pace back and forth, palms to his eyes.

"Did you know we found her car in Highland Lake? Her killer or killers drove it into the lake."

Adriano looked at Sam. "Highland Lake?" Recognition lighted his face. "We own ..." he began.

At that point, Rimmer grabbed him by the arm and yanked him toward the door. "That's enough!" he roared. "We're done here! Not another word, Mr. Moretti!"

Sam had opened a wound and turned a knife in it, but must have figured he had gotten all there was to get, at least for the time being. He said quietly, "He needs to remain in this room, Mr. Rimmer, and you can remain with him. We're done, at least for now." And he pushed the stop button on the recorder, picked it up and left, with me in his wake. I couldn't wait to get out of the room and talk *this* over.

Sam headed for the break room, where we both got cups of freshly brewed coffee and headed back to his office. "What do you think, Rhe?" he asked as soon as he shut the door behind me.

"Well, I believed Adriano when he said he didn't kill Lili. His emotion is raw and real. I saw it on the day of her funeral, but he was under tight control, with his father watching him like a hawk. No control today."

"I agree. He really didn't know how she was killed, and that last little bit that slipped out, about the family owning something? I bet it's a piece of property on Highland Lake."

"Well, something else to get Phil working on, huh? When will Adriano be released?"

"Probably tomorrow, when court is in session, unless Moretti senior pulls some strings."

"Sam, you do realize Adriano's the father of Lili's baby, right?"

"Yeah, I got that. Moretti senior should have been happy about that, another kid for his mortuary dynasty."

Something was dancing around at the edge of my thoughts, but I couldn't put my finger on it. "And now for something completely different,' I said, channeling Monte Python. "Bitsy."

"Yeah, Bitsy, who seems to be in the middle of this, right up to her sweet little neck. Imagine, using recruiting visits to pimp for the big cheese, Moretti Senior."

"Remember seeing her chatting with him at Lili's funeral? It struck me strange at the time but now it all fits. Do you have enough to bring her in?"

"Not yet. I need to speak with the other Pequod students brought in, to confirm what Zoey said and find out what other girls were involved. It could take a few days to build a case." Sam thought a moment, and then said, "Once she gets the news about the raid, she might run. I'd better put someone on her so if she does, we'll know where she's going."

"Sam, you don't know Bitsy. Her head's so far up her rear, she'd never consider fleeing. She'll just get her lawyers to create a plausible excuse and wall you off. We're going to need something irrefutable – her financials, some paperwork."

"Well, maybe when we get to the bottom of Palestra and all of its tentacles, we'll find something. The FBI should be able to get a court order to look at her financials in the meantime."

We spent a few more minutes discussing the interview, and Sam promised to call me with any developments. I headed home, feeling wrung out from all the emotion I'd witnessed and not a little worried about Bitsy. I would have given a bundle to be a fly on the wall when she heard about the raid on East Almorel, and there was no telling what she might do.

25

With Indian summer and its warmth and blazing leaf color visiting for the weekend, Will, Jack and I all enjoyed a last afternoon in the pool on Sunday afternoon, caught some sunshine, and had a barbecue outside for supper. I didn't have to return to work until midnight on Wednesday. With the prospect of a relaxing Monday at home and the warm sun and water, I felt positively blissful, especially since everything seemed to be wrapping up.

My day of relaxation was interrupted by a call from Sam to tell me the meeting between his department and the FBI agents working on the case had been moved up to the next morning. Could I make it? *You bet.*

Tuesday morning, after breakfast and a vigorous romp in bed with Will after Jack left for school, I entered the police station by 9 AM on the dot, wearing a certain glow. My single purpose was to get the investigation at the hospital started, and to do that, I had to convince them of the seriousness of what I had seen at Moretti's funeral home. When I entered the large conference room, everyone at the table stopped talking and looked at me. *Good heavens, is it that obvious?* I patted my hair in case I'd missed a spot when I combed it out. *Get real,* I told myself. *They're just waiting on my story…or admiring the cracking scabs around my mouth.*

"So where's the coffee and doughnuts?" I asked to break the silence. John and Phil raced each other to the side table where the food was located. John poured me coffee, and Phil came back with a plate of three doughnuts.

I sat down with my feast, looked at Sam and then studied the men sitting at the table, obviously FBI agents. There were two and they were a perfect Laurel and Hardy combination: one short and a little rotund, the other tall and lean, both with regulation haircuts, smooth-shaven, dressed in dark suits, white shirts, discrete ties, and wearing serious looks on their faces. Ordinarily they might have intimidated me, but not today.

Sam introduced me to them: Agents Bowers and Bongiovanni. Agent Bongiovanni was so tall he couldn't fit his legs under the table and sat sideways, but with his graying hair, he looked more mature than Bowers. I figured he was the lead agent when he said, "Relax, Mrs. Brewster. Have your coffee and when you're ready, begin with what you remember of Monday night."

I took a bite of a jelly-filled doughnut, wiped my chin where the jelly had dripped, then took a sip of coffee and a deep breath before giving them an abbreviated version of my statement. A lot of the personal details weren't necessary, so I began with being grabbed and chloroformed and waking up in the van. I told them how surprised I'd been to discover that one of the two men was Ray Little, the person wanted for the beating of Tanya Davis, and how I figured the other man, Bruce Gavoni, was the one I'd seen driving the van on the day Oliver was murdered.

After a brief description of being dumped in the freezer, I told them what I'd found on the shelves. They asked me some questions about organ and tissue trafficking, and after hopefully making a good case for what I thought Moretti was doing, I told them I'd seen the van from New Living Technologies at the hospital. I also mentioned running into Ray Little in the basement corridor, probably after making a delivery.

"All the tissues from Moretti's funeral home have to be tested," I stated forcefully. "I can guarantee you tissue harvesting in a mortuary is not done under sterile conditions, and each type of tissue has to be pre-treated in a specific way before transplantation, which I doubt was done. Add to that, the fact we have no idea whether the donors had cancer, an infection or a communicable disease at the time of death, and every recipient is at risk. The hospital *must* be warned about the real possibility that tissues obtained from New Living Technologies were contaminated. The recipients should be tested immediately!" When I finished, everyone, including the FBI agents, were murmuring in agreement.

John then stated, "We now know that Antonio Moretti is the CEO of Palestra, the company including his mortuaries, the Caribbean Queen Enterprise, East Almorel, and New Living Technologies."

What Agent Bongiovanni said next made me smile inwardly. "Because the spread of his enterprise is across several states, we've gone ahead and obtained search warrants for his various establishments. They're being searched at this moment. Any evidence - the body parts, tissues, and financials - will all go to the FBI labs for analysis. We'll let you know if we find anything that could help with your murder investigation."

"Any sign of Moretti Senior?" I asked.

"So far he's in the wind, but don't worry, we'll find him," the agent named Bowers answered. He'd been nervous since we all sat down, tapping his fingers on the table, checking his phone, and biting his nails.

I'm not so sure, I thought. *He has a lot of means with which to run.* "So what's going to happen with the hospital?" I asked the agents. "How are the patients going to be informed?"

"We'll tell the CEO of the possibility of contaminated transplant tissue immediately, but we'll need to find a paper trail to confirm it," continued Bowers. "Hopefully he'll be cooperative. It's going to take some time to find everything, but we have agents working on it right now. Mr. Moretti is going to be indicted for a long list of federal and local crimes, don't you worry," he finished in a condescending tone. I could almost hear the missing ending: *your pretty little head. I wonder if he'd passed the FBI gender sensitivity training. Do they even have that?*

"Is that all you're going to do?" I asked in frustration.

"This is where things get a little tangled, Rhe," explained Sam. "As you told me, Judge Jeffries was at Almorel the night you, ah, visited. For our guests," he said, indicating the FBI agents with his head, "he sits on the hospital board. Plus we've learned he pushed for the hiring of Dr. Montez, who is in charge of developing the hospital's transplantation program. Dr. Montez has also been a guest at Almorel, but neither of them was there when we raided it. We hope one of the young women we arrested might be able to identify them from a photo array."

Agent Bongiovanni leaned forward, placing his arms on the table, and replied, "Based on that and anything we find when we check their financials, we'll be bringing Judge Jeffries, the hospital CEO - Dr. Manning, is it? - and Dr. Montez in for questioning, probably in the next day or so. I personally doubt there will be any paper trail leading back to them, and they'll deny knowing New Living Technologies was run out of an unregulated mortuary. It's going to be a hard road to prove they were involved in the organ trafficking, unless we can find evidence they benefited financially from the arrangement."

"So what will happen with them? Nothing?" I asked indignantly.

"Again, as I said, unless we can find they got kickbacks from Moretti, I'm pretty sure we're going to lose them. However, this is going to leak out and the way things go in a situation like this, their reputations will take a hit. Dr. Montez might leave, Judge Jeffries might step down from the hospital board – we just have to let things run their course."

"Great, Montez will just go somewhere else," I replied, "and do the same thing!" Sam raised his hands palms up in a gesture that read: *Enough.*

"What about the patients?" I continued.

"We'll let you know," replied Bowers.

"My brother had an ACL repair at Sturdevant a month ago. Is it possible he got infected tissue?" asked John, whose bass voice was unusually loud and stressed. I could certainly understand his fear. When an ACL from a cadaver is used for a repair, the tissue is boiled and irradiated. Cells from the patient receiving the transplant gradually populate the collagen, creating a new ACL. *Who knows if the ACL used for the transplant was appropriately treated?*

"You won't allow Judge Jeffries to be involved in any investigation, will you?" I asked. "That would be a little like having the fox guard the henhouse."

Agent Bongiovanni faced me. "We have assigned an agent to oversee the process, and it will be run outside the chain of command in the hospital. If that's all, we need to get going on this," he said, rising to his considerable height. The other agent got up quickly and they both headed for the door.

"Thanks for your help," Sam called to their retreating backs. He then turned to me and said, "Let's get some more coffee. I want to know if you've had any thoughts on who killed Lili." Sam, John, Phil and I all got up and headed to the side table with our coffee cups for refills. I needed some more juice before another discussion like the last one, but I decided to be virtuous and didn't take another doughnut.

When we were all seated again, I sat back, sipped my coffee and said, "I think Moretti Senior decided Lili needed to be gotten rid of and paid Bruce Gavoni to do the deed. From listening to the interaction between Ray and Bruce, Ray seems to be a real wuss. There's no way he would have done it. I hope you can get Ray to roll on Bruce."

"But why would Moretti want to kill the Bianchi girl?" asked Phil. "Just because his son was having a relationship with her?" John remained silent, but from the look on his face, I was sure he already knew.

"Well, it actually *was* the relationship between Adriano and Lili," I answered. "Moretti probably didn't even notice anything at first, but something – something he sensed or noticed, something someone said to him – made him start looking and asking questions. Pretty quickly he figured out they'd gotten serious. That's when he came up to visit Lili at Pequod, something Zoey inadvertently told us at the funeral. I'll bet he told her to stop seeing Adriano, and they must have argued. He probably confronted Adriano, too."

"But why would that be a problem?" asked Phil.

I sighed. He clearly didn't get it. "Remember, Adriano and Lili were first cousins, and first cousins do not fall in love and get married, at least not in a good Catholic family. It's possible Adriano told him that Lili was pregnant. You saw Marsh's autopsy report? She was probably about five to six weeks along, certainly far enough to be aware of it and tell Adriano.

"Seeing each other and even being intimate was one thing, but the pregnancy was something else again. Moretti must have become enraged, especially if he found out *after* he'd had his talk with her and also had told Adriano to stop seeing her. Plus Lili had apparently found out about what was going on at East Almorel. That's what the initials A/EA were in her appointment book: Adriano and East Almorel. Perhaps Adriano told her. If Moretti knew that, he might have worried she'd talk. I'm thinking he asked to meet her again, maybe with Adriano, and instead sent Bruce to kill her.

"This is all conjecture, of course, but if Adriano thinks his father either killed Lili or had her killed, you're going to get a lot of information from him. He was really overwhelmed and angry when he learned how Lili was killed, and he probably made some sort of mental connection when he learned where her car'd been dumped."

"How can you be sure that it was Bruce that killed her?" This time John was asking the question.

"I can't be, but weren't his fingerprints found in Lili's house? And Moretti might not have wanted to get his hands dirty, killing a family member himself. He was such a cold bastard, sitting there at her funeral, holding his sister's hand and being so solicitous!"

After a minute of thinking about what I'd said, Sam asked "So who put the body on the soccer field? And why? Where does the hot tub figure in to this?"

"I am pretty sure Oliver put her there. I suspect he was initially hired by New Living Technologies to make the tissue deliveries, because he knew hospitals and medical environments. He wasn't dumb and I'm sure he knew the risks of bringing tissue from a mortuary. But this was big money for him. The first thing he did was buy a motorcycle he couldn't have afforded in his wildest dreams. The lure of the money must have been overwhelming.

"As an eager and apparently loyal employee, Oliver was put to the test by his employer and asked to get rid of Lili's body. Again, I doubt that Ray would have done it, even under duress, and Bruce isn't big enough to carry the body. Hell, he couldn't even lift me out of the van! But Oliver worked with bodies every day. He was a natural choice, although I'm sure this job was not something he'd ever anticipated. Maybe he was thinking about telling the police.

"So while trying to decide about that or maybe figure out how to dump the body, he put Lili in the hot tub at the beach club. At some point, he figured there was a way to avoid having to choose between those two options and took the body to the soccer field, to be found by someone else.

"I doubt he knew the hot tub was still filled with water but didn't think to drain it, and he realized his mistake in dumping her there when I came in with a sample from the tub. As a morgue assistant, he would know there was a good chance of matching the sample and the water from Lili's clothing, if not DNA. That's why he conveniently lost the sample and went back and drained the tub. To prevent me from getting another one.

"Are you sure he was the man at the soccer field?" asked Phil.

"Absolutely. The brief description we got from Paulette and Beth Smith rules out both Bruce and Ray. Ray is way too big and wouldn't have had the *cojones* to carry a dead body onto the field. Bruce is too small and wiry to heft the body and the chair."

"So Oliver dumped the body out in the open and got killed for doing it," stated Sam, more as a fact than a question.

"I'm sure of it. Hiding the body for several days, then putting it out in the open for everyone to see, was definitely not what Moretti wanted. Especially since this set our investigation in motion. Oliver was a weak link and Moretti had Bruce get him out of the way. If I hadn't shown up, maybe Bruce and Ray would have removed Oliver's body, although Bruce's method of killing left a lot to be cleaned up."

"I think Oliver suspected he was a target," added Sam. "We found evidence of hasty packing in the house. I figure he was planning to run, but Bruce got to him first."

"Even though I didn't see his face, I'm sure Bruce was the guy I saw driving away from Oliver's house the day he died," I added. "He had to be the person who killed Oliver. Ray is way too big to be the man driving that van.'

"How did Oliver's motorcycle end up at Almorel? Did Bruce take it when he murdered Oliver?" Phil asked and answered his own questions.

"Bruce probably put it in the van before he killed Oliver. If Oliver was busy packing and preoccupied with getting out of town, he might not have heard anything before Bruce showed up at the door. Maybe Bruce coveted the motorcycle; it *is* pretty snazzy. Or maybe he felt the police would go looking to see where the money came from to buy it."

Sam interjected at this point, "I'm pretty sure we can get Ray to roll on Bruce. He's already facing charges from beating Tanya, along with Rhe's kidnapping and attempted murder. I'm thinking he isn't going to want a first degree murder charge on top of that, and might talk if we can offer him something. We'll see what the DA thinks."

"So if Oliver was in charge of disposing of Lili's body, why did he leave it on the soccer field?" John asked after some thought.

"That's the sixty-four thousand dollar question. I need to learn more about Oliver, and I think I know who to ask," I answered.

Silence around the table, then "I think that'll do it," from Sam. We all nodded in agreement. Forgetting about protocol, I hugged John, Phil, and Sam before I left the room. After all, they'd saved my life.

26

I had invited Sam to dinner on Thursday night, and he showed up at our door right on time, carrying a bottle of wine. I was surprised because Sam is never on time, and I had dawdled getting dinner ready in order to accommodate him. With a little help from Paulette - well, a lot of help - I had spent the afternoon making Beef Wellington, my greatest culinary accomplishment to date. I couldn't help thinking Sam was on time because he thought the Beef Wellington would provide another disaster story to relate to eager ears at the station.

Au contraire.

Together with roasted rosemary potatoes, green beans with almonds, and a chocolate mousse for dessert, the Beef Wellington made a meal that was a smashing success, except Jack had chosen that night to play with his food. He loudly compared the Wellington to pigs in a blanket and built a wall on his plate with the potatoes, surrounding the green beans, which he didn't eat. None of that was a problem until he put a green bean up his nose, at which point I cleared his plate, thinking of things he might do with the mousse.

"You've really outdone yourself this time, Rhe," Sam commented after he had eaten everything on his plate, leaving me nothing to scrape off.

"Thanks, Sam. Sorry to deprive you of a good tale to tell John and Phil tomorrow." Sam had the sense to look a little embarrassed. "What? You think I didn't know my cooking was the stuff of legends?"

Jack ate his mousse without playing, proclaiming it the best chocolate pudding he'd ever had, and went to his room to do homework, but only after I promised to help with his latest Lego kit when he finished. Sam, Will and I remained at the table for after-dinner coffee and a little town gossip. I sensed there was something Sam was waiting to tell us, and it didn't take long before he frowned and said, "I have some news. We found Antonio Moretti today."

"Yeah? Where? In one of his caskets?" snorted Will.

"Close. He's dead."

"What? Dead? Where? How?" I leaned forward in anticipation, dropping my necklace in the mousse on my plate.

"In his Highland Lake house. He must have snuck back in there after the FBI got finished going through it. The caretaker found him this morning and called the police."

Just then Jack yelled for his Dad, and Will got up to see what the problem was. "I'll fill you in, hon," I said as he rose from his chair.

"I really don't care," Will commented as he left the kitchen. "I'm just glad he's dead."

"So, how did he die?" I asked Sam, my interest so enormous it was practically sitting on the table.

"He was shot at close range in the head. We have the bullet casing. It's a 9 mil. The bullet got mashed when it exited and went into a metal plaque on the wall, so we can't match it up with anything in the system. Maybe fingerprints on the casing will give us a hit."

"Any evidence as to who did it?"

"There was no sign of a break-in, so we think it was someone he knew."

"Wow, that makes the list of suspects pretty long – Adriano, his other son, one of the Bianchis, and how about Bitsy? Do you still have a tail on her?"

"She disappeared right after the raid on Almorel. Hasn't been at work, and no activity on her credit card according to the Fibbies."

"Have they looked for her at her parents' mountain house?"

"I never knew they had one."

"That's 'cuz you don't move in the right circles, kiddo. It's on Sugarloaf. I went up there skiing with her once. Sorry I can't tell you where it is – it was quite a while ago and I wasn't the one driving."

"Let me make a phone call." Sam took out his cell phone and stepped into the family room to make a brief call, before coming back to the kitchen to resume our conversation. I took the opportunity to clean off the dessert clinging to my necklace.

He sat down with a satisfied look on his face. "Any more of that mousse, Rhe? I sure would like some." I gave a long, semi-accusatory gaze at his expanding middle, then shook my head and went to get him another, much smaller helping. He continued, "I called Phil to get him working on finding the location. Thanks for that, Rhe."

"Any time." I took a little bow.

A pause, then Sam asked, "So what do *you* think? I mean, who might have killed Moretti."

I set the mousse in front of him and gave it a dollop of whipped cream. "I would rule out the Bianchis, they're not the type. I don't know the other Moretti son, so I can't say anything about him. My thinking is, it's either Adriano or Bitsy. Adriano has a terrific motive – his father killed the girl he loved. Bitsy's motive could also be revenge, for getting her into his schemes so deeply she might not be able to wiggle out, even with the best lawyers her money can buy. More coffee?"

"Yes, please. But that's just it, Rhe. According to what we've learned from her financials, she's practically broke."

I almost dropped the coffee pot. "What? Her father left her everything and he was loaded!"

"From what we've been able to learn, his estate took a serious bite with his wife's last illness. After she died and the estate came to Bitsy, she made some bad choices – buying the damned newspaper and pouring money into it without much return. Then, as president of her father's bank, she gave in to government pressure and issued mortgages to people who couldn't make the payments. Then she bought mortgage-backed securities. The bank is in the hole to the tune of ten million dollars."

I poured us both another cup. "So Bitsy got in bed with Antonio Moretti to pay off her debts?"

"Sure looks that way. She was also a part owner in the Caribbean Queen and made the down payment on East Almorel."

"So *she* was Moretti's deep pocket. Poor Bitsy! What a sorry end," I replied, returning the coffee pot to the counter and grabbing the Irish Cream-flavored creamer before sitting down.

"Honestly, Rhe, how can you feel sorry for her after she probably tried to have you killed?" Sam said this between mouthfuls of mousse.

I took a long sip of my flavored coffee. "Don't mistake me, Sam, I'm pissing mad and want to see her in a jail cell. But I was also thinking she had a crappy childhood, ruled by an iron-fisted, money-grubbing father and a mother who thought she was local royalty, tiara and all. They turned Bitsy into a holier-than-thou prig with an above-the-law attitude. She wasn't a pleasant kid and she's no nicer as an adult. But maybe she would have turned out differently if she'd had a normal childhood."

"Isn't that always the way? Blame the parents?"

"I know, I know, she's supposed to be a responsible adult. But I remember her childhood all too well."

"I think you're just too kind-hearted. You should get your wish, though. She's not going to avoid some serious prison time. Just how long will depend on what we can prove about her involvement in what happened to you."

"Speaking of that, what's happening with my two favorite kidnappers?"

"Interesting you should ask, since Ray rolled on Bruce. Almost immediately after we mentioned that if he could tell us about Lili's murder, we might get the DA to consider life with a possibility for parole. Turns out, it was just as you suspected. Bruce killed Lili at the request of Moretti senior. Ray had refused to touch the body, leaving Oliver the job of disposing of it. Bruce'll probably get life with no parole when all's said and done. Too bad there's no death penalty in this state. But both of them will get to know the inside of the state prison up close and personal for a long time."

"Well, that definitely makes me breathe easier about Tanya. Ray's away for life and she can get back to her own. Do you think he'll also be tried for beating her?"

"Depends on whether she and her grandfather want to pursue it. What with everything else, maybe not."

"Any news of Adriano?"

"Dunno about him. He's disappeared as well, but the FBI's looking for him."

⌒⌒

The following morning, while I was cleaning leaves out of the pool in preparation for covering it for the winter, the phone rang. I raced inside to answer it, thinking it was Sam with news of Bitsy. "Sam?" I answered breathlessly.

"No, Rhe, this is Bob Morgan."

"Bob! Good to hear from you! I kept my end of the bargain, and you got a good story with East Almorel. Now you owe me," I said with a smile on my lips at the thought of him owing me anything.

Instead of a flip response, which I'd expected, he said, "Rhe, I was wondering if you could come down to my office?" His usually warm and friendly voice had a quaver at the end of his question.

"May I ask why? I know I promised you my story once Sam okayed it, but the case is still ongoing, as you probably know."

"No, it's not that. I have some information about Bitsy you need to see."

"What do you mean? Do you know where she is? If so, you need to call Sam."

"No, it's not that, it's some things I learned when she and I were..... together. Perhaps it would help the investigation, but I'm not at all sure."

"You should still call Sam."

"I would, but I want to remain out of this, so I can at least try to be impartial when the whole story does get written. I'd like to run this info by you first. Please, Rhe? For an old friend?"

I thought it over for a quick moment. The sleuth in me was excited at the idea of perhaps finding Bitsy, and he *was* an old friend. "Okay, but understand I am heading directly to Sam if anything you show me is important. See you in 20 minutes."

I grabbed my bag and phone, and when I got in the car I called Sam because I had the feeling what Bob had to say would interest him, and I wanted to give him a heads up. No answer, so I left a voice mail telling him where I was going and why.

When I got to the Post and Sentinel, the receptionist greeted me like an old friend and told me Bob was waiting for me, repeating the directions to his office. I mounted the stairs, once again marveling at the sparkling light pouring in from the huge windows, and walked down the hall to his office. The door was closed, so I knocked, waited for an answer and when there was none, turned the knob and poked my head in and looked around. *No Bob. Crap. Hadn't he called me to come here?*

I sidled in the door. *Maybe he's in his bathroom.* I walked over to the door I'd seen open on my last visit. I knocked, and my knock pushed the door open. *Bob.* He was lying on the floor, with a spreading pool of blood beneath his head. Without thinking, I dropped my bag, bent down, and felt for a pulse. It was there, a little thin, and he was breathing. I checked his neck for injury and finding none, checked his pupils, which were normal. I did a quick survey of his head and scalp, found a single deep laceration with no depression of the skull, so I turned him on his side and grabbed some paper towels from the counter to apply pressure to his head wound. At that point, I sensed a presence in the room behind me. "Want to give me a hand here? Can you call 911?" I called, glancing over my shoulder but not seeing anyone.

Hearing no answer, I reached into my bag for my phone and only then swiveled completely around to see who was there. A familiar voice said, "I wouldn't do that if I were you," and I looked up to find the barrel of a gun about six inches from my head. Bitsy was holding it. "Don't worry, I didn't hit him hard enough to kill him. After all, I love him." She smiled at me.

"Really? Strange way to show it."

"I needed him to get you here, and he wasn't exactly co-operative. But he saw it my way in the end."

"What do you want from me?" I asked as I rose to my feet in response to an upward flick of the gun.

"What do I want? What do I want, she asks?" Bitsy's voice climbed an octave. Now that my eyes were no longer on a level with the gun, I had the chance to take a good look at her. She was a mess. The prim, trim fashionista in high heels and total control had been replaced by a short, frumpy woman swathed in wrinkled, baggy pants and a sweat shirt. I couldn't help myself, I just stared. From the dull, disheveled hair and the sour smell, I could tell she hadn't bathed in a while and her face, ashen and devoid of makeup, resembled Morticia. "What are you looking at?" she demanded.

"Your designer clothing. Why did you do this to Bob?"

"Why not? He's mine, bought and paid for, and he deserved it. He told me I disgusted him. Do you know why he did that? Because of you. He's in love with you. He's always been in love with you. Just one more thing of mine you had to have!"

At this point, I realized I was in uncharted territory – my first time with a half-crazed woman with a probably loaded gun, telling me something I hadn't known. I was flabbergasted and said the first thing that occurred to me. "He doesn't mean anything to me, Bitsy, not the way you're thinking. He's just a friend."

"He wasn't just a friend in high school, was he?"

"Good God, that was years ago. We dated for all of three weeks, and I married someone else and had a child with him."

"Did you know Bob dropped me for you?"

"When, in high school? For heaven's sake, Bob went through girls like Grant through Richmond. Surely you didn't expect he'd stay with any one girl."

"He would have with me, if you hadn't come along."

At this point, I figured I wasn't going to make her see sense, so I asked, "Why don't we sit down and talk about this?" *Whatever this was.* "Bob's got some hot water for tea. We could have some tea and talk." *Maybe I could get the gun from her? I really needed to get back to Bob.*

She snorted. "No, I don't want some tea, you whore. You always thought you were better than me – you had lots of friends, won at everything you tried, and you were smart. Well, this time you're going to find out what being smart gets you."

I stared at her, speechless. *My God, she's jealous of me! And she's only got one oar in the water!*

"You just had to tear me down, didn't you? If it weren't for you, everything would be just fine. I'd be making money to pay back the bank and no one would know anything. The paper is thriving, and Bob and I were going to get married."

That's not what he said.

"Then along you came, asking questions, snooping around, sticking that large nose of yours where it didn't belong. And now what am I left with? No money, no job, no future." Her voice was rising to a shriek. "I want to get married, have kids, just like you. But no, you just couldn't let me have that, could you? You've always hated me! And now you've gone and ruined it all!"

Just then, Bob groaned and I took my chance. I turned around, bent down and leaned over him, putting my back to Bitsy and blocking her sight of my bag, praying, praying, she wouldn't decide to pull the trigger. My heart was pounding in my ears from fear. "Get away from him!" Bitsy screeched.

"Just let me stop the bleeding. Do you want to go to prison for murder?" She paused, during which time I pressed some paper towels to his wound with one hand while simultaneously reaching into my bag with the other. *Okay, St. Jude, if there was ever a time to save a hopeless woman, it's now. Got it!* I flipped the safety.

At that moment, there was a commotion in the hallway and as I rose, I saw that Bitsy's attention had been drawn for a second to the noise. I tased her at point blank range. She fell backwards, convulsing, and the gun went off. A piece of plaster from the ceiling chipped out and grazed my cheek. I was just standing there when the office door banged open and Sam charged in, gun drawn.

He stood over Bitsy, gun trained on her, and looked at me. "My God, Rhe, she's shot you! Get an ambulance!" he yelled to someone else in the room.

I looked at Sam, put my hand to my cheek, and was surprised when it came away bloody. I smiled and pointed to the hole in the ceiling. "It's Bob who needs help. He's got a bad head wound." I turned back to take care of him.

The rest of the afternoon passed in a blur. EMS arrived, examined Bob, and put him on a gurney for the ride to the hospital. One of the techs had cleaned and bandaged my cheek, wrapping a blanket around my shoulders when I started to shake in the aftermath. Bitsy was monitored until she had recovered sufficiently and was lucid enough to acknowledge she understood when Sam Mirandized her. John cuffed her and started leading her out of the office. When she got to the door she yelled, "You're a whore, Rhe. A whore, do you hear? How long have you been doing it with Bob? I'll get you for this!" Her voice faded away as she was dragged down the hallway. *Must be setting up an insanity plea*, I thought. *Maybe she is bonkers, but she's also one smart cookie.*

Sam and I sat in Bob's office, while Phil held off curious employees outside. He'd had some hot coffee brought in and I gratefully wrapped my cold fingers around the cup, welcoming its warmth. I just couldn't seem to stop shivering. "Is there any way you can keep the details of this from Will?" I chattered at Sam.

"I can give him a sanitized version if you want. Downplay the gun."

"That would be good." I took a deep drink of the coffee and relished the heat as it wandered down to my stomach. *Better.*

"Can you tell me what happened?" he asked, and the ever present recorder popped out of his jacket. So I told him.

27

Sam was as good as his word. I called Will and told him that Bitsy had confronted me at Bob's office. When Will asked to talk to Sam, Sam confirmed my story, omitting any mention of the gun. I figured it was only a matter of time before someone else mentioned it, and sure enough, Ruthie called the house Saturday afternoon and spilled the beans while talking to Will.

The first indication something was wrong was when I heard Will pounding up the stairs to the bedroom, where I was folding a pile of wash I'd dumped on the bed. He burst in and slammed the door. "So when were you going to tell me Bitsy had a gun?" he roared.

"Oh probably never, given your reaction," I snapped back.

Will crossed the room and grabbed me by the shoulders. He was angrier than I had ever seen him, and I was truly afraid he was going to lose control and shake the life out of me. "You simply cannot continue doing this, Rhe! I won't allow it! I won't!" He shook me with each exclamation.

"I have no way of predicting when these things will happen," I shouted back. "And you have no right to dictate how I live my life! You do whatever *you* want," and here I paused, thinking about the qualms I'd had about Will's behavior the night we followed Zoey and her friends. I just couldn't help myself, and righteous anger boiled over. "Just how did you know about East Almorel and how to get there the night we followed Zoey? You've been there, haven't you? You went with that friend you told me about, what's his name? Yeah, Art Crowell, from the Bio department. That was just to throw me off, wasn't it? So, did you enjoy the hookers?" I threw this last question in his face with all the scorn I could muster.

Will dropped his hands and sank back on the bed, his face pale.

Suddenly silent and deflated, he appeared to be struggling with what to say next. "Yes, I've been there," he finally croaked out. I stepped away from him, backing into the dresser, as the reality of his words hit me. Until that moment, I was sure there was a logical explanation that didn't involve his actually being there. *You've done it now, Rhe. The truth is worse than the imagining.*

"But why? Why would you do such a thing?"

"It isn't what you think, it really isn't."

"How could you do that? Is our sex life so boring?" My mind was reeling. *My husband had made it with a hooker. How much worse could it get?*

"Give me the courtesy of an explanation, will you?" Will demanded sarcastically. I remained silent but crossed my arms in defiance. "Remember the weekend you went to the nursing convention in Boston last spring?"

"You were looking forward to spending the weekend with Jack, as I recall." My sarcasm was dripping on the floor.

"Art and I were chatting over lunch, and when I told him that I was minding the store for the weekend, he suggested we have a boy's night out on Saturday. He didn't say what we would do, just that we'd go out and have some fun. I figured we'd hit a local bar or something like that. I never even thought to ask him."

"So it was all his idea, right?"

"Yes, it was. Really, Rhe. I asked Paulette if she could watch Jack, and Art came by around eight. First we went to Hinckley's - you know that bar just off Main on Beacon Alley? -and had a couple of beers. Then Art told me he had a surprise for me, but we would have to drive. What did I know? He drove to East Almorel. Believe me, I had no idea where we were going, and Art finally told me we were going to a gambling joint that had shows with local talent. Until we got inside, I had no idea what the place was."

"So did you enjoy it? Which girl did you choose? How was the hot tub?" I poured it on.

"Rhe, you're not listening to me! It didn't take long for me to figure out what was going on there and when I did, I asked Art to take me home. When he tried to get me to stay, I called a cab. I'm not that sort of man, Rhe. You of all people should know that."

Suddenly the anger drained out of me, and I leaned back on the dresser for support, my mind a jumble of thoughts. *This is Will. You know him. You love him. He wouldn't do that...or would he? Do I really know him all that well? He certainly doesn't understand me.*

Then I realized Paulette had never said anything about watching Jack that night. "But Paulette never told me she watched Jack when I was away. Why didn't she mention it?"

"Because I told her the whole story and she promised not to say anything. Don't you understand how embarrassing it was? How could I tell you? I haven't spoken to Art since."

"But you *could* have told me! I would've understood."

"And you could've told me about the gun."

He has me there.

"What if Bitsy had killed you? Where would that leave Jack and me?" I noticed his eyes filled as he said this.

God, Rhe, you're such a fool. But so is he. Where do we go from here?

⌒⌒

The following afternoon, Paulette arrived in my kitchen before I had a chance to go out the door to visit hers. She was carrying a wrapped plate, from which was emanating a mouth-watering smell. "Voilà!" she exclaimed, removing the wrap. "A real cherry Danish, my first!"

"And of course you had to test it on the local omnivore, right?" I replied, eyeing the confection.

"Absolutely!" She set the plate down on the table and gave me her usual around-the-waist hug. "How are you? I still can't imagine how frightening it must have been facing that lunatic Bitsy, and her with a gun!"

"Hey, she was the last loose end, and things are pretty well wrapped up. I'm thinking that having a normal life might not be so bad for now." Paulette looked at me quizzically. I ignored her look and pulled two clean coffee mugs out, filled them from a fresh pot of coffee, and placed them and two plates on the table. "Do you want regular cream or some of the foo-foo stuff?" I asked her.

"Oh definitely foo-foo. Which kind do you have?"

"I have Italian crème, hazelnut, and chocolate macchiato."

"Bring on the Italian crème, let's celebrate!"

We plopped ourselves down at the kitchen table, poured on the Italian crème and helped ourselves to the Danish. I took a bite and my taste buds did a happy dance. "Paulette, you nailed this! It's wicked good. I should ask you to teach me how to make it, but I'd never be able to do it. So how about I hire you?" I said through a mouthful, with a crumby smile.

She took a long sip of coffee and gave me a satisfied grin. The thought of my fight with Will and Paulette's involvement suddenly intruded on pleasure, and I looked down at my coffee. The change in my face registered with Paulette, who has always had some secret radar when it comes to my moods, and she asked, "How are things with you and Will?'

"Not good, but I am hoping they might improve now that Lili's murder is solved."

"And how do you feel about that?"

"About the situation with Will or the case being over?"

"Both."

"Well, Will and I had the worst fight of our marriage yesterday. He blew up when he found out Bitsy threatened me with a gun."

"You hadn't told him?"

"No, because I knew he would explode. And he did."

"Have you talked with Will at all since the fight?"

There she had me, because we hadn't really said much to each other at all during the remainder of Saturday, both of us pretty much focusing on Jack. Any discussion of the case was absolutely off limits, partly to shield Jack, although no doubt he would hear all sorts of things at school. When and if he did, I would spend some time telling him what I felt he could handle and straighten out the lurid details, which were bound to circulate.

"Paulette, I asked Will about his trip to East Almorel." I gave her a pointed stare, and she flushed. "You knew about it and you didn't tell me. Why?"

"Because Will told me what happened and begged me not to say anything. He was embarrassed and afraid you wouldn't understand."

"Well, I understood it enough not to be angry, but I didn't understand why he wouldn't tell me. And *that's* the problem. Will and I are having an issue trusting each other enough to communicate the serious things. It's something we've clearly got to work on. Maybe with a professional...?"

"But things should be better now that you're not working with the police anymore, right?" She stared at me when I didn't answer. "You're *not* working with the police again, are you?"

I'd made a decision even before the confrontation with Will. "If a situation arises, then yes, I will."

"But why, Rhe? You have a family, a husband who loves you, a job – a career, really – you enjoy. Why do you want to jeopardize that?"

"Paulette, if I could put it into words, I would. I just know when I was working on solving Lili's murder, I felt, I don't know, more alive and challenged than I ever have. I can't give it up, and I don't know if Will will ever understand that."

Paulette gave me a half smile and said, "I think I know what you mean."

"The car chase?"

She nodded.

A wave of nausea suddenly hit me, and I sat back in my chair, waiting for it to pass. *Too much stress this past week*, I thought. Paulette turned her head slightly and gave me a puzzled look. "It's nothing, just tired," I replied. "On a brighter note," I continued, getting up and grabbing my bag from the counter, "let me show you something." I pulled out a small flat wallet, flipping it open to show her what was inside.

"Wow! Is that what I think it is?"

"Yup, an official police badge and a card showing that I'm a consultant. Sam gave it to me yesterday. Now when I talk to someone on official business, I can just flip them the badge!"

Just then there was a knock on the back door and when I looked around, I saw Sam standing in the garage through the glass panes. I motioned him to come in. "For heaven's sake, you don't need to stand on ceremony out there," I said as he entered. "After the past couple of weeks, you're allowed to come in unannounced!"

Sam's eyes immediately found the coffee cake on the table, and he took off his coat, putting it on the back of a chair, and sat down. "Can I have some of that?" he asked with a big grin.

"Of course," responded Paulette. "Coffee with that?"

I was already at the coffee pot, filling him a cup, and brought it and a plate and a fork back to the table. "To what do we owe your visit?"

'Well, it'll be on the news soon anyway, so I thought I might tell you in person."

"Moretti's murder?" I interjected.

"Goddammit, Rhe, how do you know these things?" Sam replied, feigning irritation. "Adriano Moretti turned himself into the police this morning. He was the one who shot and killed his father."

"Why? Because his father had something to do with Lili's murder?" Paulette asked.

"Yup. Apparently, Adriano confronted him about Lili's killing, and his father admitted to killing her. But he told Adriano that Bruce, one of the guys who kidnapped Rhe, was the one who actually did it. He must have thought if Bruce killed her, it would somehow be a lesser offense in his son's eyes."

"But why would Moretti want her killed? I thought he loved his sons. Wouldn't he want him to be happy?" Paulette hit the nail on the head, and I responded.

"It's what we discussed, Sam, right? It was a religious conviction on the father's part that Adriano and Lili, being first cousins and being intimate with each other, were committing a mortal sin. When Moretti learned Lili was pregnant, he felt he had to do something. He couldn't ask her to have an abortion, because as a Catholic, that's murder. And of course, as a Catholic, she would have refused. See the conundrum? So Moretti figured the only way to solve the problem and get rid of the family's embarrassment, was to have someone else eliminate her. He never thought Adriano would figure it out."

Sam continued, "Adriano apparently snapped, left his father, found a gun and came back and shot him." His face lit up with an idea. "It's almost a Romeo and Juliet, except that Romeo didn't die."

"What I can't understand is how Moretti got involved in pimping prostitutes and supplying tissues to hospitals taken from people he was supposed to be burying," commented Paulette thoughtfully. "Even more people may die if those transplants are contaminated. And none of this seemed to bother him."

I nodded in agreement.

After moment during which Sam scraped his plate with his fork and looked longingly at what remained of the cherry Danish, Paulette said, "I believe there are some truly evil people born into this world, and Moretti was one of them. I can't imagine how the Bianchis are handling all this." Paulette had such a good heart; it was just like her to think of Lili's parents first. She twirled a curl of hair; she was thinking about something. "So why did Oliver put the body on the soccer field?" she asked. "He could have put it anywhere to be discovered."

I didn't have an answer for her....yet.

⌒⌒

Monday, I returned to work on my normal day schedule. The staff treated me like visiting royalty, with lots of congratulations and good goings. Nancy Ennis, on the other hand, seemed alternately stiff and guilty. I asked her to have coffee with me when there was a break, and while she agreed, she didn't look happy about it.

We sat in the cafeteria, at the same table where we'd been three weeks before, and slowly stirred cream into our coffees, neither of us wanting to talk. I thought of words from the old Carly Simon song ...*there are clouds in my coffee. Clouds and dreams.* I took a deep breath and began, "Nancy, you were dating Oliver and I know you were beginning to care about him. You shouldn't be embarrassed or feel guilty about that. He had no idea how serious a business he'd gotten into. He was lured by the money. That doesn't make him inherently evil, nor you for liking him."

Tears formed in Nancy's eyes and started to trickle down her cheeks. "He was a good person, Rhe! I knew there was something going on the last few times we went out. He kept looking over his shoulder and a couple of times didn't even hear stuff I was saying to him. When I asked what was wrong, he told me not to be concerned, just something at work. I meant to talk to Marsh about it, but now it turns out that wasn't it at all. I feel guilty I didn't help him, and horrible because he was so sweet and kind to me." More tears dropped.

I reached over and took her hand. "You couldn't have helped him, Nancy, and nobody in their right mind should blame you for caring about him." I tried to comfort her but suspected it would take some time for her to work it through. I only hoped her colleagues at the hospital wouldn't judge her.

After a minute, she looked up at me and said, "The funny thing is, Rhe, Oliver really admired you. He talked a lot about you and asked me all sorts of questions about you and your family. He was really interested in how you solved the hospital robberies and more than once told me he thought you were intuitive and very brave. I even thought he had a little crush on you!"

"You're kidding, right?"

"Well, I have to admit I was a bit jealous. But it just sounds silly now that I've said it."

I shook my head, not sure how to react. "I guess I should be flattered. I really regret that I didn't get to know him better. Maybe things would have worked out differently." *Is this why Oliver had left Lili's body at the soccer field?*

⟨⟨≈⟩⟩

That night Sam appeared for dinner without an invitation, which I took to mean either he was now fine with my cooking or he was too hungry to care. We had plenty, since I had grilled a butterflied chicken with rosemary and olive oil. I even surrendered to Will's love of potatoes and made twice baked, with bacon, chives, and sour cream, but countered that with a salad. I love balancing calories. That's why it's okay to have French fries, as long as you have them with a diet Coke. For dessert, I made baked apples, which even I can't screw up. And anything is one of Jack's favorite desserts as long as there's ice cream on top.

Over dinner, we talked about mundane things and avoided anything to do with the past few weeks. Jack's soccer season was coming to an end in a week, and Sam mentioned the prediction of snow, which we hoped would hold off. Basketball season was about to start up, and Sam was coaching one of the teams. Jack gave us an animated description of his teacher, Miss Patterson, which was both scathing and funny. My son was turning into quite the comedian.

"And Miss Patterson isn't married, Uncle Sam," Jack announced. "She doesn't have kids but she sure seems to like us."

"You playing matchmaker now, Jack?" I asked.

"What's a matchmaker, Mom?"

"Never mind. You'll learn soon enough." I was silent for a while, recalling that Miss Patterson was attractive and only a few years younger than Sam.

"You're awfully quiet," Sam commented.

"Oh. Nothing. Just thinking." I was already scheming how I could get them to meet, and I swear Sam was reading my mind. He blushed.

After dinner, while Jack was finishing his homework in his room, Sam, Will and I sat at our kitchen table having post-repast coffee. I needed to tell them what I'd learned about Oliver.

"Sam, I think I know why Lili's body was left on the soccer field. You know I never considered Oliver as Lili's killer. Marsh described Oliver as a good kid and a hard worker and Marsh is a good judge of people. Plus Oliver was dating a nurse from the hospital, Nancy Ennis, and she described the same person to me. She's devastated by his death."

"But his being a good guy doesn't mean he's any less guilty of being involved in the crime," replied Sam.

"I know that, but hear me out. Oliver was good looking and charming, but in a job with no future. He saw his part time work as a way to have things he could never afford, and he spent money on Nancy and bought that fancy motorcycle. As the money kept coming, he probably saw himself moving up in the organization. And I found out something interesting from talking to both Marsh and Nancy: Oliver had an interest in me."

"Just like you to attract attention from someone like him," interjected Will. He had been largely quiet for the past several minutes but now crossed his arms and scowled.

I gave Will a warning shake of my head and continued, "He apparently had talked to Marsh at length about my solving the robberies at the hospital. According to Marsh, he was trying to get up the courage to talk to me directly, but he never did, even though I was in the morgue fairly regularly. Nancy told me much the same thing and said he'd asked a lot of questions about me and my family. She suggested he had a little crush."

"That *is* kind of creepy," interjected Sam.

"I agree, but it explains the body on the soccer field. When he was told to dispose of Lili's body, he must have figured out he was in way over his head. So he put Lili's body where he hoped *I* would find it, thinking I would be able to figure out how Lili was killed. That one action on his part helped solve Lili's murder and brought a whole lot of bad things out in the open. He must have known that as the investigation went on, there would come a point where Morretti would get nervous and blame him for everything. So Oliver decided to run, and that's why he was packing up on the day he was killed. In a way, it was a brave thing for him to do."

"If he wanted you to figure things out, then why lose the sample of water you brought in?" asked Sam.

"To buy himself the time to decide when and where to run. He didn't make it, and that's sad. So Oliver put the body on the field for me to discover and that one act set everything in motion. It doesn't excuse him, but I think he still deserves a small measure of our gratitude."

At this point, Will pushed his chair away from the table, stood up and glared at his brother. "What's up, baby brother?" Sam asked.

Seeing Will's face, I could tell that was absolutely the wrong thing to say.

"What's up? *Now* you want to know what I think? I think you're the reason for all the danger Rhe's been in. If you hadn't brought her into the investigation, none of this crap would have happened. And then her old lover Bob almost gets her killed, too." His voice got louder. "And you wanna know what else I think? I think you've been spending more time with Rhe than her own husband!" With that, he stormed out of the kitchen.

"Will!" I shouted after him. "I can't believe you said that!"

Turning to Sam, I said "I'm so sorry. Will and I have been butting heads lately, but that was way out of line. He's mad at me, but he shouldn't be taking it out on you."

"I'd better go, Rhe," Sam said rising from the table and grabbing his coat from the back of the chair.

"You know he didn't mean it, Sam."

"I'm not sure. I'll give him some time to cool off and then try to talk with him."

Will slept in his office that night.

28

The following morning, I threw up in the kitchen sink after breakfast. With everything happening in the past weeks, I figured I was run down or had caught something from an ER patient. Or maybe my cooking wasn't as good as I'd thought, although Will and Jack seemed fine. But I also lost my breakfast the morning after that.

Jack brought home a black kitten with a white chest and ears, given to him by one of his friends on the condition that his parents were okay with it. We were, and Jack named the kitten Tuxedo, Tux for short.

That weekend, I told Will that I was pregnant. I can't tell you how happy he was to hear it. I just can't tell you.